THOSE
THE FUTURE
LEFT BEHIND

THOSE
THE FUTURE
LEFT BEHIND

A Novel

Patrick Meisch

Published by SparkPress, a BookSparks imprint,
A division of SparkPoint Studio, LLC
Phoenix, Arizona, USA, 85007
www.gosparkpress.com

Published 2021
Printed in the United States of America
Print ISBN: 978-1-68463-079-0
E-ISBN: 978-1-68463-080-6
Library of Congress Control Number: 2020918799

For Steve and Christine
for teaching a young boy to dream.

1
0001 – The Gambler

"Good evening. I'm here for Mr. Chaezka on behalf of the Bureau of Fortune. He, most likely, is not expecting me."

After hearing my introduction, the young woman in the snappy gold and green vest paused for a second to look me over as concern surfaced in her expression. As she decided what the best course of action would be for her, admittedly, small part in the following performance, I surreptitiously admired her gaudy outfit before my gaze defaulted to somewhere around her shoes. Given the shoes were obviously bespoke, and the tiny rakes with which they were adorned real gold, and they alone were most likely worth more than my relatively pedestrian garb in its entirety, bestowing these outfits on a lowly greeter such as the lady before me, who was in the process of circulating her fist above her head as some sort of signal, was a tremendous show of wealth.

I glimpsed an imposing woman moving directly towards us through a crowd of revelers behind the greeter. Her outfit was all boring black except for a white button–up shirt. Even centuries from its inception, the clothing used to portray an individual employed as security has not changed much, although, in an establishment such as this, the individual marching towards me was anything but inconspicuous.

"Thank you for waiting! Ms. Alexia will be taking care of you until Mr. Chaezka is ready to receive. Please ask her anything that is on your mind, and I am sorry I was unable to assist you further."

The greeter finished with a practiced, sheepish grimace. She sidled past me on to the next guest and, as I looked back around, my eyes were met by the stern countenance of Ms. Alexia, presumed security woman extraordinaire. She turned her head to check that no one was attempting to eavesdrop, and I noticed the barely visible, yet telltale slit scar of a ComCom implant procedure rippling along her muscular neck, which lent credence to my previous presumption.

"Good evening, Collector, and with that out of the way I'll drop the bullshit and we can move on. Sound good?" Ms. Alexia asked, in a smoky voice.

"I appreciate your candor, Ms. Alexia, it seems as though you know my purpose in being here this evening."

"Candace is fine. And affirmative, but you seem to have arrived sooner than Chazz expected. He is still preparing, so he asked me if I could distract you for twenty minutes or so. So how 'bout it? Have anythin' in mind?"

"I suppose I could be distracted for a bit with a tour if you wouldn't mind taking me around. I've never been to one of these casinos before, and I hear The Govy's Rake is supposed to be the best of the best, though you don't strike me as the guiding type."

Candace emitted a short, tired laugh at this and then replied.

"I've been 'round enough to take you for a spin, I guess, and I could probably clue you into a few things the rest of these bimbos don't know about. Chazz told me to spare no expense while I 'distract' you, so it's probably the least I can do. I'll bring you to some of the best spots 'round if you tell me you'll answer a question for me when we're done. It'll be a personal one, so I understand if you turn me down . . . and I don't know if I can trust a Collector at their word."

"Though it might not assuage your misgivings to hear me say it, you can trust that I'll answer your question. Unfortunately, I doubt that I'll be welcomed back to try my luck at the tables when I am finished with my work here anyhow."

"Fair enough." She said as she gestured me over to the entrance of the main floor. "Why don't we start at the start and you can tell me if I left anything out since I'm sure you already know the lay of the land from your intel.

"These statues here," Candace began by gesturing at pairs of bronze statues cast in the likeness of Greek gods that flanked the three entry hallways into the casino proper, "combine an Old-world charm with cutting-edge tech."

Candace proceeded to demonstrate her herculean strength by tilting one of these statues over to show me the housing panel underneath.

"Inside is a GC reader, much like you'll find in typical stores, just in a purtier package."

"From where do you hail originally, Candace, if you don't mind me asking?"

"Atlanta, SER. You gonna take me away for the accent next?" She jabbed.

I chuckled one of the more genuine chuckles I had in quite some time.

"Hardly. I think standardizing the language of the business world to English was enough. Attempting to squash its accents is overkill in my opinion. I find your SER drawwwwwl to be mighty charmin'!" I offered in my best imitation of the accent. She returned a look that made me feel as though she was terribly offended and then softened up and laughed at the fleeting expression of doubt I must have shown.

"Trackin' guests has never been easier. Since the worth of the credit account you have linked to your CFOB is taken down as soon as you walk through these here doors, we know how much yer comin' in with and, hopefully, how little yer leavin' with. That's also how we knew you were trouble when you walked in. Non–standard CFOB ping. Most of the time, you would have been promptly escorted off the premises, as we only allow possible customers on the floor, but Clete, our head of visual security, said you had a different look about you and Mindy, your greeter, confirmed that and gave us the signal to move in. Speaking of which, have you noticed the walls?"

It's true that I had looked the place over as I had come in on top of the intel I had gone over tirelessly before arriving. The infrequent check–ins on my ComCom allowed me the opportunity to review if necessary, as well. I knew that cameras were ubiquitous in casinos and that this was no different here, but the way Candace put it was good enough to include in this memoir of sorts and the sight was quite spectacular, especially due to the fact that the average person wouldn't notice or appreciate the difference.

"Ain't a single place an ant could shit on this floor where we wouldn't be able to find 'im, and we'd be able to squash 'im no more than thirty seconds later. Part of the reason Chazz chose the emerald color for The Rake is that the cameras that are woven into the one-way mirror walls give off a twinkle if yer lookin' at 'em at the right angle, so he said that the walls will look like real emeralds shinin'."

"Fashion and function." I quipped. "You do have quite a spectac-ular venue."

"Do you want to see the tables?"

"Lead on!"

All of the floor employees of The Govy's Rake had been trained to glide amongst the throngs of customers with a mesmerizing, swaying motion, which made the trip to whichever table would most likely be your financial demise a pleasant experience. Candace was eschew-ing this training at the time and a perspicacious eye could see she was nervous, despite her security background. We walked along the floor, which was made of a fluffy green synth–fur, the wispiness of which reminded me of an Old–world treat I had read about known as cotton candy, which was not made of cotton. I told Candace about this musing, and she opened up a bit while a pair of personal defense drones buzzed overhead to promptly escort a newly-creditless dignitary of some kind, who was causing a ruckus behind us, off the premises.

"My great great grandpappy used to run one of those cotton candy machines in the summertime for a while. Actually, you kinda shot the bull about the Old-world look. Chazz is obsessed with the Old-world look. In fact, not just the look. I'm sure you've noticed the music." She said, gesturing around to the ceiling and wall panels in which indistinguishable microspeakers had been embedded. I had noticed.

"I've heard this kind of music only once before. When I was really little, I was playing with one of my neighbors in a unit next to our orphanage, and his grandmother would fall asleep in an old wooden chair listening to this kind of music every night. Although this song had less of . . . that," I emphasized by pointing up, "blaring digiment in it."

"That ain't no digiment," Candace said, listening to the music with her eyes closed for a few seconds and snapping. "That's the real thing. A real trumpet."

"Huh. Amusing. I thought imitations had become advanced enough to be indistinguishable in this day and age."

"Naw. Hearin' this tune every week kinda makes me sad," Candace said, her expression becoming somber for a moment, "to think about what we have lost with all the streamlinin' we've done, I mean. But I guess that's part of the reason I accepted the job here."

Candace took me past each table, most of which were at capacity with guests in various states of inebriation cursing and carousing, enumerating each game as we went: Blackjack, Choice Poker, 5-Card Draw, UTH, Skitsgy, Mahjong, Craps, Cortifo . . . The green floor and brown wood of the sides of each table made the casino look

almost like a forest, something I had yet to see in my travels but I had
heard about on the fairytale stream channels one of my caretakers,
Graciela, used to cue up for me in my youth before she went off on
her errands. As I walked through this forest, I did not sense that
any wolves were creeping up on me. No ambush. Only Candace. I
wondered why there had been no signs of resistance so far. Many of
the example cases in the BoF training vids ended when the Collector
was ambushed by a larger force, but there seemed to be no danger of
that sort, at the time.

"Do you have a favorite game?" Candace asked me.

"I've only ever gambled a little bit in makeshift parlor units. I
know about many of the games, but most of the ones I've played are
Old-world in origin. I suppose Texas Hold 'em is my favorite, but I've
not really played enough to be terribly good at it. Plus, these days
ComComs can calc part of your odds for you, so there's much less
risk."

"That's why we have readers to check for ComCom activation at
each table. You've heard about these, right? Ours are a bit more specific than the types installed in school classrooms to detect cheatin',
but they work on the same principles."

"Ah, yes, I have. Unfortunately, in the parlors where I played, while
most of the people who played were too poor to afford a ComCom,
some people were able to get their hands on devices that were similar from black market sources that would only do calcs and would
have no other functionality, so many players would be 'cheating.' I
stopped playing after watching a vid on a parlor where the house
player strangled a person to death who was suspected of cheating
using one of these types of devices, and then it turned out that she
was just really good."

"Fortunate that we won't ever make that mistake," Candace
said while showing me a table and the window-like slits where the
ComCom readers were housed. Then, she took me behind the tables

into a Pit Boss Room and showed me a screen that tracked tables. "Each unfilled circle is an empty seat at a table, green is an active player, pink is a player stepping away momentarily. If one of those circles starts flashing black and red, that's a ComCom or like calc app activation."

"What do you do if a calc app starts up?"

"ComCom and other direct calculation applications must be deactivated before a player starts playing at any table. If any accidental or intentional application reactivation occurs during the remainder of play at the table, all winnings that the user has are stripped, the user is blacklisted based on ComCom ID Number and CFOB Number and banned for life from all of Chaezka Casinos. Your ComCom can still ping paramedics and carry out any other typical functions, but if the direct calculation application is engaged, yer outta here."

"So when did the table I was just at pick up on my calc app?"

"The average scan distance is about fifteen meters. Calc app users that are on the floor but not at a table are tracked with floating blue dots on the screens that I showed you."

"Impressive. There were very few blue dots on the screen that I saw, so most of your customers are either returning or they know the rules pretty well."

"Yup. We try to run a tight ship 'round here. Anyway, I was informed that Chazz is ready to see ya' now. Are you good to go?"

"Since I arrived," I replied, checking my surroundings for the sixty-second time in the seventeenish minutes I had been on the floor. "However, I did enjoy the tour! The peek into the Pit Boss Room was completely new to me." I smiled at Candace, feeling a slight sense of remorse that I'd only spend a few more moments with her, but that's the job.

As we walked up to a personal elevator whose frame was cast in the shape of a golden lion's head, Candace waved off two more security guards that were sizing me up and they proceeded to walk the floor.

ComCom: transmit location: penthouse elevator on approach to target EndCom

"There're only three people in this building that know what you are about to do, and, when you leave, I'm going to be the only one stickin' around who is allowed to remember. I won't say a word about it for the rest of my life, and I'll go with whatever story is concocted by yer Bureau, but I do still want the answer to that question you promised me. Whatever happens next, I want you to know that Chazz is a good man, and he has taken mighty good care of us for as long as he could. You'll be free to walk out of here on my and Chazz's honor if you can trust us at our word."

I was not expecting this kind of treatment for one of my first jobs. Unfortunately, in this kind of work, it is all too common for these types of scenarios to turn into a bloodbath and I was prepared for that eventuality. A saying I had heard from a veteran of the Bureau was: "The luckiest Collector is the one who only has to collect one life per job. The unluckiest Collector is the one whose one life is collected instead."

"I certainly trust you, and I imagine I can trust Mr. Chaezka. I'll answer your question whenever you are ready to ask."

An archaic ding sounded the arrival of the elevator door, and Candace and I walked in. If she was going to betray me, this was the moment. My body tensed in response to the close-quarters environment. After she turned an old, metal key, a panel opened, and she pressed the revealed button.

"I wanted to be a Collector once," Candace sighed, "but the officers conducting my test said that I wouldn't qualify because I showed signs 'demonstrating a lack of resolve to finish a job.'" She said this last mimicking whatever monotonous government psych officer denied her. "They were right. I'd never be able to kill someone like Chazz, but you can." She looked at me holding back tears, undoubtedly out of habitual restraint. "I was angry the day they refused me, partially because my future was uncertain, partially because it made me feel like I wasn't good enough. A month and a half later, I joined a general security firm and a year or so later Chazz hired me because he wanted to take a gamble on a kid that was down on her luck. I've worked for him, with him, ever since. Sixteen years and change."

Ding. We walked into a gorgeous marble foyer. *Clack clackclack clack* the sound of our shoes as we walked up a large ballroom staircase. ComCom chatter about backup mobilizing.

"Now I know that being refused was a blessin'. So, Collector," she stopped, and I turned to face her. I can't remember her face well enough to describe her in that moment, likely due to the nervousness I felt on my first real Collection, despite all of my mental training, "my question is: Do you feel satisfied doing what you do?"

"I believe it is honestly too early for me to tell you exactly if I am satisfied or not and why. I know that probably isn't a satisfactory answer. I know that it will probably not set you at ease in any way. What I can tell you is that I have asked myself this question before, and I will never stop asking myself this question, and, by the time I am done, I can promise you that I'll have a definitive answer. . . . Will that be enough?"

Candace opened the door in front of us, and I saw a man sitting and shuffling a deck of cards behind a desk.

"I hope that it will be, for your sake," she said, softly, any sign of tears in her eyes erased.

I watched Candace walk into the room ahead of me and stop. The man at the desk put the cards down and stood up, looking directly at Candace.

"How do I look?" He asked, arms up and swiveling slightly from side to side.

"Like a million bucks." Candace crooned.

"Goodbye, Candy." He said, a tone of finality in his voice.

"Goodbye, Chazz." She returned with an air of stoicism.

Then, Candace turned around and walked past me, nodded once, donning the mask of a quivering smile, ding, and she was gone.

"Good evening, Collector!" Mr. Chaezka boomed. "Come on down!"

I proceeded into Mr. Chaezka's penthouse with trepidation, checking every corner, listening and watching with all of my being. Compared to the casino floor, his quarters were less ostentatious, though not lacking in style by any means. Candace mentioned Mr. Chaezka's love for the aesthetic of the Old-world, and he was beginning to walk over to what was, undoubtedly, one of his most prized possessions.

"Can I fix you a drink?" He asked, taking two tumblers off of an overhead rack as a bit of dust fell from one of the corners, illuminated by the soft, green light of a dingy lamp.

"I appreciate the offer, but I don't drink much other than water and the occasional soda." I scanned Mr. Chaezka's eyes for the first time. They were blue and slightly reminiscent in how they were lidded at that moment.

"I've got twenty or so different sodas in back, mostly older brands. How 'bout it?"

"The Bureau would consider it irresponsible to partake, but I'll admit I have worked up a bit of a thirst. Roy Rogers?"

"Good stuff!" Mr. Chaezka beamed. "I can't say I don't like drinking alone, but I haven't had a chance to get back behind Old Ma' here in a while due to my travels, you see."

I had seen. Mr. Chaezka hadn't been back in the NER in quite some time. In going over the travel logs pulled from his not-so-private drone, I had seen that he had been bouncing from one casino of his to another over the last two years and making stops in different resort towns along the way. Seoul then Hokkaido, Shanghai then Bangkok, Cairo then Harare, JoBurg then Rio, San Jose then Aspen, Louisville then, finally, ending up here in one of the few remaining structures in Atlantic City standing above the sea.

Mr. Chaezka put my tumbler away and slid a glass in the shape of a triangular prism less the top surface out from behind the mahogany bar and deftly filled the bottom sixteenth of its volume with grenadine as I admired the surroundings. It was evident that Mr. Chaezka was quite fond of this bar. All of the glasses were sorted by shape, hanging, where possible, from customized rack slides that curved gently in a pattern evocative of seaweed tendrils through which a mermaid had been engraved turning about to show off her elusive, shapely form. The rack was mahogany as was the bar, hence "Old Ma'," I assumed.

"Do you like the bar?" Mr. Chaezka asked, smirking as he was guessing at my answer as I slid on to one of the cushioned stools that creaked ever so slightly when I shifted my weight into a comfortable slouch.

"I think I do like it, although I have never seen anything quite like it." I tested my weight again as he slid my Roy Rogers over in front of me, just a few centimeters off stage right from the axis that would bisect my body. "And I imagine you wouldn't mind telling me more about it—?"

"HAHAHAHAHA!" Mr. Chaezka burst out. "You're slick, kid! I might as well tell someone who appreciates it a bit more. Let's see . . ."

I kept surveying the bar as Mr. Chaezka spoke. The shelves on which the liquor was stored were worked into the shape of an open clam. There were thirty–five bottles in all of various shapes and brands.

"My father was a bartender for most of his life. He used to tell me that he started drinkin' at fourteen, and he started tending a day after. There was a man in his complex that ran a bar . . ."

The spacing between each bottle and the next was almost perfect enough to make me feel more comfortable just looking at it. Order. "And so he inherited this bar, Old Ma', from that man. It's a single cut of mahogany from a country that used to be called Brazil that is now part of Nueva Amazonia, close to Rio, where I just was a while ago."

The clamshell was a fitting design for the old standard bottom-, middle-, top-shelf system Mr. Chaezka had been telling me about. There were only a few bottles on the bottom shelf, although I got a sense that these would all be top-shelf bottles if you were to be buying from the dispensary machines popular these days, which have no shelves at all but still have a sorting option labeled top, middle, and bottom, for your selection. Most of the bottles were in the middle shelves of the clam and then the numbers tapered off to leave a single bottle up by the lip. The engraving on it was in the shape of an M.

"It's eighteen feet and a quarter long, three and a half feet wide, and it rests on a piece that is four feet even deep. Another Roy Rogers? Oh! I see you're lookin' at the shelves. You sure I can't tempt you with a drink? You know the funny thing about that there M bottle?"

The bottle was about five-eighths full.

"Is it as expensive as it looks?"

"Probably more nowadays. The damn bottle cost more than the scotch itself. But the scotch is damn good."

"It's a fine looking bottle, though. The surface of the glass, when you look at it straight on, has vertices that conform to make an M shape."

Here, Mr. Chaezka came over and stood in front of me and looked at the bottle for a second.

"Sunuvabitch. I've had that bottle sittin' there for, what . . . thirteen some years. I *never* noticed that! No wonder it cost a fortune. The fuckin' bottle's an M! I always just looked at the M on the label. I thought that the scotch tasted good enough to merit the price, but this kinda eliminates some of that buyer's remorse I had at the time. You're sumthin' else, kid."

I smirked in my discomfort and looked over at one of the lamps affixed to the wall behind the shelves that bathed the clamshell in light to give it an aura of splendor that mimicked the shimmer one can see playing across the surface of the ocean while immersed within it.

"So I have only four stools at the bar because of what happened to Dad. After he was tending bar for years, he started hating some of the people who would come in. He didn't like how the times were changing the generations, and he thought they were getting ruder. My dad liked Old-world things, too, and he passed that nostalgia down to me. He liked serving drinks to a few people at a time and finding what they really liked while having a conversation or two with 'em. In his daddy's time, people would only come to these types of places for the hospitality and for extra-fine drinks that couldn't be found anywhere else. Nowadays these types of places don't exist. No one cares for the hospitality anymore and the extra-fine drinks can be shipped by drone to the highest bidder. He always used to tell me that all this advancement was making us become less personable. I think he was right. Turns out, he had been gambling every now and again with some friends to try to make himself feel better about what the world was becoming, I guess. He got into trouble, somewhat, but he told me that that was the only thing he liked as much as tending bar for respectable clientele. He said gambling gave him hope. Back to the four bar stools. He wanted to serve only to friends after he made a small fortune gambling, so he started restricting his bar to member-only, and that made him happy for a while. He said he'd never turn away a newcomer once, but he wouldn't necessarily welcome them back."

Any sign of joviality in Mr. Chaezka had seeped away by this point, and I saw through his veneer to the knot-ridden fibers that composed his history.

"Seven men from the casino that he won his fortune from came to the bar one day to have drinks. I was sitting at a corner table, polishing some glasses for him. He served them his best and thanked them for coming, even though he didn't expect such a large crowd of newcomers. They got up and swept out around the room over the next minute or so except for two guys at the bar. Then, they all pulled guns and told him that they wanted the money he cheated from them. Not all of it, but a good amount. He told them that it was gone. He spent it. He didn't tell them that he spent it on most of the aspects of this bar you see before you, thankfully, I guess. I couldn't look away from the gun a man had pulled on someone sitting next to me at a table. I heard them say they were going to kill him and all he said was 'could you do it outside, so you don't disturb my customers?' They took him outside. We all heard one shot. Thump. Scraping. Jump jets. You know the rest. Both those parties left me with something that day. My father left me Old Ma', and those thugs left me with the idea that casinos were the most powerful organizations in the world."

"Which is why you made the choice?" I finished my second Roy Rogers, the balance of which between grenadine and cola was so well-made that my taste buds never, to this day, have known a better one.

"Partially." Mr. Chaezka said, beginning to smile again. "Another Roy Rogers?"

"My thirst is quenched for now, but I'd like to hear more of your story if you wouldn't mind."

"I don't! Actually, I'm kind of happy to talk about it with you. I've only told this to a few others in my life. All of them sat at those stools. You know the most fucked up thing about it?"

Incoming transmission from Reaper 6–2, receive?

ComCom: receive last

"*Check–in.*"

ComCom: Send: "All good. Still working." EndCom

"What's that?" I replied, genuinely intrigued by the tale.

Mr. Chaezka took my glass, and it was only a glass, as he made the drink so well that he was confident enough to not include ice or a stir rod of any sort with it, cleaned it, dried it, stored it, and spot-cleaned the bar with mindlessly mechanical precision.

"After witnessing my dad die from gambling trouble, the most impactful choice I made in my life was a gamble itself. He also left me with hope and probably some bad genes that make it so I can't stay away from it. Isn't that fucked up?"

"Indeed, it is, but I've often heard people say that life is a series of gambles."

"Isn't it, though?" Mr. Chaezka asked, becoming excited.

"I think those people are certainly correct. Everything I have done this evening would certainly fall under the classification of a gamble."

"Could I entice you for one more gamble, then?" He asked, the corners of his mouth turning up, slyly.

At this, my body tensed again, but I replied.

"Perhaps."

"Wonderful!" He yelled, and a crucifix on a chain jangled out of his double-breasted, white suit as he lifted his arms, as if up to the Lord, ruffling his Sunday best slightly. "But first, I would like to offer you one more drink." He began to reach for the M-shaped bottle.

"As I said before, I don't drink. I've drank only once in my life before, out of curiosity, and never to the point of drunkenness. I can, without doubt, say that I abhor the taste of alcohol and would prefer to maintain my wits in their optimal state at all times. That said, I have always been curious as to why many people choose to imbibe such drinks, and I have often been told that many drink for the taste and most for the stupor. So, were I to entertain the notion of accepting your offer, which would be under literally the most special of circumstances, as I don't imagine I am likely to ever do this again, I would guess that the amount I would taste would not affect my wits much, and I would ask if you really feel as though it is worth tasting for a newcomer such as myself, all while ensuring that you understand that I am extremely appreciative of your offer."

At this, Mr. Chaezka turned around, bottle still in hand, and said. "That is the wordiest reply I may have ever had while tending bar. I'll tell you that I think it tastes good. But you are inexperienced in alcohol, so you may still hate it. I still think you should try it, though. I won't be insulted if you don't like it, especially since you told me you appreciate the offer."

"I am curious about the taste enough to think about it, and, since you don't know me well, I'll tell you this is almost entirely a function of trusting you, based on hearing your story, which is not something I expected to occur at all this evening."

I also trusted the cocktail of antitoxins and preventative medicines running through my system, but he didn't have to know about that.

"I didn't expect you to be so interested, either. In fact, I thought that you were just going to walk in, bang bang, and that was it. As you can see from my attire and the twenty minutes I tried to use to sort my affairs, I knew this day was comin', based on the contract, but I didn't expect you to be so prompt. Three days after my thirty-sixth, and I don't expect I'll see the fourth."

"Unfortunately, you won't, but why don't we go and enjoy that gamble about which you were speaking?"

"Deal!" Mr. Chaezka belted, pumping his fist, and removing the stopper of the bottle. "And I tell you what. I'll pour one for me now and one for you that I'll let sit here, and you can drink it later if you want or don't and it'll be no skin off my back. Just for you if you want it."

"Deal."

We walked over to Mr. Chaezka's desk and the deck of cards he was shuffling earlier. The only things on it were the deck, an open case filled with poker chips, and a data pad.

"More than any other type of gambling, I always liked poker. People will tell you that you can tell everything about a person from how they play poker, but I've played enough and seen enough to know that that's bullshit. You can barely learn anything, but it's a lot of fun to see how people react in that situation. So . . . I was wonderin' if you would honor me with a game?" Mr. Chaezka asked, and I believed that was all he wanted.

"That's it? That's the gamble?" I replied, chuckling a bit.

"That's it! I know you're a busy person, so I can limit it to three hands if you like. I just want to get one last game in before I go."

"So you're one of those rare gamblers that can enjoy a game, even if there's nothing at stake for the other player? There is nothing at stake for me, correct?"

"Well, seeing as you could've killed me any time you were here, I figured you'd be wagering some of your time against the dwindling minutes I have left. That'll make it fun enough for me, and I imagine you could enjoy the game as well. I know they wouldn't send you if you weren't going to finish the job."

"I just want to see the famous gambler play! I certainly don't know as many games as you, so how about Texas Hold 'em?"

"Sure! It's the best one anyway," Mr. Chaezka said as he gave me the deck to inspect and deal. He slid a pile of chips, equal to his own, towards me and I took a seat, anteing to match the 10 percent worth of chips he put in for a friendly game before dealing the pocket.

He peered at his cards in a practiced fashion while I held mine up, not worrying about cameras behind me, for once. Jack and eight suited in clubs. I checked. He checked. I dealt out the flop.

"How was Candy?" He asked, diverting his attention from me for the first time since I entered.

"Candace is a loyal person, at least from what I can tell. She admires you greatly, and she feels indebted to you for the gamble you took for her sake."

The flop was a three of clubs, an eight of diamonds, and a king of clubs. I checked. He checked. I dealt the turn.

"Candy is the safest bet I ever made! I'm proud of the woman she has become. I had originally planned on leaving my entire company with her, but she refused. Said she would only feel comfortable watching over this place."

Four of clubs. I bet 10 percent of my chips.

"Your first-class hospitality has been appreciated. Do you feel as though you have achieved your goals? Most of the guests on the floor seemed hopeful, and I can't sense any foul play in any of the games you have."

"I think you've got it, kid. Fold. Most of my casinos have been operating the way I dreamed. There are always a few power struggles here and there at the ones I haven't visited in a while, but they shape up quickly when my senior members show up. The only trouble I ever had was from a hitman that was hired by the casino I won my capital from. Candy saw to that, though."

I gathered my chips, shuffled the deck, handed it to him, and put in my ante.

"I thought the Bureau had a No Kill Mandate on all of our Blanks. If you would have informed us of this earlier, we would have snuffed that establishment out."

"I thought about it, but I didn't want you all sniffing around any earlier than you needed to be. That was only three months after I made the choice. I took you all up on your offer to be able to gamble for quite some time, but, back then, I was still reckless. I took the fortune and I bet it on a couple of hands of 50,000 GC–a–hand blackjack. Beat the dealer's bust the first time after doubling down and blackjacked the second! It was the luckiest I ever felt. Now, The Rake brings in about a tenth of a percent of the NER government's revenue through our 30 percent 'dues.'"

He cracked a smile at this. Still no bargaining. No real grief, either.

I cut, and he anted and dealt the pocket. I had pocket nines, diamond and I can't remember the other suit. I raised the ante and he called.

"Given you found out the identity of those who hired the hitman, I could still file a reconciliation order if you give me a name."

The flop was a pair of twos and a queen. He checked. I checked.

"Candy made me swear that I would do just that if she ever got a sense that this could happen again, but most people don't try to violate NKMs. I don't need to sew any more death on my way out."

The turn was a seven. He bet the ante. I called. I was wary of a slow roll, but I had little to lose if I lost the hand.

"Are you enjoying the game?"

"Very much so. I wish I could have played with you more back when I was younger!"

He dealt the river. My old friend the Jack of clubs. He checked. I checked in case he happened to have a pocket two. He had two-pair at the showdown sevens and twos, and he laughed when I tossed my nines over his sevens.

"Risky business, there," he said, wincing.

"When in Rome, as they used to say."

I slid my chips over, slightly pleased that I was beating such a renowned gambler.

ComCom: Send: Reaper 6-2: 10-minute warning. EndCom

"Rome is a shithole these days. I was there three or so years back. Now that the Vatican sees less use and the rebellions destroyed so many of their architectural marvels, tourism has gone down the drain. A great deal of their lower class has migrated to Aria Bloc to the North East. So many monuments and churches destroyed." A conflicted look crept across his visage.

I dealt what would be our last pocket after he anted. His poker face was flawless. I had the three of hearts and a king of spades. I checked. He checked.

"I saw your crucifix earlier. Art thou a religious man?"

He emitted a weary grunt at this before replying. "My dad was one of the last real Christians. Devout, I mean. I've tried to be, but it's hard when you are away from the community so much."

He pulled his crucifix out and ran its chain through his fingers while he looked at the flop, which was a three of diamonds, a three of spades, and a ten of clubs. He only ever looked at his cards once, whereas I would check mine every once in a while, as if to ensure that my king hadn't vacated the throne to become a wandering joker. I bet twice the ante.

"People only believe in what they see these days, like on those things," he said, pointing derisively at my data pad. "But it's the things we can't see that'll matter the most in life . . . and in death. The times have changed. I loved the Old–world my grampy used to talk about and its old values, but I can't see much of those anymore. New world. New values. New god in machines."

He called like it was nothing. I became wary and went over the outs again.

"I'll divulge one thought to you that I can't seem to quiet."

"What's that, Collector?"

The turn was an ace of hearts. No flush potential. Security, to some degree, as I didn't think he had an ace. I bet twice the ante once again to scare him off. Another call. There was no flush potential, but there was straight potential. He had a few sensible outs, but his risk-loving personality made this estimation much more difficult.

"I expected more resistance from you."

"What? In the game? This is still anyone's hand!" He beamed.

"In the Collection," I replied, perplexed.

"Oh, but that is the essence of gambling," he said, looking directly at me. "If there is no risk, then there is no feeling of triumph. I wouldn't have had nearly as much fun all this time if there were no one to come and end it at some point. That's common sense. You've gambled before, and you don't even understand that?"

"This is one Hell of a gamble, though," I said, with consternation.

"That's right! It was one Hell of a gamble!" He crowed, ecstatically, his expression that of a salesman trying to convince me to buy in.

I guess that was the hallmark difference between us.

The last river he would ever see was a seven of diamonds, a useless, hopeless card that would be meaningless in the impending showdown.

I bet twice the ante one final time. He smiled and folded.

"That was fun!" He chirped, his face struggling to return to one full of expression as if the poker face he had worn for so long in his life was the more comfortable of the two.

"I'm glad you could enjoy one last game, but I expected to lose at least a hand. I suppose your luck is running out."

"Nah. I think it's stronger than ever, and I'm gonna need it. All of the gambling I have done in my life is nothing compared to the bet I've been trying to make . . . that I'm about to make," Mr. Chaezka replied, setting his crucifix on top of his fold and looking at me with what I truly hoped was an expression of prescient wisdom. A nigh-unbelievable faith, from my perspective. Still, there was hope some-where in my mind.

I knew he was ready. I walked over to him as he checked his suit one more time. As he settled himself in his desk chair, a beautiful wing–backed mahogany masterpiece upholstered with green leather, I showed him, already figuring his choice, my Einherjar Industries R–45 pistol in my right hand and an injection gauntlet with a newly spun-up syringe on my left. He pointed to my left, his face softening somewhat in relief.

"How do I look?" He asked as I inspected him for one last indication of resistance, paying extra attention to his extremities.

"Like 20,000 GC," I replied, as I shook his outstretched hand and punched the injection into his shoulder.

Mr. Chaezka's wide smile faded somewhat as he grew unconscious in seconds. He was dead two minutes and eighteen seconds later.

ComCom: Send: Reaper 6–2: "Collection confirmed." EndCom

I turned to leave and the glittering gold of Mr. Chaezka's crucifix caught my eye. I walked over to the desk, picked it up and ran its chain through my fingers. Then, I set it aside and looked at his hand. It was the three of clubs and the ten of diamonds. I found myself smirking uncontrollably.

I hope your last gamble pays off as handsomely as would have that hand.

I took a seat at Old Ma' and looked at the amber color of the drink Mr. Chaezka had poured me, as it rippled in response to my weight. I measured my curiosity, as I have so many times before, and relented. I nodded at the drink, admired the ambiance once more, almost sensing the chill of the waters of the mesopelagic benthic regions, swiveled off the stool and walked to the elevator.

Some things don't change with such facility, but you have given me hope.

2.

Interlude – The Post–Mechanized World

"Constant improvement in technology brings increasing prosperity to humanity."

This has been a resonant theme throughout history. Mr. Chaezka's fondness of the Old–world impacted me early on in my career and, as you can see in its twilight, reflection on this idea and its limitations still has as strong a hold as ever on my psyche.

Despite what I may have learned from my studies of ancient through postmodern through post-mechanized history, I remain skeptical of this theme, at least from a holistic standpoint. Perhaps this is due to my career requiring me to consistently wade through the afterbirth of these nascent improvements, but these words ring hollow in the same way as does the tune "history is written by the victors," a ring full of discordant exceptions. When one invents a paradigm–shifting technology, rarely are the first thoughts thereafter ones of caution related to the eventualities that will, one day, cause the suffering of many. I'd like to think that the nuclear weapons of the 1900s would be an exception to this idea, but I can't help but to think that many of their inventors were primarily holding images in their minds of the prosperity their own people might experience in the wake of the devastation they would wreak as they tinkered away in undisclosed locations, inventing the demise of others.

Should these ramblings that I feel compelled to write down in half-minded rebellion ever become a part of history in their own right, a history I hope to be at once more calculating and compassionate than its predecessors, I feel as though I would be remiss to continue recounting my selfish microcosms of experience without describing the World-state, albeit however briefly, should other counts of history be restricted.

As technology steadily improved throughout the 2000s, the consequences that had been put on the rear-searer during times of invention began to rear their ugly heads. I learned in my BoF training that the people of that time brushed off ideas like the earth's realistic carrying capacity, and global warming, and extinction of pollinators in order to continue pursuing their hedonistic lives. The prevailing rationale at the time was one of the majority of humanity mindlessly yielding to notions of instant gratification, as we have always been one of the more intemperate organisms. "It's not my problem," many would say. "I'll be dead before that happens . . ." the surreptitious thoughts of others. As one of the generations that remain to clean up the mess, my pleas for moderation will never reach the perpetrators of these problems, and it's quite possible they will be lost on the current generation as well.

The population surge associated with improvements in technology coupled with the compounding scarcity of resources plaguing our present era has made the disparity between the upper and the lower classes starker than ever. It's ironic to think that the only organizations that are radical enough to really address these matters are required to put a throttle on, arguably, our most precious resource, the lives of our fellow humans, and, while I happen to work for one such organization, I am still dissatisfied with the associated cost. I, too, am avaricious in that I want everything to work out for the best, and it is this greed that drove us to create all the marvels that are now ensuring incredibly fulfilling lives for many, but too many are born in hopes of having a chance at one of these lives. Until a few years ago, we, as a species, didn't have the mind to deny these aspirations. Really, I guess we still don't have the power to definitively deny a birth, but some governments of the blocs have pioneered a way to limit the longevity of one.

Providing you with a distillation of the slew of mechanical innovations of the 2100s that will exemplify the ideals of the times might be a useful exercise before I continue with my tales of the Bureau of Fortune and its affected.

Improvements in medical technology have allowed those of us with means to design our children for success at the genetic level. This has not been realized at quite the level imagined in the late 1900s, but a small amount of improvement coupled with a massive population has allowed those fortunate enough to dabble in the genetic composition of their offspring the ability to afford said offspring slight competitive advantages that might increase the likelihood of this child becoming the next gravball superstar, the next vid vixen, or the next scientist to invent such a polarizing technology as the one from which his or her allelic advantages were spawned. These chimeras, as they are often called in derogation, frequently endure bullying, perpetrated almost exclusively by the jealous have–nots, from a young age if they so happen to have a recognizable phenotype. However, most of these alterations go undetected until the situation from which their owner may benefit arises.

Of course, the procedures are prohibitively expensive for the majority of the population, but many will embrace their greed, the genes for which have yet to be isolated and may not even exist, and strive for a career that will allow them to make enough GCs to nudge their children's fates in a predetermined direction.

Parents of children with exceedingly rare and possibly lucrative novel genetic mutations are scouted a few weeks after birth and are offered a large sum of GCs in order to submit their child to the isolation process used to dedicate said gene to a genetic augmentation company. These GACs attempt to outcompete one another by adding the next exclusive gene that might be popular enough to begin a fad. Their advertisements can be found bannering the peripheries of myriad information spaces and their products are desperately sought after by celebrities who wish for another fifteen seconds of fame and their followers who would wish for a semblance of the same. Incidentally, my orphanage papers noted that I was a first-gen test subject of an iris coloration design experiment whose irises were tinged with lilac–pigment–producing cells, which were isolated from a person with a rare form of albinism. This footnote was the only information my irresponsible overseer saw fit to include in the receptacle in which I had been abandoned after verifying the success of the operation soon after my birth.

This tech, technically known as pIGD, or pre–Implantation Genetic Design, and amusingly referred to as "plastic surgery on steroids," demonstrates some of the prevailing sentiments of those on the cutting–edge of medical science at the time. General improvements to medical care have caused many diseases to go the way of smallpox, and the life expectancy for the average SWR—or South West Region of the Formerly–United States—bloc resident, the standard at the time, though not the average, to become a whopping ninety-two years for males and ninety-seven years for females. Lest you revere our abilities at the time you may be reading this, a universal "cure" for cancer remains elusive.

Late in the 2000s, the Retail Automation Program was well on its way to dominating most of the big box retailers of the time. When the self–service checkout machine was invented, it started off as somewhat of a novelty. For a few shoppers, it was convenient to buy a few items by quickly scanning them through and leaving so as not to have to wait in line behind someone with a cart full of items. But it turned out that people liked using these machines more and more over the years to the point that two machines became four, then a store would take out a few unused checkout lanes to make room for another two machines. Where those lanes would usually have to be manned by people during busy times for the store, now one attendant could man four or even eight machines depending on how adept he or she happened to be at swiping cards and touching screens.

As the general shopper became more and more familiar with these machines, fewer attendants were necessary to run a bank of machines and stores continued to drop checkout lanes for machines. Machines could serve more people and a store only had to pay for a machine once plus the electricity used to run it and occasional maintenance. Eventually, the industry proceeded to the point where it was cheaper to buy a new machine if it broke than it would be to hire, train, and pay a new cashier. The machines had no need for training as they were programmed and came that way upon delivery. Many stores began being designed from the ground up around the idea of the SSCM to the point where one could walk in and out of a store with one's desired items without ever taking out a form of payment or speaking to anyone. By 2080, almost every single store that had initially resisted the movement would only have a few checkout lanes manned by people, and those lanes had become the new novelty. Those grass roots have grown to the point that, these days, we can order almost anything we want from an e-market in a few seconds and a drone flies it over farm and field to us in less than a day.

Drone automation is popular enough to detail another of its applications, as the drone exemplifies the postmechanized world as the workhorse of industry, not unlike the drone ant in service of its queen. They are many, they are adaptable, and they are taken for granted.

Great strides have been made in the field of agricultural technology due to drone engineering. "Agridrone—Let us sew the seed, pluck the weed, and spread the feed. You just open the box!" was

the slogan of the idea initially and the inventors reaped a dispro-
portionate amount to the value of the innovation they had grown.
Agriculture has always been one of the cornerstones of civilization;
people working the land to produce enough on which to live and to
provide for others. Mechanization has always been about removing
people from the equation. Back in the day—an expression used to
fondly look back on simpler times—one or a couple of farmers used
to farm a few different crops. They would care for the land, watch
the skies for storms, sense when to plant and when to harvest, and
raise and process different forms of livestock. Now, the countryside
is awhiz with a new type of farmer that can till the soil, sew the seed,
water and fertilize, and they have sensors for things like temperature,
humidity, and wind speed.

The standard Agridrone does most of your fieldwork for you for
plant–based systems with the vanilla software. Operations can set
up automation for mowing, baling, raking, and almost every other
function you could desire. There are also automated operations for
livestock farms that will raise and slaughter any type of animal
for which you can program an execution, and it won't have second
thoughts when the animals look at them for the last time either. It's
efficiency in its most brutal sense. Furthermore, these inventions
have been coupled with regular drone shipping lines so whatever is
produced from "your" farm can be shipped automatically as well. In
essence, farmers have become like the SSCM attendants in stores in
that one farmer, who has taken a couple of classes in automative processes, can run the equivalent of eight farms from the Old–world and
keep all the profits. When automation turned this corner, the farmers that were quick-witted traded in their tractors for key interfaces
and invested in an Agridrone control room. It was not uncommon
to see new farmers or, occasionally, VCs moving around the countryside offering enormous amounts of GCs in hopes of buying as
many fields as possible. Farmers don't pace the fields much anymore.

Instead, they monitor their drone routes from data pads in whatever comfortable lodgings they choose.

If it is true that eras in technology can be distinguished by the forms of communication used by the masses, then we are certainly on the cusp of a new one. Ancient civilizations thought writing on clay tablets was a big deal in preserving knowledge through the ages. The invention of the telegraph and the subsequent telephone allowed us to communicate, on an unprecedented scale of distance, greetings to a friend or orders to a soldier. The invention of the cellular phone made business and pleasure communications easier to accomplish on the go in the hectic lives of those living around the turn of the twenty-first century. Then came the smartphone. This pocket–sized computing device is the only form of technology mentioned here that still exists as some semblance of itself in the current era.

Soon after its conception, the smartphone rounded out the list when one would name the basic necessities of life, that is to say if one happened to be of the millennial or later generations. Its power as a status symbol was such that it was not uncommon to see parents who were living well below the poverty line buying smartphones for their children so that they could go to school and show it to their friends in order to jump one more hurdle in the socialization competition.

It was estimated that, at the time, water and food were still plentiful enough within much of the world, and one could feed a child for a month on what was known as a "low–cost plan" at around the equivalent of 6 GC, or 300 "American dollars" as the preeminent currency of the time was known. The average "poor" child at the time could be clothed for less than 0.4 GCs a month if one were to shop at the thriftier venues. Many of these children, at least by first-world standards, could find some form of shelter on a periodic basis and worse yet is that one could see caretakers of these children talking away on smartphones on a bench under the eaves of a building somewhere in the city while their children shivered and complained of hunger at the feet of these so-called "guardians," who would rather chat in comfort than cook or clothe.

The cost of running a smartphone line at the time for an individual was estimated to be around 0.8 GCs a month. Needfull to say, one could have clothed a child to better ward off the cold for less than what one would pay for the difference between "smart" and regular phone service, most of which happened to be for the privilege to access the internet via an ever–growing selection of applications. If application use on phones was anything like the typical equivalent waste–of–thought internet–use applications of today, then these consumers were making horribly irresponsible choices in the preservation of the lives of their progeny.

Many of these forms of technology were initially created in order to bring us, as a people, closer together, but, somewhere along the spectrum, we advanced past the point of caring as much about the people behind the voices as the voices themselves. Our onphone, online personas rendered ourselves the simulacra. Unfortunately, these interactions that were initially deemed anomalous as a social bug that would eventually be repaired along with their encoded counterparts in the iteration of the device known as the "smart" phone were only left to swarm and bring about a plague over the following decades that would serve to exacerbate other precursors to social reclusivity. Now, genuine, face-to-face interlocution is a rarity due to the ubiquity of digital displays, but one that I seek through my career, to a degree. The typical resident of the world finds interpersonal interaction stressful without the aid of the social filter that is the screen. Phones and their human wielders were becoming inseparable and now their equivalent can literally be found within us. Our dependency on these devices will prove deleterious one day, but, much like non-technological cancer, their lurking dangers may not be discovered until too late.

The hallmark communication technology of our emerging

technological age is one that makes the smartphone appear quite dumb by comparison. While the initial trappings of what would eventually become the smartphone were compiled in the now–silicon–less valley of the SWR, it was their erstwhile competitors in a place known as South Korea that pioneered the tech and Japan, now Shin–Japan, which eventually appropriated the tech, along with its country of origin. To the standard consumer, it is a cellular device, now intertwined with one's actual cells, that allows one immediate messaging to another, akin to a phone. Routed through a data pad, it can also be used to control most of the devices you might employ in your household or place of work that run on compatible receivers. To the military consumer, it is an all–in–one communications package. The Complete Communications Company is proud to present the ComCom. Its mascot is adorable, its processor is powerful, and its consumer is insatiable.

The ComCom is a neural implant that was only made possible after advances in artificial limbs had arrived at the long–sought pinnacle of their development. Drawing on the funding of military amputee research groups the world over provided by companies looking to jump on the PR bandwagon, neuroengineers arrived at a breakthrough in the chemi–electrical mapping of synapses between traditional computing circuits and those of the human body. We still have yet to achieve perfect integration in a number of applications, but people who have lost limbs and have clean amputations can now receive installations of artificial limbs that are at least representative in function to the original limb and, in some ways, superior. The superiority of these functions in the initial states of testing intrigued other labs that began researching cybercellular improvements, but these labs were quickly rebuffed by a transnational mandate that required many of these operations to be shut down. As the years went by, much like the inception, restriction, and progression of stem cell research, regulations slackened greatly. These labs were undeniably relocated to military black sites as evidenced by a number of cyber-ceullularly-enhanced soldiers showing up about six years later in the Bengali Federation's annexation of Cambodia. These modifications are quickly becoming the newest competitive edge for military and paramilitary troops. Civilians have access to a number of operations, at next-to-prohibitive costs, pending licenses, for a few cybercellular enhancements besides limb replacements and augmentations. The ComCom is one of the best-selling and least-restricted devices available to the public.

In an operation that takes less than two hours to complete, the cost of which varies based on your choice of installer, the 24 GC implant is set just behind your ear of choice for easy access replacement of its battery, the lifespan of which is about eight years. Then, after mapping of your neural pathways is completed at a surcharge, the circuitry is interwoven with the neurons you utilize for speaking, listening, and comprehension.

The mandatory training to be logged in advance of the operation for your permit on ComCom Command is tested immediately upon waking up in a specialized environment. In order to work a ComCom, you must master a form of split-thinking where you are only attempting to give commands to your ComCom as opposed to your friend, or your body, or any other entity. This split-thinking only needs to be mastered while you are awake, as ComComs are programmed to enter a dormant state as you sleep. During your training, you are brought into a facility that looks a lot like a pet shelter, albeit with soundproof cages for the dogs. All of the dogs that are present have been rescued from their environments, although some facilities have been closed down due to allegations of the "rescuing" occurring from illegitimate sectors, such as little Aisla's room in unit 5E. These dogs are then all conditioned to help train you to become a worthy ComCom owner. Every dog is named ComCom and every dog will respond to your basic dog-friendly commands. They can't message Jormy about what you want for dinner, but they can sit. You are trained to speak with the dogs only in a commanding tone, as that is exactly what you will do when thinking your ComCom through its functions. If you pass, you are issued a provisional license, and you qualify for a ComCom operation.

Unlike the dogs, you can name your ComCom anything you like during its calibration period, although you are strongly cautioned to name it something unique. If you happen to want to be friends with someone of the same name as your ComCom after your calibration has finished, you either have to change your ComCom name, change your friend, or never deviate from the nickname you give said friend. People in upper–class social circles often have numerous nicknames if their regular name happens to be common due to this conflict. Horror stories abound regarding people who chose to name their ComCom "Jon" in the alpha stages of clinical trials, one of which had some of his neural pathways fried due to poor responses when the implant overloaded during a session in which the test subject told his coworker, presumably named Jon, "go fuck yourself!"

Security and impulse control software updates have tightened since then, but we are really only just out of the beta phase of the production and issues turn up every month or so. There are even dedicated groups of ill–advised, aristocratic adolescents that stream their attempts at finding glitches in the software and the "humorous" results that follow. *Only* three of the top five streaming groups have had members die during testing!

From a paramilitary standpoint, the ComCom is vital to staying in contact with one's organization. MilSpec ComComs allow the user access to all forms of radio wave communication and are even rumored to be powerful enough for laser–based communications, but that has not yet been released. However, and with whomever you want to communicate, the ComCom finds a way. For each form of contact, you must know the identity of the terminal to which you are trying to connect, whether that be another agent or the biometric security system on a vault. Negotiating security is the hard part, which requires authentication before contact in order to transmit. The typical user needs to give an ID number to someone before contact can be made between said terminal and a ComCom, similar to a phone number.

A few military entities, and the Bureau, have developed a parser technology that tracks these authentication codes along with some form of identification information within tens of kilometers of where the parser is mounted allowing the agents of said organization a leg up in "data acquisition assaults," or hacking, in laymen's terms, if they can get in close to the target. When this information released to the public, spending on personal anti–ID–acquisition security suites increased exponentially. They aren't nearly as good as they are marketed to be and nearly 99.9 percent of those purchasing the suites will never be targeted anyway. It is the greatest racket industry of which I can think, but I guess those buying are investing in mental security more than anything else.

The Bureau condones minor interdepartmental hacks on April Fool's day as an exercise to increase morale, although if you go too far you are blacklisted. One of my co–Collectors hacked my auto-vac system in my unit and programmed it to suck the sheets off my bed. In playful revenge, I hacked his third-party music filter on his ComCom to play one of the more awful songs I could find on his playlist for three cycles while fixing his cochlear attenuation setting at an uncomfortable volume. Apparently, others thought this was an inappropriate response in terms of magnitude.

ComCom chatter on certain channels is almost unceasing in the Bureau to the point that I have been reprimanded in my work occasionally for being "cavalier in ComCom etiquette." When I am on–mission, I try to tune out most ComCom communiqués to the point that I only interact on direct commands from a handler or when giving status updates myself. Fortunately, my record is one that conveyed professionalism from the early stages of training, so the flak I receive from other Collectors on this issue is usually quelled by my performance marks in my mission completion rating, a form of gamification devised by the Bureau to improve performance of the Collectors through competition. The benefits I accrue through my target acquiescence scores far outweigh the marks I lose through "ComCom autism," a more-or-less fitting accusation levied against me by a certain Collector on a mission involving a hostage negotiation in which I forcibly overruled his attempt of remote negotiating through me. Call me Old world–fashioned, but I prefer to conduct most of my conversations in person, where possible.

The _____ of Fortune program originated as a system to offer the prosperity produced by these technological advances to anyone at a price. People wanted to experience the incredible lives enriched by another technological renaissance, but the insatiable greed of people coupled with the hope that one's children might be able to experience even better lives has effectively bottlenecked the human species. Only so many of us can fit through the opening, and the size of the bottle itself is created by a comparatively few ultra–rich and, undoubtedly, ultra–greedy individuals.

This program, run by the Bureau of Fortune, or BoF for short, was initially conceived as an austere attempt at a checks and balances system for the burgeoning population, the dwindling resources, and the inexorable mechanization that were, just before the turn of the twenty-second century, threatening the overall quality of an average human life in many parts of the world. It was first enacted by the ChinoSoviet economic bloc with reported successes of increasing the overall quality of a comrade's life. This improvement was quantified by government–tallied social surveys that use an index to rate perceived happiness of the individual six months into the program compared to happiness before joining with the knowledge that their

lives were, essentially, just cut in half. Within the first year, approximately 9 percent of the eligible population of the bloc elected to par-
ticipate in the program, which could have been inflated somewhat
compared to the percentage of non–communist–ruled participants
that might join up in future BoF–affiliated regions. After CS bloc
advertising firms worked on promoting the program throughout
the inaugural year, the participation rate increased from 9 percent
to 14 percent in year two. Their published eligible population range
was from sixteen years old to thirty-six years old with termination
of life set for around forty years of age. With the world following
the progress of the program into year three, the participation rate
climbed to 19 percent of eligible participants and this percentage
held into year four.

"Fill the blank with any dream you want to become reality!"
While the slogan of the program wasn't particularly snappy, it spread
like wildfire across the Asian continent. Soon, the neighboring
inhabitants of the Bengali Federation were clambering up the steps
of Parliament in Mumbai to beg the candidates running for prime
minister to consider including a proposal for the formation of a BoF
in their platforms. The candidate who won at the time garnered
the swing votes necessary to do so on exactly this proposal. Three
months later, a BoF was granting wishes to 15 percent of the nation's
eighteen-year-olds, as the new range of eligibility set forth with the
government's tentative trial period was that one could seek a fortune
starting as early as eighteen years old and up to age thirty–six, with
termination of life set for around thirty–six years of age. Fast–forward five years from then and Neuva Amazonia, the United Kingdom,
and all three American Regions had incorporated a BoF into their
governments. Notable holdouts at the time were the Canadian and
Oceanic blocs. Apparently, Bureaus offered a freedom of choice that
people around the world sought as an escape from mediocrity.

I am most familiar with the NER's BoF, given it is my formal

Bureau of employment, and so I'll continue to elucidate the machinations of a Bureau through this biased lens.

As mechanization continued revolutionizing global economies, neighboring countries with good trade relations began unifying on a level unseen since the colonization of the British Empire in order to better regulate and improve the integration of a mechanized society. A standard currency, the General Credit, was proposed at this time by the newly sovereign German bloc, to make these unifications easier for the affected populace. The proposal was accepted across the globe and the German bloc was elected to create and maintain the infrastructure for its regulation. Some countries such as China and the former Soviet Union fragments unified due to similar governmental values, countries in Central America unified under this guise as well but then fell apart due to cartel squabbles, and the United States split into three, relatively autonomous regions.

The tradeoff for mechanizing a region, given it had to be heavily regulated by the government, was that all companies running on a mechanized platform based on machine–to–person job displacement ratios had to yield between 16 to 20 percent of their increase in net profits to the government responsible for regulating the business in question. Ten to 12 percent of these taxes would go directly to BoFs if they happened to be present in the governmental structure. However, this heavy tax did not make most CEOs think twice about mechanizing, as the estimated increase to net profits for a "humanely mechanized company" was around 31 percent, meaning a company mechanized under these constraints would stand to gain at least an 11 percent growth when all was said and done. Funding from this and other taxes are some of the means by which the Bureaus can continue to operate.

Initially, around 60 percent of mechanized regions had BoFs. After the above–mentioned laws were passed by the UK's Department of Mechanization, they were incorporated by almost all mechanized regions worldwide and the outcry for BoF inclusion reached fever pitch to the point that only 1.5 percent of mechanized regions in the world do not yield taxes that go directly to a BoF. If mechanization was the new industrial world order, then the multitude of soon-to-be-displaced citizens decided they would rather have a Bureau around than not. These taxes alone are sufficient to grant fortunes to more than 1.7 times the normal population of fortune–seekers of BoF–affiliated regions. To give an idea of this in the NER, the current normal population of fortune seekers has stabilized to include around 16 percent of the people who turn eighteen each year, which has remained remarkably constant through the twenty-one years since the NER approved a BoF. The rest of the normal population is not usually tracked as rigorously, as the number of eighteen-year-olds that sign up each year dwarfs the total number of all other ages combined in the eligible age range of eighteen to thirty-six. Analysts of the program say that the response they receive the most on surveys at the time of application as to why eighteen-year-olds choose to sign up as soon as possible, some going so far as to sign up on their birthdays before celebrating with friends and family, is that they want to "get their full money's worth," although really they should be substituting "life's" for "money's" as that is the currency with which they are paying.

These days, with how competitive jobs that are carried out by "flesh-workers," as is the sardonic term employed for the non–mechanized worker by the youth, have become due to the sheer number of competitors, tracking for jobs occurs even before secondary school. Very few college programs exist as they did in the early 2000s now that much of the material once taught in lecture halls and laboratories is consumed via data pad by kids as they microwave their dinners. Gone are the days where one could enter a university without having decided a major as you should have that down by freshman year of secondary or you will be engaging in an expensive waste of time. An applicant to med school should have volunteered in a hospital since age twelve and should have research completed, ideally in technological applications of medical sciences, by age eighteen, before attending a two–year undergraduate feeder program specifically catered to medical science programs. For want of classes in patient care, many of the MDs spit out from these programs these days are nigh indistinguishable from the machines with which they work. The realm of business is an even colder mistress and one who holds very few degrees.

After examining these conditions in my time, it's no wonder that the government of the NER condones offering the _____ of Fortune program at such a young age. To compete in these working conditions, one must attain mental adulthood at the same time as the onset of its sexual counterpart. An unpublished reason as to why the Bureau keeps the approximate termination of life window at thirty-six years old is because of the resultant delay in the biological goal of said maturity. Due to increased effectiveness, education, and regulation of birth control, the average age at which women bear children has increased to thirty-seven years old, worldwide.

If predictions are to be believed, the alleviation of the challenges the _____ of Fortune Program was designed to check will become apparent as early as 2180. This is the estimated time that the population of the world should dip below its carrying capacity, given Bureaus aren't shut down, among a number of other factors.

Fortunes can be awarded to any human person that: desires one, can give an estimate of the amount desired and the general purpose for acquiring said fortune, isn't already above the luxury line set by the government, and can pass the psych eval. The psych screening consists of a regular medical exam, paid for by the applicant out of pocket, as well as a full psychiatric evaluation that is used to render candidates that might negatively affect the Bureau either physically or relationally with the public ineligible. This form of processing has decreased the likelihood of individuals acquiring fortunes that could eventually be used for something deemed particularly unsightly in the public's eye, such as purchasing weapons for mass murder while initially seeking the fortune under pretenses as mundane as "shopping." While the resulting loss of life in these circumstances would fulfill the ultimate goal of the Bureau quicker than might buying a thousand cute new pairs of boots, the Bureau wouldn't last long if its image were frequently tarnished through events that might work to dispel its aura of control. The killing that the Bureau accomplishes is sophisticated, personalized, orchestrated, even, not garish and wanton. We have a reputation to keep, after all.

After learning a bit more about the World–state, you might be curious as to why I chose to work for the Bureau. I suppose I can provide this answer now, in hopes that you won't think less of me for it, but the answer to Candace's question will have to wait some time yet. I am still ruminating on that quandary even as I collate these thoughts.

Honestly, if I think back to the very beginning, I believe the main reason I became a Collector was out of a sense of disenchantment with what the world had become. I was raised on romantic stories of what life used to be like a century ago. Resources were still plentiful. Many of those who wanted for something wanted for a paltry amount of that something compared to today. Monarch butterflies used to wend their way across the States on their annual migration en masse before deforestation rendered them functionally extinct. There was space enough for all. Technology hadn't yet bred the perverted arrogance instilled in every child upon registration of the service to his or her data pad. People used to talk face to face, frequently, about all sorts of topics. Society was more genuine. These stories poisoned me against my own generation and literally doomed a select few of those that came before and many more that followed.

I was lost. My voice was drowned in the cacophony of my peers.

My thoughts were stifled, and the embers of my dreams were smothered. As I turned eighteen and thought about making the choice to seek a fortune in order to attempt to attain some semblance of fulfillment, some quality that might set me apart from the masses, only a few thoughts remained in my mind about my future. The two that surfaced from the quagmire of my consciousness, slowly extricating themselves from the morass of immature uncertainty, as an agent from the Bureau approached me with what she purported to be a "unique opportunity," really one of 16,200 offered to others in the NER that year, were: "I wish we could turn back the time of the biological clock so that fewer people could exist to enjoy greater prosperity," and "I wish I could have more meaningful conversations with people." I had no sense of purpose, and I had hope that conversations with a few people of quality, yet another resource in which I found our society deficient, could inspire one within me.

After Collector H 24K06 approached me before my equivalent of a secondary school graduation and convinced me to take the Bureau of Fortune Aptitude Battery, or BFAB, as the culmination of two year's worth of covert, on–again–off–again scouting, and as a favor to repay her for treating me to, admittedly, the greatest gustatory experience I could ever hope to derive from grilled meat, I was assessed to be an "exceptionally qualified" candidate for the Collector division of the Bureau. H 24K06, or Seeker 06, as was her call sign, must have thought she gave one hell of a pitch when I immediately told her I would enroll in the Collector Program upon her conclusion of the list of perks associated with working for the Bureau as a Collector. In truth, it wasn't a hard sell. I knew from screen three of the BFAB that it would be worth a shot. This screen displayed the Bureau's mission statement: "To offer opportunity to all, regardless of socioeconomic background, to pursue dreams on an accelerated timeline."

While this mission might appear, at first glance, to be a support for people who would otherwise be unable to live out their most sought-after aspirations, given their current lot in life, I saw it as something more. I realized this statement was a parallel to the former of my two salient thoughts around the time of my recruitment, only bereft of a romantic wish. While the biological clock of humanity would keep on ticking, as ever, this solution would propose an alternate face to the clock. One with fewer numbers, fewer rotations, and fewer minutes one might live. One might experience more prosperity, but will fade out of existence sooner than initially thought as a consequence. This, in turn, may leave space for others to flourish as flowers rather than as weeds. These others would be less numerous, but more beautiful. A morbid thought, I know, but this is the chain of causality that enslaved my cogitations. It revitalized a hope that I had thought long dead, namely: that while I may not be able to experience the prosperity of the tales on which I was raised, nor might my possible daughter, nor might my possible daughter's daughter, perhaps, one day, one of my line might be so lucky.

While most people who are scouted for Collector candidacy join because of the perks—chief of which is access to something akin to a fortune, replete with a number of conditions, while still being able to live out a normal lifespan without fear of Collection for yourself—I believe the reason I joined was because the unlikely chance to be able to further one of those two thoughts, or fervent wishes, really, was too tantalizing to repudiate. The reason I remained in the employ of the Bureau was due to the fulfillment of the latter of these two wishes, which precipitated as the product of a chance thought to be even less likely to bear fruit, as a result of a gamble, if you will. My first Collection, the sole spin of the wheel on which I would judge whether or not this "career" would be a calling as opposed to just a culling, happened to be with a man who convinced me that genuine conversation was not just a thing of the past, of legend, and it continues to serve as the closest thing to an act of God, or divine intervention, or astronomical convergence that I might ever witness. The reason I have continued my work as a Collector is that, more than any other time, you will find that genuine, meaningful conversation can exist just before the existence of one of those conversing is about to cease.

3

0012 – The Escapist

I shifted in the front seat of the Bureau car in order to stretch out my shoulders as the seat back contorted from lounge mode to default around me. Dropping the window tint in order to take in the spectacular view of the skyscraper trees on the second floor and above balconies cascading out from the high-rises, like the eaves of a willow, over the streets of Kyoto, I waved to an elderly lady who was enjoying the sunset in her massage chair that barely fit within one such enclosure and was surprised to see that she waved back. The last time I attempted such a greeting, I was met with a glare that evoked every possible crease around the glarer's eyes to form an expression that conveyed unmistakable contempt. A few units later, a boy paused for a second after catching a baseball to jump up and down to get my attention. I inclined my head to acknowledge him, and he laughed and acted like he was going to hurl the ball at me, pulled back at the last second, and then threw the ball over the car to a girl standing on the balcony across the way. I gave him my best imitation pout, and he laughed hard enough to miss the ball on the return throw, which struck him in the thigh, rolled off the balcony, and triggered a low-frequency ping in the car's proximity warning suite. Unfortunately, I couldn't afford to compromise my position to toss it back to him, but I thought about it.

After getting sick of the autobrake kicking in every two seconds due to the higher-than-forecasted vehicle density on the thoroughfare, I ordered the car to parallel park on the closest sidewalk using a nearby planter in place of another vehicle as the guide.

Incoming transmission from Orbit 3–9, tagged handling, receive?

ComCom: receive last

"We saw that you engaged a manual–park command in your car approximately .97 kilometers from your planned drop point. Everything okay?"

ComCom: Send: "All good. Jaunty traffic is annoying me, so I'll walk the rest of the way following the same directions as the car." PendCom

"Acknowledged. Routing a sniper drone wing to provide overwatch. Paint as you please."

ComCom: Send: "Appreciated, but most likely unnecessary. I'll re–ping on Collection." EndCom

My HUD accommodated for the glare from the reddening sun reflecting off a nearby fountain as the car doors swung open, and I kicked aside a few soda cans before approving the return route for the car on my data pad. Walking in the bike lane to avoid the bustling crowds coming out of some of the area's best dining venues, I couldn't help being pulled on to the curb for a few seconds in pursuit of an enticing scent of what seemed to be authentic eel sliders. Glimpsing the name of the offending establishment, I executed a few taps on my data pad to place an order for carry out to be ready in forty-five minutes and felt my forearm vibrate with the payment confirmation.

I tried to tune into my surroundings a bit more after closing the notification of my drone escort arrival. Guardians were ushering their kids inside as the sun slipped over the crests of the buildings in order to obey curfew, and foot traffic was decreasing a bit as well as salarymen stumbled through the doors of their regular bars to avoid their familial and other obligations just a little longer. This part of town was historically a red-light district dating back to the ninth century, and its premodern roots of pleasure have taken hold and blossomed into a beautiful concrete forest of hypermodern bliss of all kinds. The area has a reputation of doing everything to the extreme. Food, drink, play, and pleasure. This fact is known only to me by way of the statement furnished by the dossier of my Collectee, which touted his establishment as the preeminent purveyor of the pornographic experience and claimed that it was important for him to be at the center of the district for historical inspiration.

The right portion of my left forearm vibrated to direct me around the final turn on the approach to the Takamagahara. In Japanese folklore, Takamagahara was said to be the lofty dwelling of the gods, reachable only by a floating bridge. I was both amused and disenchanted when I arrived at the entrance to my destination to find it no more than a staircase with a sign flashing the name of the club and a down arrow in alternating pink and yellow neon text. Furthermore, I was sure that when I entered, I would only see one god exalted in idolization, and that one born of human lust for the flesh rather than the graces of the divine. There was a preponderance of people lining up on the staircase in hopes of gaining admission to these holy grounds. Pardoning my way through these devotees, I met with little resistance. Once a Collector is identified by a sea of people a power is bestowed upon them, not unlike the power granted to Moses, although a Collector doesn't usually have to lift a hand to part the sea. Unlike Moses, I was not leading a people from a plagued to a promised land; I was taking a promised person from a land he had plagued. Not only did the masses on the stairs press themselves against the wall to avoid my person, but, by the time I clomped down the last step, there was only one person left in the well.

"I'm afraid I am bad for business," I said to the bouncer with a helpless shrug of my shoulders. "You can be going now if you would like."

The henchman-of-sorts displayed a fleeting sense of loyalty by thinking it over as his eyes turned down to the corner of the table next to him and the stun baton taped to its underside that my sniper drones had already flagged on my threat detection software. And then he walked around me, giving me as much room as possible and never taking his eyes off of my left hand, and, by the sound of his footsteps, ran up the stairs.

"I assume the door is unlocked?!" I yelled after him before turning around, disappointed at the lack of hospitality.

I gingerly pushed the old, hinged door open and immediately began to see why the place was known as the Garden of Hedon. It was beautiful, despite the lurking depravity. Unfortunately, the dedication to ancient Japanese design extended only to the architecture, landscaping, and lighting, and not to the people milling about. Only the greeters at the desk for checking out equipment and authenticating to a room were clad in the traditional garments and effects of geisha. Patrons could easily be distinguished by the VR interfaces they were carrying or, sometimes, already wearing, from the registration desk to their rooms on either side of a meandering stream over which bridges had been built and lit by not red, but purple lanterns.

From what I had read on the briefing, only the foyer area in which I was standing was actually decorated in this traditional manner. Once one exited to the outer hallways flanked with rooms, one was "hosted" in a space that was barely larger than a roomy bathroom. Obviously, one could pay for the deluxe package that allowed ample room for moving around during the planned activities, in which case you got a room the size of a standard unit kitchen. All of the rooms were equipped with the same standard mattress, with fitted sheet, cushioned chair, and table. Everything else requested to play part in the festivities had to be carted in by attendants, including the modified androanes of various masses and configurations. The trappings of the rooms themselves were relatively meager, but the experience was enriched by whichever VR parameters you selected. The architect designed the rooms to come in only two sizes and two floor plans so that the VR set could map whatever fantasy you chose to inhabit to the space provided.

I strolled up to the registration desk to start my adventure. One of the attendants saw my uniform and complimented me on my attention to detail.

"Wow! I've only seen a Collector in real life a couple of times, but your outfit looks just like one! The overcoat is the same length, you made a Bureau hologo replica, which must've been hard with all the computer stuff to make it, and you even have an injection gauntlet! But you're not wearing the hat! Oh well. It's still pretty convincing! So, you are obviously doing a Collector/Collectee fantasy, but what room are you in? Can I get a reg number from you?"

At this point, I was mulling over whether I thought this exchange was humorous or not as I looked at the other attendant, who was pulling on the cuff of the one who had just been "taking care of me." I smiled at her a little uncomfortably, and she whispered into her coworker's ear and, I assume, told her to go in back for a second because that's just what she did. I admired the bow on the first attendant's sash as she turned around to leave, which was adorned with branches blooming with white cherry blossoms on a sky-blue background. It was a perfect bow.

"Did you tie that for her?" I asked, stifling a laugh.

"No. She actually took care of that part herself." My capable new attendant replied, with a grin that faded all too quickly. "I know you are the real thing, since I've seen one of you do your work before."

"I'm sorry you have had to go through that. Usually, we try to be circumspect in our Collections, but I know too many of us don't care who may be watching. Was the collected close to you?"

"Friend's stepdad, but not really. I know you aren't here for our craft, so what can I do for you?"

"All you need do is point me in the direction of your proprietor. Hopefully, I'll be done in no more than half an hour, and you can carry on with your day."

"Good for me, I guess. I've been lookin' for a reason to leave this place, and this is as good as any. I imagine you can guess where he might be."

"Assuming it is really as simple as you think, then I'd guess somewhere in the palace looming over those walls in back."

"You got it." The young woman sighed. "He's not really smart or motivated enough to hide himself anyway. I'll unlock the door to the gate in the wall in a bit, you go through that, then you walk around to the back of the palace, go up the stairs there. The code to the door pad is 6969 . . . actually. He'll have one to three bodyguards in there and, possibly, up to three-ish androns. The bodyguards are armed."

"You have been exceptionally cooperative for someone who is about to possibly have her place of work shut down. Do you bear him ill will? Has he mistreated you?"

"Nope, but he made the choice." She inflected matter-of-factly. "Plus, I've only been working here because it was one of the first jobs I could find to pay the bills, and I have been too complacent to try for something else."

"What are some of the other things you have thought about doing?" I asked, curious, but also knowing she saved me a lot of time through her concise instructions. "Maybe I could help you out . . ."

"Kate," she gestured back at the curtains behind her, "and I have thought about working on the human relations side of e-banking, but we have never had the slick look that a lot of those companies are looking for."

"You two seem like a good team or, at least, you could carry her on the way to becoming a good team." I looked up a couple of e-banking firms in the area on my data pad to find only two that had customer service position vacancies. "It's kind of a boring job, you know, you two would basically be mascots to try to pull in new customers."

ComCom: Send: Orbit 3-9: "Request for closest data pad hack authentication for mission data acquisition" PendCom

"That kind of job makes Kate happy. She loves people, even though she can be a bit naïve, and Kate being happy makes me happy."

"Authentication code for that terminal is SV56Q62"

ComCom: Send: "Thanks, Orbit" EndCom

"I've just sent information to your data pad about a place to which you and Kate should apply. Do it while I am still here since you won't be getting any business," I tossed a portable beacon that emits the Bureau's flipping coin hologo used to warn people of a Collection in progress over by the door at this point, "for the rest of the day anyway. I have a connection there. Can you tell me your first and last and Kate's last name?"

"Huh. Will do . . . I'm Mara Andersson and Kate's last name is Elsinger. I'll go get that gate for you now . . . and thanks, I guess?" She said, looking back over her shoulder as she ducked behind the curtain.

I decided to take another look through the foyer as I made my way to the gate, because a tenth of this Mikail Zilnich's fortune must have gone into the attention to the detail paid to its construction. The ceiling and upper walls of the area were composed of a single molded LCD on which a harvest moon illuminated a sky teeming with stars and gnats. A few clouds could be seen rolling by now and again and the sounds of cicadas and the crackling of torches lulled people further into the illusion. Since I had arrived, the sun had set, and the pink and orange skies of the country with them. I walked along the pathway made of pounded dirt in between what must have been the furrows of a cart that were traced indelibly along the winding way. They were too precise to cause me to worry about the possibility of impeding merchants who might be bringing goods to the castle in the background, though I did wonder if someone would eventually come and whisk away my footprints. The scent of cherry blossom permeated the air with a tinge of decaying leaves, which disappointed me slightly as a research oversight. The weeping willows, Japanese maples, and katsura that were interspersed according to a pattern of Feng Shui were petrified at the peak brilliance of their fall senescence. The cherry blossoms that were more numerous around the bridges were displaying their pink and white petals, some of which were actually programmed to fall, fluttering to the ground below. The overall contrast between the two was impossibly brilliant. I strolled over to a katsura to admire the bark, and I was able to smell a hint of caramel emanating from the ridges cut into the wood. At least he nailed that part. Realizing I had no estimate of what it cost to make one of these fake trees, I tried to commit the question to memory so I might ask it in conversation later. Then, I strolled back out of fall and into spring without ever feeling the bite of the winter chill in order to run my hand along the banister of one of the footbridges.

The wooden footbridges were painted red, and they must have been finished with a hand brush in order to fit the environment. The flaking of the paint here and there was a charming touch as well. The *thunk* sounds of my footsteps gave way to the trickle of the stream and the sharper *thok* of a shishi-odoshi as I leaned over one of the banisters to scrutinize the koi swimming below. Their colors ranged from white to black to orange, speckled and splotched, and a few solid gold. Their swimming pattern was irregular enough to warrant further testing, so I leaned down and stretched my left arm through the railings and extended my index finger into the water. No change. I began to trace around in an infinite pattern. Still nothing. Growing dissatisfied, I immersed my arm, past the data pad, and began splashing it around vigorously. I had never felt so ignored. There was only one more test I could conduct. I walked over to one of the stands that provided complimentary, traditional festival foods and asked for some dango, with the sauce, as they had no other option. I crested the bridge once more, pinched off a piece of one of the dumplings, surveyed my surroundings to make sure no one but the cameras would be watching, and lofted it into the largest aggregation of the creatures, hoping to witness the long–awaited melee of motion, but, alas, to no avail. I had never seen koi turn down food, or bits of paper masquerading as food, or dirt. They are gluttonous creatures, almost as much as the clientele that were keeping their distance from my childish attempts at science. A silver lining in all this came by way of an abbreviated laugh I thought I detected coming from behind the gate to the castle, which would have been a welcomed demonstration of mirth from the rather demure Mara Andersson.

The last sight I beheld on my trek through the Kyoto mountainside was the castle. It was a stunning edifice built almost entirely of wood, after the traditional fashion. A quick scan from my data pad revealed that it was modeled after the main keep of Matsumoto Castle, which resided in what was historic Nagano Prefecture as opposed to Kyoto Prefecture. Comparing the dimensions revealed that the scale was approximately 1:5, which was decently impressive, all things considered, but that ratio only held true for the exterior.

Walking up to the recently unlocked gate in the stone wall preceding the castle, I wrestled with whether or not I appreciated the collection of inconsistencies present in this depiction of a "historically accurate" red light district and about whether or not the typical patron noticed or cared. I felt a tinge of sadness at the fact that most of the people present on a regular basis might only appreciate the attempted dedication once in a fleeting state of awareness before their senses would be overloaded with the less-subtle locales of the anticipated VR experience. There was a bitter sense of longing about the design that forced me to recall my experiences with my first Collection, and I could tell, before ever meeting Mr. Zilnich, that he wished to leave the world above ground behind.

Incoming transmission from D, receive?

ComCom: receive last

"Heya, I saw you were on-mission, but I was wondering if we were still on for tonight?"

ComCom: Send: "I heard you were in the area as well, so I ordered dinner, pick up twenty-five minutes or so from now. I could drone over fifteen minutes later?" PendCom

"Don't worry about it. I finished early. I'm on the Shinkansen to get away from the collar for a bit, headed to you."

ComCom: Send: "I'll send you an address to a nice rooftop place of which I know. Meet there?" PendCom

"So, by order, I bet you won't be treating me to steak, huh?"

ComCom: Send: "Regretfully, no. However, I'll try to expose you to more of the cultural cuisine of the area. Kyoto is lovely this time of year, and you'd be missing out if we had American everywhere." PendCom

"Mmmmmhm. They do drinks there?"

ComCom: Send: "They do. It's most of what they do, so they're amenable to outside food." PendCom

"Sounds like a good time! See ya'!"

ComCom: Send: "Until then" EndCom

I tossed an imisphere over the wall, activated it, scrolled it around the perimeter and saw nothing worrisome on my data pad. Checking the area for electrical current higher than background turned up nothing as well. I nudged the gate open slowly, peered around it, hand on my EinIn, proceeded through, closed the gate, and recovered my imisphere, reanchoring it on a polarity pad on my left thigh. Following Mara's instructions, I walked around back to see the proposed entry stairway. Ascending the wooden stairs while attempting not to make them creak as much as possible, out of habit, I noticed that this part of the castle was not kept up nearly as well as the rest of it. Gouges in the wall had gone unrepaired and a blemish from the residue of some kind of orange fluid had yet to be covered up. I took the skewer from the dango I had eaten and threw it into the combustible waste receptacle, the only one I had seen in the area, near the padlocked door, next to which were a number of carelessly mislaid candy wrappers. Punching in the entry code, I marveled at how juvenile this man must have been at age thirty–six. Still, I was looking forward to the conversation we would have, as ever.

Inside, I noticed three pairs of shoes in a container by the door. I repressed an inkling to follow the custom and remove my own. Regulation deemed that inappropriate as "even a Collector's boots contain proprietary technology that should, under no circumstances, fall into the hands of the civilian." I suppose a terrain analysis suite, perspiration wicking, stun contacts, magnetic anchorings, and hot drop repulsers warrant the advised security. The shoes of the three others were less kitted but arguably more stylish. The floor of the hall-way looked as though it had been recently waxed and not a drop of moisture could be found on its surface. I doubt the staff was running up and down on all fours to clean it, but I wouldn't be surprised if Mr. Zilnich required this for thematic resonance.

At the end of the hallway was a sliding door through which emanated the soft glow of more paper lanterns. I could hear clicking sounds every so often as I prepared to breach, if necessary, though it would be a shame to destroy the door. Scanning for active terminals revealed four in use and more on standby.

ComCom: Send: Orbit 3-9: "Prepped for Collection. Initiating post-transmission. Request for authentication to nearest active ComCom terminals to avoid collateral loss of life." PendCom

"Good to have you back. Working request . . . Authentication codes sent to your data pad prepped for one-touch transmission ordered in increasing distance from your current terminal location. Good hunting."

ComCom: Send: "Thanks. Commencing Collection. Await CC Ping." EndCom

I readied my HUD for targeting, pulled up an app for flash-bang activation in the corner of my data pad, switched the safety of my EinIn from off to three-shot burst but left it anchored to the polarity pad on my right thigh, slid the door open, and introduced myself.

"Good evening, all, or konbanwa, as they used to say. I'm here for Mr. Zilnich on behalf of the BoF."

Before me stood one burly man, one equally burly woman, and, though not technically standing, as he was reclining in a VR–compatible interface chair further in back, one lanky, bearded man wearing a hooded, pink sweatshirt, white boxers, and sandals. Having seen enough to make an educated guess, I activated the two closest proximity authentication codes.

ComCom: Send: Nearest cleared ComCom terminals: "Halt! This is a Bureau-sanctioned Collection. Should you desire not to be collected as collateral, follow these instructions. The Collector before you is the one contacting you via ComCom. I will gesture upwards to confirm. If you wish to comply, mimic the gesture." PendCom

I gently shook my right fist in the air twice. Both of the attendants followed suit.

ComCom: Send: "Thank you for agreeing to comply. I will now ask you to submit to individual inspections in order to relieve you of threats. Gesture to comply." PendCom

Both gestured.

ComCom: Send: "Please kneel, with your hands together above your head. Respond to the following interrogative: Can the Collectee hear us right now?" PendCom

"No." The woman said. The man shook his head as well.

EndCom

"I figured as much based on the complexity of his interface, but I decided to be careful. I apologize for the curtness of my process, and I don't mean to alarm you. Thank you for agreeing to comply, and we should have you both out of here as soon as possible, pending Mr. Zilnich's interactions. I'll now remove any weaponry from you as a precaution. Then, I will have you act as your typical roles when I converse with Mr. Zilnich. The only difference is that I would like you to ignore any commands he may give you that might be considered offensive and or hostile and defer to me."

"Why don't you just shoot him right now?" The man asked.

"I suppose that's primarily for my own selfish reasons, though, partially, it's because I would hate to die in my sleep without seeing it coming and that extends to his current . . . state."

"I would too." The woman chirped, her voice struggling to return to its normal register due to the stressful scenario.

"I don't know if he'd mind much." The man continued.

I walked over behind the man, keeping an eye on the woman's hands all the while.

"May I?" I asked, trying to calm the mood.

"Pistol on the left hip, safety is on, two clips on the right hip."

I removed the declared items and patted him down for good measure, pleased to find he was an honest young man of around twenty-four years. I then overly quietly back stepped to a table that was just behind, below, and to the right of my clueless Collectee's peripheral range and placed them there, ejecting the loaded clip, unchambering the first round and sliding it back into the clip.

"Don't worry! I was just unloading your partner's gun," I said in response to a wince from the older woman.

"Thank god." She sighed in relief.

"This is some archaic weaponry you all possess here." I probed. "Your employer must not have expected you to use it."

"Fifteen years and we've only ever had to fire a couple of warning shots, right, Bob?"

"S'right. Plus, not everyone can fork over the GCs for Einherjars. What's so good about them anyway? My gun shoots, your gun shoots a little better?"

"Well, if you want the side-by-side. My EinIn has a 36 + 0 shot capacity per clip. Your Berretta has a 15 + 1. Muzzle velocity is higher on the Berretta, but only slightly. My EinIn will never jam under normal firing use. Its grip biometrically locks the trigger to my and up to three other users' handprints. Its profile can be synced with my HUD to track bullet count and other data. However, the trade-mark difference would be the auto–corrective firing setting. When you first sync with an EinIn model, you have to practice firing with it for about ninety minutes in a couple of different sessions in order to calibrate the ACF. Most of this is trying to make sure that you hold the ergonomic grip the same way every time when firing, even under stress. Once the calibration is finished, the ACF ensures that recoil from each separate bullet on the three-shot burst is directionally counterbalanced by the expulsion of the gas used to fire them. It's a lovely application of the Law of Conservation of Momentum that produces a spread between the three bullets of no more than 1.5 cm from a distance of twelve meters or less."

"So you like guns a lot?" The woman quavered.

"I appreciate precision."

The hair on the back of the woman's neck was still standing up slightly as I walked behind her.

"Your turn now, if I may?" I asked.

"Go right ahead! I'm fitted with the same archaic setup just opposite hip." She emitted a nervous laugh.

I repeated the previous process, without expounding further on my weaponry. Then, I walked back out in front of them.

"Thanks again, you two. It's rare to see those hired in your business relinquish their arms so readily and, though practiced, I don't relish firefights. Might I have your names?"

"I'm Carmen." The woman replied, rising to her feet in response to my gesture to do so, her face relaxing as her breathing slowed.

"Bob. And let me add that it's kind of embarrassing to be taken down to my knees by a kid your age. How old are you anyway?"

"Ah. I do get that one a lot. Nineteen. And you?"

"Twenty-eight and half. Half-birthday was just yesterday," he replied, rubbing the back of his neck.

I frowned at the inaccuracy of my guess. "Well, you don't look a day older than twenty-four. So how deep is he in? Full dive? His ComCom is off." I gestured with a thumb over towards Zilnich.

"He does this fourteen-hours a day scheduled around mealtimes and basic hygiene, so he gets up to eat and shit and he usually just sleeps in the same chair, but occasionally goes to bed upstairs," Bob said, with a perplexed look.

"Are either of you related to him or is this just a job like with the ladies outside?"

"Just a job for me," Carmen replied. "Until someone like you shows up, I get to read or stream, sometimes we play games, right, Bob?"

"Yeah. It's a leisurely lifestyle that pays the bills." He said, smirking at Carmen "But it's over now."

They both hung their heads a bit at this.

"Did he inform you that he was a Blank?" I asked, reading the answer from their faces before they gave words to it.

"Nah," Carmen said, after clearing her throat a bit. "We barely ever talked other than his typical requests. I guess I never really wondered how he did all this, either."

"Well, I'm sorry this had to affect you in this fashion. After this, I'll talk to the Bureau about whether or not we can revise the clause associated with informing employees paid on fortune earnings about Blank status, but I can't promise anything will change."

"We'd appreciate you tryin'," Bob said, sobering up a bit more.

"You both seem capable, so I think you'll be able to find employment after this. There's always another rich person to protect. We'll seize any remainder of his fortune, but you both will be paid through the end of the month, and it's only the third today. We can get this show on the road here in a bit so you can get back home a little early. Any questions before we proceed?"

"Nope."

"Nope."

"Okay. Two things. Please, I implore you, do not make any sudden movements near the guns and remember to defer to me, but act like you are still his. Go ahead and bring him out in your typical fashion."

Bob went over to Zilnich's left side, stood behind him, and firmly tapped his shoulder twice.

"What?!" My Collectee bellowed. "My real–time says it's only 9:17! I'm gonna stay in longer!"

"This is pretty important," Bob asserted. "You're going to want to pull all the way out for this."

Zilnich shifted in his chair, grunting in dissatisfaction all the while, tapped the release on the right side of his interface, paused his R, flipped up the visual and audio peripherals, and rubbed his eyes. He opened them slightly to accommodate for the lighting change, then opened them fully. I dug into my pack as he was doing this to pull out the bottle of tainted plum wine I had brought for the occasion. I set it down on another table that had a couple of spare parts for his setup and some data pads on it.

"Who the hell are you?" Zilnich groaned. "We don't cater to fantasies in The Keep. You need to keep all of that in the room with your assigned caretakers. Get out of here."

After expending the time to tell me this in what I was beginning to think was a titanic effort on his part from his tone, he made a motion towards his peripherals again. Most unappealing. I became annoyed.

"Unbelievable." I began. "Twice in one day, one hour even. Tell me Mikhail Zilnich, Blank status initiated October 29th of just over eighteen years ago, blood type O-negative, clinically depressed, currently recovering from a mild case of scurvy, doomed to die in less than twenty minutes, do I really look so inexperienced as to be here to partake in one of your perverted peddlings? Moreover, is said fantasy really so popular? If so, I don't quite understand the appeal."

At this, Zilnich looked down and away for a few seconds, sufficiently abashed, but the sentiment didn't last long.

"Pretty good acting, but can you prove it?"

"Are you really so far gone that everything else in your life seems trivial or false? I don't feel the need to prove my identity, currently, but in due time. Until then, I had hoped to be cordial, as I do like to enjoy these moments as much as possible, out of reverence for the life that you seem to have squandered."

"What did you have in mind? I'm a little too busy enjoying myself to talk to a Govy dog." He fixed me with a bloodshot stare, and I examined the bags under his eyes.

"Perhaps one of the simpler pleasures to loosen your tongue." I turned the label of the bottle towards him. "I'm given to understand that this is your favorite among alcoholic beverages? I had this specially prepared with a toxin that will kill you slowly, but surely enough, while you escape into the bliss within the bottle. What do you think?"

"Maybe later. I've got a couple more checkpoints to get through first."

Zilnich flounced back into his chair, dropped and activated his peripherals, in practiced fashion, and began diving again. Carmen looked at me like this was expected. Bob paled and looked a little more horrified.

"Sometimes I can't stomach this little punk." He said, pinching his nasolacrimal ducts and shaking his head softly from side to side.

"Can you bring him out once more for me? I'd like to see how he reacts this time."

"Carmen?" Bob asked.

"Okay."

Carmen changed places with Bob and squeezed Zilnich's shoulder.

He flipped up his audio peripherals but left the visual engaged and kept playing.

"What? Every second you pull me back into this world hurts my brain!" He barked.

"Sorry, Mikey, but I don't think the Collector is going to wait on you."

"That is accurate, Mr. Zilnich. I usually like to set aside time to spend in conversation with my Collectees, but I don't have time to waste."

"Hold on. Hold on. Hold on!" Zilnich pleaded. "I'm almost done. Just a few more checkpoints."

He dropped his audio peripherals and reengaged.

"I just have two questions for you two before I let you go. First, the koi are fake, right?"

"I'm sorry?" Bob asked.

"Outside? In the stream?" Carmen asked.

"Right. The koi swimming outside. They're fake?"

"Oh." Bob caught on. "Yeah, they're fake. We've never replaced a single one."

"I figured. Pollinators have been mechanized so why not pleasure organisms? And the third pair of shoes in the entryway. To whom do they belong?"

"Those are Tracie's. She normally works upstairs, but she just forgot to bring them out with her last night. She's kind of gotten used to walking around the whole place barefoot." Carmen explained.

"Got it. I didn't think I sensed anyone else in the area. Well, thanks again for cooperating. You don't need to be here to see this. Please exit through the entryway and out of the establishment entirely. The clerical staff will be able to handle the rest of the evening, and my cleanup and decommissioning team will arrive soon."

I stepped aside to let them pass. They began to walk by.

"Oh!" Carmen exclaimed. "I forgot my data pad! Can I still go get it? It's just on the table there."

"Of course. Couldn't make it without *that*."

ComCom: Send: Orbit 3-9: "Orbit. Please lock down all other data pad terminals within twenty meters and unlock again in twenty minutes." PendCom

"Working . . . done. Twenty-minute countdown . . . mark."

ComCom: Send: "Thanks." EndCom

Bob turned to wait as Carmen retrieved her data pad.

"Those are locked down for a while. Security and all."

"You seem a bit deflated from when you entered," Bob noticed. "You good?"

"Just a wasted opportunity is all . . . Have a good life, you two."

They exited through the sliding door together and slid it back into place. I walked up to Mr. Zilnich and studied him one more time in the flickering light of the lanterns. His caretakers must have completed their work with diligence, as people in his state usually show greater signs of physical stress. Only his mental state was emaciated from his insalubrious pastimes. I removed the bullets from one of the Beretta clips, one by one, and dropped them to the ground, slid the empty clip into one of the guns, cocked the slide, and cleared the side table of the remaining clutter. I pulled the table within reach of Zilnich's right hand, and placed the gun on it, only centimeters from his twitching appendage, and well within his field of vision. Then, I walked to the other side of him and squeezed his shoulder, as I had seen Carmen do. He tapped his head setup twice and lifted the visual peripheral this time, looked puzzled, then flipped up his left audio peripheral. I could hear the background music coursing through the speakers.

"The Collector's gone?" he asked, relief mixing with incredulity.

"Not quite," I said, stepping out from behind him. "I think it's time to come back to reality and die with some dignity."

At last, his pupils dilated in panic, and his neck snapped around in desperation. He surveyed the environment. I was sure he saw the gun on the table.

"I don't like this reality . . ." he whispered. He flipped his peripherals down and tapped back in.

I walked towards the door, turned and unanchored, fired a burst through the articulated arm connecting his visual peripheral to the head mount, turned and reanchored, sent the CC ping, and wondered if this could have been my fate if not for a BFAB aptitude rating.

In that, we are alike.

4
0134 – The Refugee

My data pad vibrated and displayed a topographical map of the desert below, a sphere estimating the current location of the target, and alpha and beta drop points several kilometers closer to my current location. I double tapped the beta drop point to confirm and immediately felt the drone swing to port and begin its descent. Tapping the release on the safety harness, I stood up and turned around as the straps snapped back into the wall of the hold and I unanchored my SMG from the overhead storage rack and began walking towards my designated drop port, anchoring the weapon to my lower back in its compacted setting. Two swipes to display the swing arc trajectory of the drop and I tapped my data pad to the drop port computer to sync up. After watching the timer on my data pad tick down to thirty-seconds to drop, I bent down and turned the dial on my boots to ready them and I set my thrust inputs to track eye movement through my HUD and the curling of my finger leads.

ComCom: Send: D: "Dropping to you in thirty" PendCom

I felt my wrist vibrate the forty-meter warning as the drone leveled, and I watched the timer tick down.

"See you soon!"

I snapped to attention and chuckled as the drop port jettisoned me. Quickly scanning, I immediately fixed my vision to the ground, just below the ridgeline of a derelict dam. I rotated my left palm up and my right palm down, clenched both fists to activate the drop repulsers, curled my left fingers to correct my initial axis, which was slightly left leaning, released, clenched just before touch down to create a cushion that stirred up the sand below, and I dropped the last half-meter and relaxed my knees as I contacted the ground.

"Niiiiiiice! You totally stuck that landing!"

Collection Commander Darianna slammed the door of the shed in which she had been squatting and came out jerking her balaclava down to grin at me.

"The first time I dropped, I didn't clench cushion and I fractured my right tibia on a rock." She grimaced and then peeped at me out of the corner of her eye to get a laugh. I was too busy admiring her dust-smeared outfit, wondering how long she had been waiting around for my arrival, to offer one.

"C'mon! You're not nervous, are you? You're never nervous! I know this is your first recon and all . . . so it's understandable," she said, bending down with her hands on her hips and wrenching her neck upwards to get a glimpse of my downturned expression. As her magnetic stare finally pulled my pupils up, I baited her in and reanimated.

"I'm fine!" I snickered. "I was only trying to compose myself after seeing how ridiculous you appear with that rag over your face!"

"Ugh!" She spat, playfully aghast. "I thought it looked ravishing! Doesn't the contrast between the red and white on it bring out my eyes?"

"Hahaha! Red and white bring out green? You always look ravishing, but with that you only look radishing."

"Mean." She simpered. "Well, good luck getting Collection details out of me now!"

She began to stalk off back towards the shed, and I caught up to her right side.

"Were you waiting here for me overlong?"

"Were you worried? You know, it's my job to worry about you, not the other way around, right?"

I guess it's only not my job in that I don't get paid for it when I worry.

"I know how you are burdened with impatience and all."

"Truth. Only about a day and a half since the Collection window opened up and you were authorized, but I had the others to keep me company until this morning. I was beginning to think they wouldn't let me have you all to myself for your first recon."

"Technically, you don't, given the others."

Daria grabbed her pack off of a hook inside the shed and began walking me over to our mechanical counterparts for the mission.

"It's my command, so they'll be good to you." She assured me.

"So, ColCom Daria, if that is the role you will be playing in this exciting new production of 'Our Day Job,' now on the Broadway Stream, shall we talk mission?"

"Take a look at these, understudy!"

She made a sweeping gesture over towards one wall and a couple of crouching, metallic men. These ambulatory automatons were yet-to-be-released Ground Combat Drones, on loan from a couple of labs working under the NERDoD for field testing. Daria's recon unit was selected as one of three in the NER Bureau to work with them, given the harsh environment in which it was currently active, and their authorization to engage in paramilitary activities. Somehow, she was able to incinerate the red tape behind allowing me to pair with one, even though it was only my first mission on a recon squad. She told me the proffered justification was for the labs to have the opportunity to compile data on new user integration and that I was a competitive fit, a sentiment that I have yet to tease apart as flattering or insulting.

The GCDs were extremely impressive, from an engineering standpoint. As Daria divulged more and more of their capabilities, my appreciation for mechanization increased slightly, much to my chagrin. Each of the members of Daria's squad had been paired, on and off, with one for about a week. They have mimic movement settings that allow the drone to follow you, drone–see–drone–do style, over variable tether distances that can be set and changed on the fly. So, were one so inclined to climb a ladder, the drone would mimic every motion you completed, wrung by wrung, until it was standing behind you at the top, assuming you had ordered it to stow its weapon. I learned this outside of the shack during Daria's obstacle course training, for which she had chosen the dam as the venue. My drone even did the thumbs up I flashed to Daria as I reached the top of one of the platforms along the dam's control room.

These particular drones were fitted as snipers. They could be fitted with a few different types of drone–compatible, and hybrid person/drone–compatible rifles. Currently, they were fitted with hybrid Sortriche Fabrications anti-personnel electromagnetic induction sniper rifles, a rugged design that had been battle tested by all sorts of warfare-inclined groups across the ever-expanding deserts of the world over the last two years since its inception. Every self-respecting warlord from the area, which happened to be Cameroon of the West African Bloc, to Cape Agulhas has at least one of these models, either in his hands or on his mantelpiece, in order to demonstrate wealth and power. Really, they should have the whole drone in their treasure rooms, but I have found most warlords have too much testosterone to "let machine men do their killing for them."

The drones are set up to work in tandem with up to seven others on a closed network, as of right now. The sniper drones not only sync their rifle vectors, but they sync telemetry data, and these particular models are programmed to triangulate an ideal sniping solution for a designated primary sniper within the squad. Each drone has probes that read humidity, wind speed, altitude, and accommodate for gravity based on firing data input for your selected rifle. Basically, two-plus drones on a team will line up a target and transmit targeting data to another drone, which takes the shot. This is all accomplished while the operators of the drones survey within the reliable signal communication distance of the network. One complication on our end, given our status as operators within a non–military entity, was that a Collector was required to take the final shot, as opposed to an unmanned drone, but the NERDoD still appreciated the feedback.

The versatility between being able to have these types of drones mimic, run routes on auto pilot, or be inhabited by operators as a battlefield proxy has rekindled discussions in warfare ethics circles regarding how killing has become too easy and too impersonal. Do we really have so many lives to spare that we would prefer to send flesh and blood into a war zone than metal and circuits? We are told by the Bureau that we are not technically engaging in warfare during Collections, so we shouldn't think about these aspects of the missions, as they are irrelevant. For Daria, that has been enough. I am dissatisfied. I, for one, appreciated the idea that this drone might have received fire in my place on this Collection. I am aware that the cost of running one of these drones is so high that they will not supplant most troops in the wars to come. I like to think that this invention was another means to preserve the lives of those precious to me, though I know the Bureau views the GCD as an effective way to take the lives of those indebted to them.

Daria and I took a break from calibration drills and, as I watched some of the water she was drinking from her pack dribble down her chin, my mind wandered back to our target. The dossier I perused on the flight over was more speculative than most, given most of the data on Ami Sekibo was collected after age twenty-two from Bureau surveys. Most of her life had been spent as a child soldier in these areas in defense of a part of Lake Chad.

Increasing aridity in the region and desertification encroaching further on some of the fringe civilizations of the Sahara compounding with the already overdrawn status of potable water sources served to spark water wars in a number of African regions about thirty years ago that have continued somewhat into today. While politicians of more civilized nations bickered over how to justly ration the water left on the continent, warlords went right to the sources and began staking their claims. You might be surprised to find how quickly people rally under these unelected leaders at the promise of access to a necessity of life. You might be more surprised to find that not all rallied make the cut. Somewhere along the line, the smartest of warlords learned that there is a delicate balance between the number of people needing water and the number needed to defend the water. They are always looking to recruit more children to fill out their buffer population, which is an estimation of the number of troops that will die in a month in defense of the water source. Parents would willingly surrender their children to this lifestyle if it meant that they might be able to get the water that the parents could not provide. Warlords are happy to take these children in. Children are smaller, require less, are less likely to incite a rebellion, and they can shoot just about as well as an adult, given training on modern weapon platforms. Ami happened to be one of these children who was let go by her family when they could no longer get enough water to support all three of them and the roving warlord in the region would not accept adult recruits.

"You're probably almost done calibrating. You ready to get back out there?" Daria asked.

"I'm ready when you are. I was just reevaluating the Collectee's history."

"Oh yeah! We haven't talked about that yet. Kind of a shitty situation, huh?" She asked, leading me into further contemplation. "Did you hear about the tactical reality they used on them?"

"Was that in the dossier? I was only able to scan it because I came immediately from a previous Collection—"

"One of the footnotes. Well," Daria began as I shifted to support myself better against a board that had been kicked slightly more inwards in the wall of the shed, "you know about the tactical reality applications that we use through VR for some of our training sims? A couple of these guys, including the warlord who took Sekibo in, have acquired the resources to train some of their troops through VR stations. Apparently, they sell some of the water they have to truck their newest set of recruits to these mobile stations that are set up in the desert and they subject the kids to these sims that train them to shoot better and quicker and it desensitizes them to violence more thoroughly as well."

"What? Through the same types of theories behind video games desensitizing children to violence?"

"Exactly." Daria clenched her jaw for a bit. "But they keep the kids dehydrated the whole time. They only get water to drink when they complete particularly gruesome levels without showing any restraint. Apparently, the malaise the kids are in during the dehydrated state decreases their inhibitions, and they also torture them."

"And that's the state they recall when they are told to shoot at the kids fighting on the other side." I finished.

"That's not even the worst of it." Daria continued, her face growing paler. "That's not even the biggest motivator. They teach them that it's us or them from the beginning. At the facilities, the kids are split up into two different groups . . ."

"Wow." My voice cracked into a whisper. I appreciated the water I drank to soothe my throat more in that moment than at any other time in my life.

"You always catch on quick. There isn't a kid who isn't ready to be a cold-blooded killer that gets trucked out on the winning team. I heard they don't even give them the guns to start. Some throttle each other to death before they even get to the armory in the middle of the arena."

"You ever feel like those developers are the ones we should be killing?" I asked.

"Not our assignment. In fact, most of the leaders of the world seem content to sit back and watch the continent tear itself apart. I'm glad I've only been here for a week, and I'm even more glad that you'll only need to be here until tomorrow, hopefully."

"Well, you were the one who ordered me here. I could have been on another recon op Stateside, Collecting some dilettante at a gala or something like that, if it weren't for you!" I smiled at her, warmly.

"And have some other bitch watching your back? You wish! You know you don't play well with others the first time. I need to take care of you. I'm pretty sure you aren't going to take to the recon lifestyle, but a good review is important to solidify your reputation, and I won't have someone else screwing that up for you."

She nodded, definitively, after saying this. I tracked her bangs as they jumped across her eyebrows. Then, she slid her helmet back on over her raven, bobtailed hair after sliding the hair tie off of her purple partial side ponytail to shoot it at my chest in one, smooth motion.

"Good shot. Center of mass. Too bad you can't shoot a rifle that well." I teased, cocking my eyebrow in anticipation of the response.

"Meh muh muh MEH meh muh. Go pair up, smart ass."

I turned around, feeling triumphant, barely hearing her laugh through her nose twice, as I did, and I pocketed the hair tie, in case she needed it later.

The noon sun marked the end of my training session with my GCD, and Daria informed the rest of her unit that we were en route. I felt the thrum of the climate control suite in my chest plate radiate through my ribs as it began adjusting for the increase in temperature as we dropped into the parched riverbed and began trekking northeast. Daria's preoccupation with status updates to the rest of the group allowed me a few quiet moments to appreciate the beauty of the desert.

It was the end of May and before monsoon season. The air was horribly dry, but the winds stirred the sands in patterns that entranced me for a full twenty minutes, though a few of these minutes were lost fantasizing about my next meal since the ripples in the sand reminded me of steam coming off the insta–lunch I ate between missions the previous day. A few meters away, a dung beetle rolled its nursery over the crest of a lesser dune and then the sphere of excrement entrapped one of its limbs as it began rolling down the leeward side. That wasn't the most perilous part of the plummet. As fate would have it, my rough estimation of the imperiled insect's path put it right under Daria's right boot in a few strides, and she was looking over her shoulder as she continued to receive updates on the target's activities over the past six hours. As opposed to interrupting her via raising my voice, I kicked my feet up from a trudge to a jog, after un–tethering my GCD, and I nudged her slightly off course, unperturbed by the possibility of rebuke, which never came, as I turned my head to watch the dung beetle tumble by. Watching the pairing come to a halt, I realized I admired the dung beetle for its ingenuity. Initially, I had classified the insect as imperiled, but the appropriate adjective would have been intrepid. The speed and dexterity with which the beetle extricated itself from the excrement could only be described as impressive and the entire dune rolling process must have been intentional. I quietly applauded the performance in my mind and admired the energy economics of the dung beetle's choice of transportation.

Re-tethering my GCD, I ascended to the apex of one of the larger dunes in the area to gaze off towards the alpha rally point. It seemed, based on the distance to the point on my data pad, that the area should have been in sight, but I definitely couldn't make out the position of the rest of the unit on the sand-swept wasteland. Daria skated up next to me and bent down to dial in her boots. I did the same. Then, she jumped and began repulsing down the slope. I was curious to see how her GCD would react, given they weren't equipped with repulsers. It mimicked the jump. Then, it ran down the dunes at the same speed as Daria, never stumbling once. She pirouetted around at the bottom, folded her hands under her chest, and started tapping her foot, mock glancing at her data pad and cocking her head to the right, looking up at me, extra smug.

After spending a bit of our trek tinkering with the GCD applications on my data pad, I had been wanting to test out a couple of the limits of the GCD, so I bent down and dialed off my boots, glimpsing Daria cocking her head to the left, looking puzzled. Then, I raised my arms in a carrying posture and wink–locked my GCD's arms via my HUD controls. I flicked to zoom in the topographical map and traced a route on my data pad from my marker to half-a-meter in front of Daria's, copy/pasted it to the GCD's route tab, untethered the GCD into standby mode, jumped into its arms while tapping on load–bearing settings, feeling the mechanized joints accommodate my weight, and then I activated the route at a running speed of 12 kph. Halfway down the dune, I shifted in my prince's arms and snapped a couple of pics of Daria's dropped jaw, making the one in which she wasn't blinking the wallpaper of my data pad and sending it to her as well. At the bottom of the dune, I vaulted out of the GCD's arms, returned it to default, and then retethered it, positioning it to proposition Daria for a fist bump, which she returned, and then she turned around and we started walking again. I was not as practiced as the dung beetle, but I felt I did well enough.

It was difficult to focus on the endemic scenery for the remainder of the approach. Aside from the lives struggling to eke out an existence in the barren landscape, the marvels were unchanging and grew tiresome after a while, an inevitability of the impatience bred into me. More dunes, same blue sky, a few scrubs scattered across the vista, the enduring heat on my cheeks where the helmet conditioners couldn't quite cover. As magnificent as the Sahara was, Daria was still the most alluring part of its expanse. I found this was always the case of locales, regardless of the backdrop. Her strident figure, hips listing with each step as she traipsed across the dunes, the flex mesh of her leggings adding less than a centimeter of girth in exchange for a wealth of protection to her lean and shapely thighs, the gentle slope of her lower back, contours concealed by anchored grenades in a few spots, the balletic dip of her nimble shoulder as she glanced back to check up on me were all graceful facets of her low–mod–percentage form.

"Don't get too comfortable back there! You're going to be the point Collector and primary sniper when we collect so you can spend your time leering at the target."

She always knew.

"I was wondering if I'd be able to listen to your lilting voice again before too long! Is the rest of the squad ready?"

Her voice was one of her loveliest qualities. Her expressive abilities were such that every sentence would end in minute inflections that could drive a point home or could leave you pendent on the probability of her giving life to another word. I've told her that she is wasted on recon because she doesn't have the opportunity to lull targets into quiescence. She's told me that she chose the recon business due to the sightseeing and to be able to get as far away from where she came from as possible.

"They've been on overwatch all day, so they're probably champing at the bit to get on with it. If you want to get into their good graces, try to wrap this one up quickly."

"How quick is quickly in the recon business?"

"By tonight would be nice! Her best–killed–by date is the thirtieth. We'd be able to take one of the next two days in the Collection window off as comp time. I could take you to Abu Dhabi?"

"Expedited it is!"

Our data pad markers began to overlap with the alpha rally point on my screen, and I shot Daria an aporetic look.

"Chill out. This one's an Old-world trick," she said, allaying my consternation.

Daria shuffled around in the sand a bit and I heard a muffled clink where some of the sand was a bit darker, as a result of being turned up a few times. She bent down, grabbed a chain from under the sand, tapped on her data pad twice, patiently watched the screen for a bit, and began pulling the chain. A crack opened up a few meters from us as a pair of doors began swinging up and out of the desert floor, sifting the sand off their sides as they did.

"Need to refill water?" Daria was reaching back to feel her pack as she asked me.

"I might as well. I suppose I'd also like to take a look inside this . . . smuggler's hole."

"Very good! How'd you know?" She began bouncing on her heels.

"The lone date palm tree outside is most likely fake, given the paucity of water in this region of the desert. If there is any water around, it is either run in at exorbitant cost through drones or trucks or comes by way of the monsoon, the volume of which is not sufficient to sustain biomass of that magnitude. People in this corner of the world can barely scrimp for enough water to get by as it is. Therefore, I figured it was a marker. For what was the hole used?"

"We don't know. It was abandoned when we happened upon it. We were running our route, and Giselle picked it up after being alerted by her subterranean scans. Our target is only six clicks over this dune, and we were going to position ourselves around this area anyway, so we had to sweep it to secure perimeter, but it has been nice for the others to get out of the sun for a while."

We descended down the ramp and into the hole. I could make out one person reclining on the ground and another peering out at me from behind an alcove in the faint light of the planterns affixed to the walls, casting their soft, blue, bioluminescent light to all but the very corners of the confined cavity.

After we untethered our GCDs into standby, Daria skipped ahead and leapt towards the reclining figure, her hair brushing against the ceiling as she almost clocked herself on it, coming down right next to its anterior with a force sufficient to send the resulting clap of her boots echoing through the chamber and out the doors.

"Really?" The gravelly voice coming from the recliner groaned, stirring from its slumber.

"Oh, yeah, okay. Go back to sleep. Didn't you want to get this over?" Lezgo!" She softly kicked the man on the ground in his side and then she bounced over to the peeping person and play punched the air in front of her.

Daria's rallying abilities were second to many when it came to consideration, but first–rate in their annoyance. My fingers ran out of wall to trace, and I stepped behind her towards the center of the cross–shaped room. At the end of the long pathway, there were jugs of water and other rations neatly stacked. In the right arm, the weapons were resting, cradled by the cracks in the rock. The left arm had caved in a bit, so it was unused and two GCDs had their backs turned to it.

Daria walked behind me as I proceeded to the water and refilled my pack and I turned around and did the same for her, hefting a new jug up, uncapping, and propping it against my knee as she crouched down and stored her empty jug. We turned around and the other two were picking up their weapons. Daria walked over to the man and pointed over her shoulder at him with a thumb.

"This is Seeker 13, Chance. He's big, tall, and outgripes them all!" She smiled, obviously pleased at her rhyme, one that I could see was recycled by Chance's bemused expression.

The hulking figure, who had to hunch down to not graze his head on the two-meter-high ceiling, extended a hand toward me in greeting, and I could see his well-toned extensor digitorum ripple as he turned his wrist over. I sized him up as I looked up to meet his gaze and I figured he had about an eighth of a meter on me in height and easily forty or so kilos on me in mass, the hefty majority of which was muscular. I willingly submitted my right hand to his vice grip.

"Daria didn't import you from the graviron when she joined up, did she? Ping me once if she is holding you hostage." I cracked the joke. He did not crack up.

"Sorry, Collector. I think this particular job has not been up my alley. I've been in the desert before, but I have never liked it. As ColCom said, let's just try to get this done fast, huh?" He grumbled as he released my hand and went over to inspect his GCD.

"I thought it was good." A whisper from Daria consoled as she glided past me to alight on the shoulder of the young woman who was looking squarely at my right kidney.

"This," Daria nudged her head into the crook of the young woman's neck and tried to lift it up as it lolled off to the right, eyes still affixed on my renal region, "is Seeker, c'mon," she crooned as she steadied the lolling head with her right glove, propping it up to stare now at my collarbone, "Seeker, there, 18, Giselle."

"Okay okay. I'll look. Just get off." Giselle consented, with a lingering Australian accent. She did as she said, and I saw she was an eyemera as well, only second gen with gray irises as opposed to my lilac.

"Put 'er there, Seeker there!" I snaked my hand over towards her, trying again at joviality.

Giselle looked down and away and then hesitantly brushed my open palm with her three longest fingers on her right hand.

"Heh heh." Giselle let slip.

"Whoah! Nice!" Daria exclaimed. "Gis is a bit antisocial, so that was actually pretty huge!"

"You were right," Giselle stated.

"What about?" I replied.

"Ah. That was for me, actually." Daria said, looking down towards the top of Giselle's straight, shoulder–length, red hair. "And we won't be talking more about that right now, right, Gis?"

Giselle seemed to acquiesce to Daria's singsong demand as she dragged her gaze across my face again on her way to her GCD.

"You said *whispering* was your favorite *whispering* those eyes." Giselle murmured to Daria in passing as they began preparing themselves.

"She doesn't strike me as antisocial." I offered.

"This is peculiar. Normally, she is all screens and no speeches. I think it's because we've talked about you before."

"Hah! More like I've listened about you before . . . a lot." Giselle chirped.

"Camera feed just picked up movement outside the warehouse. I'm going up if any of you gabbers want to follow." Chance shouldered his pack and led his GCD out the doors.

"Alright, we're going." Daria aimed a venomous look at Giselle, who stuck her tongue out in response.

Giselle clomped her GCD out on a preset route and walked past me, head down.

"I like your eyes too. Did you pick them yourself?" I inquired.

She picked her head up a bit at this and I thought I saw a hint of a smile as she passed, but I received no verbal corroboration.

"Seriously weird," Daria said to herself as she ground some caked sand from one of her boots off against the wall next to me. "She is really never like this. I know you have a way with some people, but Chance is usually more sociable than Gis, and you saw what he is like."

"Maybe I just got lucky? Maybe she's more comfortable when she's around you."

"It's a good thing, actually! I'm happy about it! These missions can really wear on her sometimes."

"You two seem to get along quite well. Perhaps she senses that we do as well and that sets her at ease?"

"That might be it. Well? Good to go? You are supposed to be the primary Collector here."

I finished tethering my GCD and walked up behind Daria's, gesturing overdramatically with my mechanical shadow.

"After you."

We climbed back out, and I immediately longed for the shade as Daria reset her balaclava and the torrid wind buffeted my cheeks. We regrouped with the rest of Seeker Squad and moved into our designated prone positions matching the formations listed on our data pads at the top of the dune facing southeast towards a group of warehouses. Daria had us cease any active ComCom connections, and we all authenticated to helmet squad chat and checked our coms by testing the priority on the companion app.

"Okay, people let's get into it." Daria began. "Chance? Overwatch details?"

"Target has been in and around these dilapidated warehouses throughout the entirety of our operation. She exits, rarely, to receive drone drops of unknown goods. Data we have analyzed from GPS uplinks have shown that she receives drone drops daily, but she has certain goods trucked in by caravan every five days around 6:00 p.m. WAT. We are currently anticipating that caravan. The second largest warehouse, which she has holed up in since a few weeks before the Collection window opened, is completely locked down with two exceptions, which are the double garage doors and a sliding door in the top two corners of each wall, which I have never seen open, but are most likely covering windows. Drone vids have confirmed that the target is currently within said warehouse unless tunnels exist between them. If this is the case, they did not show up on subT scans.

Thermal imaging can't discriminate through the insulation in the warehouse. One concern is that shipments of food seem too plentiful for one person so others may exist within the compound, though no one other than Sekibo has been visualized. The other is that there are a number of cameras around the compound and a few privately registered drones have been in the area, though, if she has been anticipating our arrival, she has not shown it in any way. Drone tracking shows a truck heading this way, ETA 6:02 WAT, nineteen and change minutes from now."

Chance shifted in his position to look through the scope array of his own rifle at the compound.

"Good!" Daria chimed in. "Giselle, how are the GCDs doing? All ready to go?"

"GCDs are nominal. Routes have been planned and overlays have been mapped to your data pads. All sensors are active, and ping is good. Primary sniper is currently designated to your GCD for transfer to the primary Collector pending approval from your HUD or data pad. Our triangulation pattern is centered on the average area Sekibo stands in to receive her goods from the back of the truck. Ready to sync routes on your go."

"Sounds like we're ready." I watched Daria breathe deeply to calm herself as she prepared to start the Collection. "Let 'em loose!"

With a few taps, Giselle ran the routes of the GCDs and each one took off towards its destination. Chance's arrived at its location northeast of the garage doors two minutes before the truck arrived. Daria's and Giselle's swung right, and Giselle's took the long route. I lost control of mine temporarily, as Giselle was technically the master of all of the GCDs, and it crawled up next to us and leveled its rifle, peering over the crest of the dune.

"It's all yours, Collector," Giselle told me, and I saw the scroll across my HUD notifying me of the transfer of authority.

I began pulling out my inhabitation controller for the GCD as I slid back down the dune, syncing it to and flipping down my visual peripheral while adding the audio input feed from my GCD to the squad uplink and setting an audio output toggle to the controller. The truck marked on our data pads started coasting towards its goal. Then, Giselle gasped.

"My GCD just went offline! Anyone have a visual?"

"It just rag dolled," Daria said. "Probably a pulse mine. Shit!"

"Truck just backed up to the doors." Chance updated. "It's self-driving. Sekibo's not coming out. I think she knows. We should have just fucking OSd this place! I think she knows!"

"Gis run an alternate triangulation solution." Daria barked. "Chance, you said yourself that there's too much food coming for one person, and we don't orbital strike. You're not in the fucking army anymore so stop acting like that's a realistic option. We're here for Sekibo, only Sekibo, and she's going down without the possibility of civie casualties."

Daria was an incredible leader when circumstances precipitated tensions.

"I'm about to inhabit. Waiting on a firing solution, but is anyone else picking up a local radio transmission?" I asked.

Everyone confirmed.

"The window! My GCD feed shows the window opening!" Daria screamed.

Then, a cachunk sound emanated from the window and the dune behind Daria's GCD shifted a bit as a projectile drilled into it.

"It's a rail rifle! Giselle move that GCD!" Chance ordered.

"I'm already running a scramble pattern." She replied. "Daria, can you inhabit and run it down? We might have to get UCaP on this one now that the element of surprise has been lost."

"I'm getting ready!" Daria replied.

"On second thought . . . " Giselle sighed. "Don't bother. Its leg just got blown off. Lucky shot."

The crack of Chance's Kernopf HE rifle, echoing from his new position a few dunes away, was followed by a distant explosion and faint crashing sounds a few seconds later.

"Rail rifle's down." Chance exhaled.

In my brief time working for the Bureau, I had taken a small amount of solace from a training session that taught us about our mortal security. When Bureaus had first been established, Collectees had often attempted to kill their Collectors, thinking that they might be able to get away with it and somehow retain their fortunes, or that they might be able to eke out another few moments of life on the run. The latter of these thoughts was true; though the quality of the life would drastically decrease due to the shunning one would receive from the purveyors of the comforts one used to know as a result of being blacklisted and stripped of all wealth, Bureau–granted or otherwise. The Bureau would then pursue you to the ends of the earth with a group of their most brutal agents and often dispatch you in a publicly broadcasted execution as opposed to the quiet end well–behaved Collectees received. By the time the NER Bureau had been founded, attempts at this futile form of resistance had become almost inconceivable.

When Daria's humanoid GCD was dismembered, that solace simmered away on the desert winds as that particular kernel of Bureau conditioning shriveled within my central processor, and I rebooted to my most dependable program of self-preservation. I dropped out of the squad chat and ordered my ComCom to receive the local radio hail I had picked up earlier, gating the transmission through my data pad companion app.

"Can you hear me? . . . Can you hear me?" The voice asked.

I held to transmit. "Good afternoon. Ms. Sekibo, I presume?" Then, I released.

"You . . . can hear me? What is a pray soom?"

Her language seemed fragmented. I attempted to condescend appropriately.

"Do not worry about that. Are you Ami Sekibo?"

"Yes. I am Ami. Are you Collector? Can we talk?" Her speech quickened in panic.

"Yes. I am the Collector for you. But I don't know if we can talk. You are shooting at my drones. You would shoot at me."

"Can we talk . . . no guns?"

"I don't know if we could. You seem too violent. I'm scared you would shoot me."

"We can talk. No guns. I come out. How many with you?"

This was a worrisome question.

"Only me and my drones to keep me safe from your guns. You would have shot me if I came out."

At this point, I heard someone running over the dune, and I commanded my ComCom to drop the signal. Daria crumpled to her knees next to me.

"What are you doing?!" She whisper-yelled at me.

I raised my finger to my pursed lips and implored her with my eyes. Then, I reestablished contact.

"Hello? Does it work?" Sekibo was asking.

"Sorry. How many with you? I don't want others to shoot me."

"No others with me. Only me. I come out to you. No guns." She seemed to be choking up.

"I send a drone out no guns. You talk to me through my drone."

"What you mean threeew?"

"You talk to drone. Drone talk to me. We talk. No guns."

"Okay."

"Okay?"

"Okay."

"Okay. I walk drone out. You come see drone. When I say. Okay?"

"Okay."

"Wait." I released my finger.

"Daria? I've got a hunch," I said, forcibly.

"Now? If you go for this and you mess up, I can't clean up your mess. Who are you talking to? I can't read your brain, idiot!"

"I'll take responsibility. It's Sekibo. Can you transfer the primary sniping designation to my HUD and not to my GCD?"

"Yup. Why?"

"You will see why. Your GCD's sensors should still be intact. Can you also swivel the head of your GCD to watch this location?" I tapped a marker down in front of the side of the warehouse on my data pad map and copied it to all of the squad's maps.

"Okay. Hold on."

I ordered my GCD to release its weapon, and I grabbed it and authenticated it to my HUD. Then, I ordered the GCD into maintenance mode, looked up the location of its sensor suite and telemetry integration chip in the schematics and I ripped it and patched it into my helmet. All the drone network sensory inputs were green. The reboot went fine as well. Adaptable models.

"Done." Daria walked on her knees in front of me, grabbed the bottom of my helmet and yanked it up and my eyes came with it. "Are you sure you can do this?"

"Remember my target acquiescence scores?" I asked her, balking a bit at the intensity of her gaze.

"They're unparalleled." She blinked, still detaining me.

"I'll admit that they are about to be tested, but all I need do is get her to walk out. I vow that I will still collect her. Order your team to stand down. If they fire, it will decimate my plan."

She released me at this point, and I rose from my supine position.

"If you miss, you're buying me dinner, and we won't be eating in the UAE."

"I'll buy you dinner either way. If I miss, I'll buy you the restaurant."

I told Sekibo to go as I dispatched my GCD to the point I had mapped at a walk, so as not to incite trepidation. I rejoined the squad chat temporarily as I prepared the Sortriche to fire from my distance to said point.

"Giselle. Could you reposition Chance's GCD to triangulate on the point I mapped with Daria's downed and my GCDs' sensor suites?" I requested.

"Already on it." She replied, monotonously. "Daria told us what you're planning. I wish I had popcorn . . ."

"It's not all that crazy an idea, honestly." Chance assured. "People used to do this all the time from this distance back in the day without GCD assistance or EI round guidance. Just a couple of guys and a rifle. I just don't know why you aren't shooting her now. Here she is."

The garage doors had opened up, and Sekibo was looking out from behind one at the drone that was still walking to the meeting point.

"Please excuse my pernicious penchant for vicariating through my victims. I like to get to know them before I blow holes in them. An indulgence, I know, but one that may save NERDoD a few GCs in this instance," I replied, acerbically.

"Triangulation is set. Good luck, Collector." Giselle wished.

"Ugh, you better be as good as Darianna says. It's all on you. Don't screw us." Chance exhorted.

"I can smell the butter on my lobster already." Daria prodded. "Get along."

I dropped my ComCom out of the group chat and connected to my GCD's audio input and output feeds through my helmet as it stopped in place, waiting for Sekibo. Then, I flipped down the visual peripheral and synced only our heads through my data pad. Looking through the drone, I scrutinized Sekibo as she vigilantly scanned her surroundings once more before wandering out. She was short, maybe a little over a meter and a half in height. Sunglasses were shading her eyes, but the telltale pink scars corrugating her right cheek from her prominent zygomatic process down to her clavicle confirmed most of what I needed to know. I ran a voiceprint pairing while speaking with her on the radio, but it seemed we had no reliable records of her raspy speech. I started up a facial biometric scan through the GCD as she stood at attention a few paces away from the drone to mollify my last qualm. It turned up thirty-six points of Ami Sekibo. Her meticulously shaved head helped.

"It's not fair." Sekibo began.

"Some elaboration . . . uh . . . start again. What is not fair?"

"I had to get fortune to . . . live, but I don't want fortune anymore."

"That is not how this works, Ami. You signed docs. You lived better with the fortune. You will be collected. That is fair. You chose." I explained, my tone devoid of sympathy.

"You do not get. Understand." She paused for a second and looked down, exhaling tremulously. "I was girl soldier. They torture me. Sixteen years. After I get old . . . enough? I and thirteen other childs run from compound in Chad to WAB, to get fortune to make me safe. I and one other boy only ones that make it. I did not want to kill anymore. But refugee fortunes smaller than regular. All I wanted was a home. Before you came I real eyes that to keep living, I will have to keep killing. I kill there in compound or I kill here, or I die here. I only get fortune for fourteen years. Short four years."

"Not everyone," I stepped in, "gets eighteen years. But you chose. It's true that pursuant to the Refugee Clause of the West African Bloc's Bureau of Fortune Contract you are entitled to a diminished fortune range—"

"Half or less normal!" She seethed.

"Right, that—"

"How is that fair?!"

"It's fair because you were not a citizen of a Bureau–affiliated region. You not from Bureau country."

"I never chose that!" She hanged her head and swung it like a pendulum back and forth, dislodging her sunglasses slightly. She looked back up, without straightening them. "I stopped killing kids. Kids that didn't have . . . enough . . . water. Kids that didn't have enough food. But I still get small fortune? I saved people when I stopped killing! Why don't I get a treat for that? Why does Bureau not treat me nice?"

"You want the truth? The Bureau doesn't care about those kids. They don't really care about you. The reason . . ." I retracted my fangs and swallowed the venom in my voice. "The only reason they gave you a fortune is because it makes them look good to others. People like the Bureau if they give people in your circ—people like you fortunes, but you are nothing to them. It would be easier for the Bureau, for the world without enough water," I unconsciously took my hands off my rifle to gesture, forgetting that my locked GCD would not oblige my attempt, "if all of those children you saved . . . were dead. It would be easier for them if you die now as well, instead of living many years more."

After hearing this, Sekibo took a few seconds to process, then her shoulders slumped, her hands relaxed in helplessness, and she broke down into a sob. I found myself sighing as I watched her chest heave in grief. I allowed her a few more moments of mourning. The sobs abated over the next two or so minutes, and she looked my drone over in disgust.

"You will not face me." She croaked. "My killer will not face me! Are we really so . . . beneath you that you can't do that?" She flung her arms up in her lamentation.

"I wish I could. I wish I had the courage, but I value my life too greatly to attempt to meet with you, to speak with you, face to face. You cannot see it, but I am agonizing over your remonstrance . . . I wish I could, but this is all I can do. Did you not enjoy your life at all? Did the fortune not make things better at all?" I pleaded, seeking exoneration from my misgivings.

Sekibo wrung her hands as she stared into the bleak, expressionless cameras of my GCD before replying.

"Fortune made things a little better, yes. I had water. I had food. I could buy all of this." She swiveled on her hips as she motioned around at the warehouses. "But my child life was taken from me. The fortune was a curse that let me trade one . . . terror for another. When I was a girl, I spend my whole life worrying about when I would die. I flee to try to leave that behind, but I need fortune to live. Once I get fortune, things were good for a time. Then, the feeling come back. I go back to worrying. I look over my shoulder everywhere. I need cameras everywhere. I could not live because I worry when I would die. Waiting for this moment."

"Did you like any part at all?"

I was taken aback as she laughed here, and I was not sure if she was becoming hysterical until a fond smile showed her ragged teeth.

"I liked sushi. I ate sushi as much as I could." She pointed over at the truck. "That's what's in there and some other things. But most of my . . . experiences were . . . not filled up all the way?"

"Empty? Hollow?"

"Yes. Hollow." Her expression slid back into melancholy.

"At least that was better than nothing," I said, more to myself than to Sekibo.

I flipped up my visual peripheral and aligned my rifle with the constricting circles and pulsing lines of my HUD sniping trajectory.

"Better than nothing . . . yes . . . but I wanted to be born with everything. Like you. I should been. It's not fair."

"I apologize for that misfortune."

I adjusted once more on the triangulation data, exhaled, and fired.

You are right. However, we don't deal in the fairness of one's contract, and this world does not accommodate fair. Few flowers can bloom in the desert.

I flipped my visual peripheral down once more and felt a hand on my pack as I examined Sekibo's lifeless body and the blood smears it left on the sand where it fell. I rotated my stiff shoulder as I released the rifle and tapped my GCD to return to a three-meter tether.

ComCom: Send: Seeker 06, Seeker 13, Seeker 18: CC ping EndCom

I pushed myself to my feet as Daria sent our location for drone extraction. Giselle was standing in front of me pointing at her data pad, and I transferred her all of my GCD data and she took control of the drone again.

"Tough one. We'll take care of the rest," she said, flickering her eyes past mine before looking back down at her data pad and walking away.

Incoming transmission from Seeker 18, receive?

ComCom: receive last

"Why do you do this to yourself?"

ComCom: Send: "Someone should . . . I think." PendCom

"Take care."

"Extraction is about eighteen minutes away. Will food cheer you up?" Daria tried.

I realized I must have been wearing my conflict on my countenance. I stopped replaying Sekibo's audio recordings and I managed a smile.

"I am famished," I admitted. "How about sushi?"

"In the UAE?!" Daria shifted back into gear. "It's going to be hard to find a good place!"

"I'll start searching. We've got a few minutes anyway."

"Okay. Are you good? I was going to go dig ol' one leg out of the dune, but I can stick around if you want . . ."

"I'll be fine. I'll have at least an adequate place picked out when you return."

"Nah. Giselle says she's got it. I'll help!" She plopped down next to me, facing away from the sun that was setting over the dunes to brilliant effect.

Incoming transmission from Seeker 13, receive?

ComCom: receive last

"Just wanted to update you on the cleanup, since you dropped out of the squad chat. Sekibo's warehouse is clear. No other signs of life. Pretty typical safe house, if a bit on the luxurious side. Lots of stuffed animals around and toys like that. There was only one other rail rifle directly opposite the one we decommed. Hell of a shot you had, but there's something messed up about how you do things. How the ColCom handles you, I have no idea. Doesn't sit right with me."

ComCom: Send: "I know. Apologies." PendCom

"Let me know a couple of weeks in advance the next time you are going to be working with us, and I can think about how we can work out the kinks."

ComCom: Send: "I appreciate that. However, I don't think an encore is likely. Thanks for your assistance, Chance." EndCom

Daria leaned over and showed me a place on her data pad.
"Sorry, I was . . ." I pointed at my left temple.
"It's fine and stop apologizing! You did well today. The GCDs were acceptable losses and you collected as you said. You were the one who was supposed to take her out, per your rotation requirements. The methods might have been unorthodox within the Bureau, but you played to your strengths. I know I would have liked to go out that way as opposed to cowering behind closed doors. Maybe that's why I let you go for it. Most of my team's targets don't get that privilege."

She took her helmet off and dropped her balaclava, bending her head down to catch my eye, in a bid to raise my spirits, her bangs getting in the way. I unsealed a pocket, pulled out her hair tie, and launched it at her hand. She managed to corral it with her thumb.

"Thanks for continuing to bet on me. I know it is not easy."

We sat for a while until the extraction drones showed up. Daria debriefed with the rest of the squad. Chance was heading back to the WAB Bureau, and Giselle was going to meet with NERDoD after taking a day off in Morocco. The hull of our ride slid open to receive us and I repulsed in after Daria. As we walked to our seats, Daria sent the coordinates for the sushi place she picked out for approval. The drone rerouted and was set to drop us off on a landing pad of the thirty-sixth floor of Vintrey Tower One in Abu Dhabi. Access codes to our rooms were sent along with a generous check-in window as well.

"I'll send my report in some time tomorrow, but what did you think of your recon rotation? I liked having you along! It was nice to spend time together on the job."

"As much as I yearn to be able to work with you again, I don't think I am suited for recon detachments. They are too impersonal for my liking."

"I figured."

Daria yawned, made herself comfortable across the seats, and nestled her head on my lap. I leaned back against my seat and propped my head against a support beam as I absentmindedly ran my fingers through her hair, waiting for the hum of the engines to lull me to sleep as I gazed once more on to the shimmering sea of sand below, bathed in the colors of the most variegated sunset I had ever had the privilege of beholding. And yet, the deepest crimson spreading over the infinite grains of the Sahara had not been shed by the sun, but by my own hands.

5
0956 – The Matrons

"Your window is open, and Onniheim Orphanage has been noti-fied of your pending arrival and the restrictions placed on their Ascension Ritual. Your request for an extension has been approved, and your PTO has been charged sixteen hours. Your updated PTO balance is 24.25 days. Will there be anything else, Collector?"

ComCom: Send: "That will be all." EndCom

I rose to my feet from the commudrone stop, which had been my refuge from the frigid Rovaniemi winds for the last two hours, as quietly as possible so as not to disturb my like–minded, home-less companion. I was only about half finished with the first of two self-heating hot chocolates I had bought for the wait on my approval, but the heat from the reaction used to warm my beverage to an ideal drinking temperature had long since seeped away. I gently lifted the right arm of the old man lying on his side under the bench, back turned towards the entrance to better ward off any gusts that might find their way inside the shelter, and nestled both the unfinished and the unopened cans in the crook between his left bicep and his chest. He stirred a bit as I readjusted his shabby blanket over his shoulder and backed away, hoping my ersatz sub-stitute for a teddy bear might bring him some comfort. I checked to ensure I had retrieved all of my effects and crunched out into the December snow.

Bracing myself against the breeze as flurries of flakes swirled along the path in front of me, I began to question my elected form of approach, wondering if disturbing the quiet streets of the early evening of this part of the world with a Bureau car might have been the better choice. My data pad reminded me that the orphanage was only a few blocks away, and I felt content in my volition as I rounded a corner and descried some children marveling at a decrepit clock post. One of the three younglings, covered toe to top in purple, puffy, insulated clothes, save for the face, whirled around to look at me, expecting the arrival of, I assumed, yet another child and backpedaled into his friend in shock who also turned around to meet me.

"S–sgoin'?" The unwitting lookout chattered, though from fear or the chill I was unsure.

"Sgoin' boys?" I mimicked their vernacular in hopes of setting them at ease.

The final youth still had yet to turn around, and the lookout hit her, harder than he might have intended, on the shoulder twice. As she turned, the lookout signed to her and she looked up at me, her eyes widening. This was certainly fear. It seemed as though the populace of the area was not nearly as accustomed to Collector sightings as most of my other experiences. This was probably a result of the recent changes to the Bureau in the area. The kids must not have been older than nine. I knelt down in the snow in hopes of seeming less intimidating.

"I'm afraid I never learned sign language. Can you keep signing to her, so she understands I'm not here to hurt you or get you into trouble?" I asked the lookout. He nodded and signed. The girl seemed relieved, but there was still a hint of distrust in her eyes.

"May I have your names?" I continued.

The lookout forgot to sign quickly enough, and the girl tugged on his sleeve.

"I'm Matti." The lookout replied. Then, he pointed at the girl. "This is Johanna."

"Eero." The other boy chimed in. "You're a Collector, huh?"

Johanna signed to Matti and looked at me, inquisitive.

"Johanna wants to know what your name is," Matti said.

"Collector will be fine for this interaction. Security measures don't allow me to give out my name. Apologies. I know this is quite rude." I shrugged my shoulders and gave them a look of helplessness.

Matti paused for a bit, mulling over his translation, and he signed. Johanna laughed quietly and perked up a bit.

"You just made fun of me, didn't you?" I stared daggers at Matti. Then I broke into a smirk as a look of horror leapt across his face.

"You do know sign language!" He accused me, outstretched, mittened index finger and all. Eero looked at Matti, then at me, mouth agape. I laughed.

"Not quite," I responded, recomposing myself. "I know expressions. I know the slight movements of your faces. Your body language. You three obviously know each other quite well and that helps eliminate some of the guesswork involved."

"Woah!" Eero exclaimed.

"That said," I tapped my HUD array and waggled my data pad in front of them, "I could always scan all of the signs you make, but I'd rather trust you for the rest of our conversation. How does that sound?"

"Hahahaha! The Collector got you!" Eero slapped Matti on the back.

"Okay," Matti consented, his face reddening.

"So what are you all up to?" I looked around the miniature park, surrounded by apartment buildings so the only exit was behind me.

I shifted off to the side a bit to make it seem like I was not guarding their only path of escape.

"We always meet here before we go play before dinner is done," Matti replied, fingers moving to relay the message.

"At this clock? Do you all live around here?"

"Yeah, but we won't tell you where. For security reasons." Matti straightened up, trying to imitate my pose as he said this. I chuckled at the retort.

"Very good! You could make a fine Collector one day."

Johanna kicked her boots in the snow, impatiently waiting for Matti to catch up. I looked at her, pointed at her, and I tapped behind my ear at my ComCom implantation site, then I curled the fingers on my left hand into a question mark for her to see, tilting my head and raising my eyebrows to convey curiosity. She lifted up her hands and dropped her hood momentarily to swivel her head from side to side, brown ponytail sliding across her shoulders, as she did. Then, she shook her head no and signed apologetically.

"What did you call this place? A clock?" Eero asked.

I studied his face for a second. Then, I responded, pointing at the lamppost, atop which a numberless, luminous, clock face had been affixed.

"That is a clock, not this whole place. Have you never before seen a clock?"

They all turned to look up at the clock, which had twelve glowing, pink bars to symbolize the hours and a sturdy, metal hand that was still moving, but only one. The glass surface that would have protected its face had been shattered, judging by the jagged pieces jutting out from the rim. I was glad that the children were too short to be able to touch the face, though I imagine passersby hadn't given the forlorn object the time of day in quite some time, much less sought the very same knowledge from its swiveling aspect. Looking at the anchorage point for the base of the clock hands, it seemed as though the second hand had fallen off long ago, but the hour hand had miraculously clung on, determined to fulfill its duty to the last. I walked up and examined the anchorage point to check its durability. The design was dual layered and the outer ring that would have once held the second hand had been compromised. The tiny chink could have been made by a rock or a hailstone, but I didn't suspect tampering. Luckily, the missing second hand was also second in importance. Most people that might have still used the clock would have preferred to estimate by the hour anyway, but that wouldn't quite do for my lesson.

"I can teach you all how to use the clock if you'd like." I turned around to see that the children had all gathered behind me to see what I had been doing.

"I know how to use a clock," Matti said. "Look. It's . . . 5:15." He pulled his left glove down and his sleeve up to show me his data pad screen.

"That is a digital clock." I gestured. "This is an analog clock."

"Nobody uses those anymore, though," Eero told me, incredulously.

"That is, for the most part, true." I conceded. "The advent of screens and the digital watch saw to that. You don't have to learn if you don't wish. It's just another piece of knowledge."

Matti finished signing and Johanna looked at him. Then, she pointed at Eero and Matti signed, conveying what Eero said as opposed to what I had said. She looked at me, her spring green eyes a reminder of that abbreviated season between the winter snows and the nigh ceaseless summer sunlight of the Laplands. She signed, emphatically.

"Johanna wants to learn. I'll learn too. Eero?"

Eero wiped his nose with the back of his glove and sat down in the snow.

"Okay. Will it take long, though?" He asked, scratching his lower back.

"I'll teach you the basics, and you can practice by looking it up on your data pad sometime if you want. Sound good?"

"Fine, but my mom wanted me home at 6:15 for dinner." Eero groaned.

"She always wants you home so early!" Matti complained.

"Well, when we are done, you might be able to estimate how much time you'll have left for play," I coaxed.

"I can just ask Matti. He always knows with his data pad."

"You'll be able to know by yourself, though it won't be quite as accurate."

"Hmmmm. Okay. Last time Matti was sick, my dad took away my games cuz I got home late, so if he's sick again, I can use the clock to not have that happen?"

"You could, more or less."

"Apt! Okay, let's do it!"

Matti sprawled on top of Eero's legs, making himself comfortable, and Johanna sat cross legged in the snow as I walked over to one of the pine trees ringing around the complex to find a makeshift second hand in the form of a branch. I noted that the fear the children displayed when we had first met had vanished, and I appreciated another opportunity to test my skills, though in a less daunting environment. Childish skepticism is an easy barrier to surmount. Target skepticism is a bit more mature and not nearly as transient. I rummaged in the glistening, freshly fallen snow below the base of one of the pines in the lantern-lit plaza, inspiring the invigorating scent of the sap, and found a suitable instrument.

"Tell Johanna that I don't know how she can sit like that so easily!" I called over to Matti as I strolled back to them. "I was never able to sit cross legged for more than a few seconds without becoming uncomfortable."

She looked at me and beamed, then gracefully rose to her feet without the aid of her hands and slowly lowered herself back down into her previous position, signing all the while.

"She says she's a dancer, a folk dancer." Matti translated.

I clapped my hands together and looked at her, impressed. I was glad to see that, unlike archaic representations of time, some elder traditions had not been forgotten.

"Let's begin. Do you all know fractions?"

Eero and Matti nodded, and Johanna quickly followed.

Kudos, Finnish education.

I lectured for the next eighteen minutes while gesticulating between the children and the marks on the clock face with my left hand and my second hand. It seemed as though all of them were following along, though Matti didn't begin participating with fervor until Johanna began asking questions. Overall, they seemed to be picking up the ideas quite well and my spontaneous endeavor in public relations seemed to be succeeding.

"So, Eero, if your mother requires you to be home at 6:15 and we will be finishing our lesson after about ten more minutes of practice, assuming you answer this question correctly, how much time will you have left to play with your friends if the current time is this?"

I moved the second stick to mark the current time of day.

"Oh! I know!" Matti said, raising his hand, which Johanna quickly wrestled into submission with her right arm while pointing at Eero with her left.

"Ummm. Seven multiplied by five is thirty-five, minus about . . . two is . . . 5:33. Uhhh. Forty-two minutes! About!"

"Well done."

"I knew it first!" Matti jeered.

"So! And you looked at your data pad! I saw you!" Eero yelled.

"Matti. If you're so smart, you should spend time helping others around you become smarter as opposed to spending it self-validating," I upbraided.

"What do you mean? I can't even drive yet. Plus, most autos park themselves."

"Validating, not valeting. Stop bragging and help Eero become as fast as you."

A tug forced Matti to pause for a moment and sign what had happened, and Johanna seemed to agree with my challenge.

"Can I count on you to help Eero and Johanna practice when I am gone?"

Matti looked from me to the other two, signed, and then nodded, puffing himself up a bit more under his puffy coat as Johanna smiled at him.

"Lovely. Now, let's practice a bit more . . ."

I detected the sounds of heavy footsteps trudging on some of the hard-packed snow around the corner of the complex's surrounding path, and I instinctively dropped my instrument of education to free up my hand for one of destruction, pausing its swing next to my right thigh.

"I thought I heard yelling over here!" A man's voice called out as he rounded the corner, covered in orange outerwear, except for his mustachioed mouth. "Are you kids okay?"

"Uncle Niilo!" Matti greeted, as he rolled off of Eero. "Look who we met! It's a—"

"Kids! Get away from there!" The protective parent roared. "That's a Collector!"

"We know! We—" Matti tried.

"Now! You should not be here, Collector! These ones are too young for you to take, or have you 'misidentified' your target as well?"

I retracted my right hand so as not to exacerbate the bombastic man's expostulations and I pointed behind Johanna, who had not yet turned around so that she might notice her liberator.

"What does he mean, Collector?" Eero asked as he prepared to leave.

"He means to be stereotypical and snide, but he is attending to your best interests," I replied with the right words for the wrong audience. "Sorry. He's right. You all should get along. You wanted to go play anyway."

"Are you here to take someone? One of us? I thought Collectors only killed adults. Are you here to kill someone?" Eero asked, fear resurfacing in his mien as he backed away from me.

"Technically, I am not going to be killing this time, which is a rarity. I am also not here for any of you. I was only seeking another conversation and to do my part to try to ensure that your generation does not end up like his." I jerked my head towards the unflinching uncle.

Eero turned around and trudged a few paces before looking over his shoulder as Matti came back to grab Johanna's hand to lead her away.

"You don't seem like someone who would kill," Eero said, with an inflection of doubt that he squashed by the end of his consolation.

"I feel as though I thought that at some point as well . . ." I searched.

"Let's go kids! Why are you taking so long! That Collector is dangerous!" Niilo's voice reverberated off the walls of the U–shaped building. I could see tints being dropped in a few windows now.

I looked at Johanna, who would not leave with Matti until I saw what she was doing. She was signing.

"What is she saying?" I asked Matti, looking up at his uncle to read the impatience in his twitching chin.

"She says she's sorry you are treated like this. Now we have to go."

Matti turned around and tugged Johanna behind him. I swiped my data pad and began searching for a video translator for English to sign language. I watched carefully and mimicked a few times.

"What are you doing, Collector? Can't you just leave us alone?! We're going! You don't need to call your dogs!" Niilo assured, his voice quavering.

I shut out Niilo's vocalizations of his perturbations and stared into the back of Johanna's hood, waiting, hoping. Eero had already rounded the corner, and Niilo turned to leave as Matti caught up to his side. Johanna shrugged Matti's hand off and slowed her pace a bit. I checked the vid one more time and looked up as she turned to round the corner and stopped to look at me. I waved then looked at my data pad and signed as best I could while trying to will the words from my mind to hers.

You all be better than him . . . Better than me.

She nodded and left, and I believed they could. Wishing I had been allotted more of that ephemeral resource on which I had been lecturing so recently to better inculcate my desires to some of the more promising members of the next generation I had met in some time, I set out along my route to the orphanage knowing that the residents living around my erstwhile classroom would not be judging me by the knowledge I had just imparted, or the demeanor with which I had done so, so much as by the attitude of my next twenty steps. I kept my head down and slowed my pace, looking for all the world as though the chastisement I had received had caused me to reconsider my position as one of the vilified vagrants of the Bureau. Turning on to step twenty-one, I was backstage eagerly looking forward to my next conversations as I wondered what would be different now that, for once, I would not be pulling the trigger or pushing the plunger to punctuate its end.

Onniheim Orphanage is a specially regulated entity within the Bureau in that it was erected as a monumental admission of fallibility. A few decades back, the fledgling Bureau instated in the region at the peoples' behest was almost torn from its nest as recompense for a grave miscalculation. An immature Collector, more so than me, was on her second mission. The unredacted mission debrief released to the Collector branches for training purposes showed she followed protocols well. Frequent ComCom check-ins, proceeded through the mission at pace, cornered the target through the use of imaging and audio taps, and she used one of her three elected means of dispatch, an unmodified EinIn SMG 4SB, to finish the target upon sighting. Her primary oversight was one that only a rook would have made in the moment. She fired without conversing with the target.

While I admit I have a predilection for performing this part of my job to the point of gluttony, all Collectors are supposed to engage their targets in conversation, where possible, and it was certainly possible in this instance, in order to better ID before DD, which is to say one better be positive, beyond a reasonable doubt, before dealing death.

For most cases of Collection, she would have walked out and on to the next mission without incident. I'm sure she thought exactly that as she turned around and sent her CC ping while exiting the premises of the wrong apartment for her rather ruthless execution. Waiting for her victim to sequester himself from society in his apartment was a call that the Bureau would approve every time. Not noticing the fact that the unit number was two less than the unit listed on the target's paperwork while breaching the door would not be.

When the results from the cleanup crew arrived, DNA analysis confirmed that she had collected the target's monozygotic twin. When the actual target went over to have supper with his brother and found the cleanup crew, he bolted to the authorities before another Collection window could be approved. The public outrage was great enough to threaten a pruning of the new Bureau branch. Though misCollections like this have certainly occurred throughout the sordid history of the Bureau, few have been so publicly exposed, and fewer left the Bureau with so little ground on which to stand in their own defense.

Discussions were held on all governmental levels, and it was certain that the Bureau would have to do something incredible in order to atone from a PR standpoint. A life for a life would not be enough to set the local community at ease, much less those critiquing on an international scale. The original target was pardoned, something that had never before occurred in the history of the Bureau under these types of circumstances. Higher ups felt they might as well outdo themselves in order to increase the likelihood of this storm blowing over as expeditiously as possible, so they attempted to build up the community through a grant of sorts that might distract the locals from the Bureau's ignominy. However, they would not budge on the principle that someone would have to pay for the fortune involved in the construction and upkeep of this penance of a property.

A young woman, seeking an end to the strife and a return of the vaunted peace of her hometown, volunteered on the condition that she would be able to run the orphanage without frequent Bureau interaction once a contract had been signed. She only wanted to see us upon violation of contract and at time of Collection. The woman was twenty-six years old, a steal for the Bureau. They agreed. Thus, Onniheim Orphanage was constructed in propitiation, the young woman became its first Matron, enough children were served over the years for most of Rovaniemi to forgive the Bureau for its transgression, and I elected to mediate the Ascension of its third Matron and the Collection of its second.

The wrought iron gates of the outer wall swung open for me as I approached the property and nodded to the cameras. Walking up the long drive, I passed a young boy who was shoveling to clear my way as well as a Domestidrone model doing the same, only more efficiently and with fewer harrumphs. Both greeted me as I passed. I checked the time and spent some more of it to marvel at the architecture of the orphanage.

The exterior of the building was crafted to evoke themes of the Victorian Gothic architectural style that belied the hypermodern interior glimpsed through the frosty panes of a square-latticed angled bay window on the first floor. The brickwork alternated from white to black every six courses excepting gray bricks set proximately to triple windows. This coupled with the silvered roofing emphasized

the motif of polychromy. The quoins running up the corners alternated colors with their laterally associated courses to stunning
effect. The eight high-peaked gables were trimmed with snaking
bargeboards shaped after some of the famous fells of the Laplands.
Rinceaux shaped as pine branches wound across the divides between
floors. The structure was sternly symmetrical, with three super-ter-
ranean floors not counting attic space. The only aspect marring the
view, a single dented cap in one of the six quadruple flue chimneys,
transfixed me for a few seconds and I wondered if they actually used
fireplaces. A few snowflakes fluttered down from the balustrades as I
kicked my boots a bit on the steps under the portico protruding over
the main entrance, and I proceeded to rap my knuckles on the oaken
doors. I looked up at the arched transom into which the name of the
orphanage had been carved and sent an arrival ping to my handler.

A young woman of approximately eighteen years dropped the
tint of the window of the left door and peered out at me as I saluted
her by tapping my visor and turning over my wrist with a slight bow
to indicate I was at her service, and, in this unusual Collection, I
literally happened to be. She tapped a keypad inside, and the left door
slid above the transom with a muffled pneumatic hiss.

"Welcome, Collector. We have been expecting you. You're late for
tweenmeal, but early for supper. May I take anything in or out for
you?"

The woman welcomed me with a fluent curtsey that rustled her
maroon and black diamonded skirt slightly, one hand occupied with
the pinching of the black lace ruffles at the end of the garment and
the other restraining her black and white diamonded, knotless tie to
her chest below the platinum mag tie clip encrusted with eight rubies
that glittered in the direct light of the atrium.

"That won't be necessary, Matron–Prospect, but I appreciate the
unexpected expectation and welcome. I can see I will be in good care
with your company."

I tilted my head a bit while flipping my right index and middle fingers up to request her return to ease. She tossed her lengthy, platinum blonde, sideswept sheet of bangs over her right shoulder as she straightened and stood at the ready.

"Milla is my name if it pleases you to call me by it. Your quarters are on the third floor with mine, should you like to retire immediately . . ."

Her punchy voice trailed off as she glanced at a pair of girls who were ascending the stairs and a look of disdain portended her correction.

"Sanna!" Milla trilled and the girl immediately whirled about and her climbing partner did as well, tripping a bit on the next step up, as they had been linked at the arms, unwittingly hiding my guess at the offense from Milla's view. Milla widened her powder blue eyes and outstretched her neck in her exasperation and the girl stiffened.

"The both of you are embarrassing me in front of our guest, but you, in particular, need to improve your appearance! What have you done wrong?" Milla thawed her icy tone a bit as she asked the question.

Sanna and her companion descended, unlinking their arms and setting them at their sides as they sullenly walked in front of Milla, who folded her arms to assume a practiced disciplinary posture of dissatisfaction. Sanna looked up first to reply.

"We're sorry, Milla. We did not greet our guest appropriately. May we do so now?" Sanna asked, looking to make amends.

"You may do so after composing your appearance. Aina? Can you help Sanna identify what she is obviously missing?"

Aina stretched her left arm out and tugged twice on her companion's white, ruffled, uniform blouse while Milla spun to show her a well tucked exemplar. Sanna blushed, and she turned directly towards me as she reached back and pulled quickly with her left hand and plunged her right down her lumbar to tuck the tail of the blouse appropriately. Then, she traced her fingers around her waist to feel out any other possible errors, and she seemed satisfied.

"Hello, Collector! Welcome to Onniheim Orphanage!" Sanna greeted, and Aina joined in.

"Good evening, young ladies. If all of your peers comport themselves as you have just now, I'm sure I will enjoy my stay. As you were, now," I assured.

The two girls looked at Milla for permission, and she waved them on with a reserved smile and a wink of pride.

"Where were we?" Milla reengaged, asking what I was sure was a superfluous question as a segue for my own comfort. "Your quarters. Would you like to retire until supper?"

"I'm sure I'll find them accommodating, but later. I'm intrigued by your operation, and I would be most interested to meet more of the orphans and learn more about how you will be running the place. I'm told that the Ascension Ceremony is scheduled for tomorrow afternoon, so I have cleared my schedule until then. This is a unique experience among my Collections, and I'd very much like to take in as much as I can."

"Well, supper will sound in about forty minutes, I'll have to attend to the Matron ten minutes prior, but I have the next half an hour or so free. Would you like to sit somewhere? I'd be happy to answer any questions you may have in the meantime, should they be in my knowledge to answer, but most of the orphans are currently streaming classes so they will be indisposed. I'd be happy to take you on a tour in the morning to meet some of them!"

"That all sounds delightful. Perhaps our seating arrangements will answer my first question? Do you happen to have a traditional fireplace?" I asked, tempering my excitement, as I had only ever heard about them in stories.

"We do have exactly one. The first Matron requested that it be included in the floor plan because she enjoyed basking in the heat when she would come in from the elements. She said it helped ease her illness. Isn't that peculiar? This way."

"Illness?" I questioned, as Milla clicked around the corner of the entrance to one of the hallways behind the ballroom staircase leading up to the second floor in her maroon flats.

"The first matron, Eevi, suffered from cancer. If she weren't collected, she said that her estimate was not longer than two more years after the beginning of her window; at least, that's what she told Matron Kirsi," Milla replied as if reading from a textbook.

We proceeded down the hallway, and I counted four doors total, two on each side, before we reached the terminus where the fireplace was located. There were four, black leather, wingback chairs organized in an arc facing the fixture. The mantel of the fireplace was a screen that was depicting snowfall in a forest and a reindeer would bound across the tree line every now and again.

"The Bureau really must have wanted to close this deal quickly if the first Matron had cancer. It is highly unusual for them to grant a fortune to someone who is afflicted with a terminal disease or disorder. Then again, I suppose the only other circumstances I can recall in which they would have done so have centered around PR scandals."

Milla directed me to the chair left of center and she looked surprised for a moment, but that was only due to her picking something out of the eyelashes above her left eye. She opened a compartment in the wall next to the mantel and pulled out some wood, kindling, and a lighter. She had her hands full, so I offered to help and brought the wood over to the firebox above the raised hearth and set it in, piling the logs together. She followed behind quickly and inserted kindling into the cracks between the logs, and I backed away, realizing I had been allowing her to come too close for my typical interactions. There was an air about her that set me at ease, which stemmed from her capability. I did not find her threatening in any way. She seemed to exude a sense of caring, which I initially detected in her interactions with the children. She was stern but caring. I handed her the stoker from the compartment, and she pushed another log into place and lit the kindling.

"The way Matron Kirsi tells it, the Bureau took records from a local doctor when they evaluated Matron Eevi, but the doctor falsified her information. The Bureau found out after the Collection window closed, and they didn't even punish the doctor. Kirsi says they just wanted to wash their hands of the situation entirely, but everyone reveres Eevi as someone who pulled a fast one on the Bureau." Milla finished stoking the fire and she was smiling, wistfully.

"You wouldn't be trying to do the same somehow, would you? I haven't sensed any deception or treachery in you yet, but I'll admit that smile of yours would normally be considered worrisome in my line of work, not that I don't sport them myself on occasion."

I blinked a bit at the heat and moved my chair back slightly as she flattened her skirt and sat in the one to my right.

"I don't think the Bureau would make the same mistake twice. Don't worry. I initially resented my 'fate,' but I have grown to accept it, enjoy it, even. I only smile like that when I think of how courageous the Matrons before me must have been to take on this role. I don't think I have the same courage. I just don't want to disappoint the other children. It's really only cowardice that drives me." Milla confessed, looking down her black stockings at the shoe she was dangling off of her right hallux, one of the only glimpses I had at her repressed childhood.

"You are no less a coward than I. It is my charge to take the lives of others in order to maintain my own lifespan, because I was not strong enough or confident enough to try to take a risk. I just happened to have the aptitude to fit into this niche. At least your sacrifice is altruistic. Though, tomorrow evening my charge will fall to you in another concession of the Bureau in this indemnification. I have been informed that your first Matron, Eevi, required this barbarism to be included in the contract between her and the Bureau. Do you know why?" I asked, turning my chair to face her while she draped her legs over the left arm of hers and stared at me with her head resting on the right arm.

"I bet you know some of my most intimate secrets. Things that I may have only ever told one person or never even spoke about at all." She began, managing a smile that I took to be meretricious as her tone suddenly shifted. "I bet you could tell what I'm wearing," she unfastened one of the mag buttons affixing her tie under the collar of her blouse, "under this . . ." she tugged at her lapel and I looked away. "I bet you know the name of my first friend, what I ate yesterday, my grade in my economics class." She sighed. "Look at me, please. I won't go any further."

I looked back and her blouse only had the top two buttons undone, but she had kicked off her shoes entirely.

"Do you know all those things? Tell me. I have been looking forward to talking with you because I have tried to get into the mind-state we think you Collectors have over the past week in order to help me with the task I have at hand, but you aren't like the descriptions I've heard from people around here." She stretched her right arm behind her head to better prop it up in order to meet my eyes.

"Do you mean that to be complimentary? From my limited sample size, I can say that enough time has passed that the children around here don't immediately decry Collectors. The fear is there, but it is an uneducated fear and one that can be allayed. The elders, on the other hand, they have yet to forget. You still strike me as a child, though one who is ready to become an adult. You seem to possess the requisite responsibility, and you are thoughtful enough to take care of the others and to make this choice. To answer your initial question, I don't know the undergarments you happened to put on today, but I do know your measurements are 32-22-30; your favorite food is strawberry yogurt; you perform adequately in economics, but

you could perform better if you weren't so busy with your duties as
Matron-Prospect. I know your polydactyly was illegally corrected by
a surgery facilitated through a distant relation when you were seven,
but not before you earned the nickname Milla Manyfingers. I know
many other things besides but none of those things really allow me
to know you, which is why I appreciate the privilege to bask in this
environ, as your first Matron once did, though I suffer mentally from
a different illness entirely, conversing with you."

"That's why." Milla asserted. "You are not the norm, and I doubt
you ever will be within the Bureau. Eevi saw the Bureau for what it
was when they tried to placate us with Onniheim. She saw the opportunity to better the lives of people around her, and she took it. She
cared about those close to her when the Bureau never could. She saw
the people, not just the numbers. She wanted that same courtesy to
be extended to her at the end, to be killed by someone who cared,
someone who knew who she was and what she had done, and someone who could carry on the same responsibility, not some randomly
assigned Collector."

The crackling of the logs was the only sound we could hear for
a time as we contemplated the fate that awaited Milla. She shifted
to sitting with her head in her hands, and she was breathing a little
heavier. I remained silent until I saw a tear run down her wrist.

"I try to provide the same service in a way, through my conversations. The Bureau is the judge and jury, and they would . . . I would
. . . have me play the executioner, though, more often than not, I find
my time is spent in confession and consolation. Someone I hold dear
once told me that I could have found the same kind of work in the
church seventy years back. I told her that the pay wasn't as good and
more people these days are looking for a way out of their struggles
through money as opposed to faith. Hence, here I am. But you are in
a position that puts my job to shame. I can really only get to know
someone I will collect in a few moments before completing my task,

as the clock is always ticking for the Bureau and I can't stop the hands. But you, you have had the privilege of getting to know the Matron for, what, the past twelve or so years that you can remember? I think I can see the reasoning behind this Ascension Ceremony now. Do you think Matron Kirsi would prefer you doing it in the end? I'd still be happy to converse with her for my part, but I think, were I to be in her situation, I would prefer you do it as well."

Milla nodded and she picked up her head.

"I think . . ." She paused to compose herself, wiping the tears from her eyes, smearing her mascara a bit as she did. "I think she would. But it's hard. These women are my heroes. They've done so much for these children in a time that would forsake them."

"And you could do the same for a future generation, but only if you wish to." I finished.

"I do. I want to make that difference," she resolved.

"It appears you are ready, though it's about a day too soon." I stifled a sneeze while checking my data pad for the time. "About two minutes until you have to attend to the Matron, though I suppose this conversation didn't proceed quite as planned, but that is the beauty of it!" I bent down a bit in my chair to catch Milla's eye, as Daria had done with me so many times in hopes of cheering me up, and Milla recovered.

"You didn't really go the way I had planned either. I can answer more of your questions tomorrow during the tour, and I promise I'll be less of an emotional wreck. Today has been . . . difficult for me. The Matron would like to speak to you this evening after supper, but she will not be able to do much with you tomorrow, you understand."

"Of course."

"She also wanted me to give you my ComCom ID so that you can keep in touch with me should you require anything. She told me to tell you that she would have given you her own, but she 'despises those infernal contraptions!'"

"Appreciated," I replied as I authenticated a one-way contact to her ComCom as she recited her ID. "I won't bother you too much."

"Well, if you follow the children, they'll take you to the dining hall. Otherwise, it is on the second floor through the middle doorway. You can, but probably won't miss it. I'll see you at the table in a few. Oh . . ." She looked at the fireplace.

"I'll take care of it. You have done more than enough. Thank you."

Milla got up, fixed her attire appropriately for a model resident, and clicked down the hall. I spread the logs apart in the firebox after enjoying the heat for a time, turned them a bit to smother them somewhat with the ashes present, affixed a camera dot to the underside of the mantel and synced it with my data pad, and closed the grate.

A two–tone ring sounded from the speaker in the corner of the room three times to notify the residents that it was time for supper, judging by the children trickling out from the rooms in the hallway. I followed a boy down the black vinyl flooring, noticing that his appearance was slightly different than Milla's. The coloring and patterning of all his clothes matched except for the cuffs of his pants, which were white. I accelerated past the child, who was lagging behind his hall mates a bit due to a difficult decision he was making on his data pad for a game he was playing. He mustered a greeting as I passed by, and I returned the greeting in kind. The two other children exiting from the hallway in front of me, a girl and another boy, also had white markings, the girl's skirt lace and the boy's cuffs. Two children from the mirrored hallway on the opposite side of the ballroom staircase climbing the stairs with me were also branded with the white. I surveyed their ties, remembering one of the outfit aspects by which I had identified Milla as the Matron-Prospect, and I noticed that besides the white coloring of the lace and cuffs, each of these children had tie clips encrusted with a single ruby, as opposed to Milla's eight. I peeled away from the confluence of children heading into the main hallway to lean on one of the walls and watch the children descending from the third to the second floor via the two, mirrored, curving wing staircases as well as those coming down the hallways of the second floor. Only two children arrived from the second-floor hallways, both with maroon trimming, and four children descended from the lofty heights of the third floor. The children from the third floor were trimmed with black, except for one, who looked quite out of place walking next to Milla, sullying the pattern I had been tracking with his white. His hunched shoulders and downturned eyes along with Milla's occasional monitoring glances suggested that he had been scolded recently.

"Run along, now," Milla said as she patted the boy on his way, and he hurried into the hallway after the stragglers with another apology.

"Hello again!" Milla greeted, with a playful look of bewilderment at her underpercenter's antics. "They always figure out new ways to get up to trouble!"

"Trouble?" I wheedled, as I turned to match Milla's stride.

"That one, Geir, has had a crush on one of our 2–percenters since he got here, and he keeps trying to win him over through his skill with robotics. So, he rigged up a teddy bear to follow his crush around, but he didn't program a way for it to open the boy's room door barring his advance, so Geir went up to help the little guy out and was spotted by one of the floor residents, so I had to talk with him a bit."

"Well, at least he is applying himself, or, at least, his robotic minions!" I japed, imitating the bear.

"That's true. Hungry?" She inquired, as we reached the dining room.

"Oh yes, though I am leery of the smorgasbord that awaits. In my travels, I have yet to dine in this region of the world, and I am notoriously finicky about my nutriment." I expressed, baring my apprehension.

"We do tend to eat traditional fare often. I could always have some of the residents eating instant get something for you—"

"No, no. That would be too boorish by a half. I'll make do as long as there is . . ." I began to scan the long table, which had offerings repeated in triplicate, for my prey of choice. "Ah! Bread and butter!"

"Are you sure?" Milla directed me around to the right side of the twenty-five–chair table, inflecting to suggest that might not be enough. "That would be a meager meal for a guest. We rarely have them, after all, guests, not meals."

"I've grown accustomed to making do on the meager, though I'll dabble in a few of the other dishes if you don't mind. I am seeing some others about which I am curious. Rest assured, this will be more hospitable a hosting than I have had in quite some time, so please do not disparage your dining any further on my account."

We reached the head of the table and Milla pulled my chair out, her chair opposite out, and then she proceeded to the head chair, pulled it out and the chatter in the room ceased. Then, she pushed the head chair back in as the rest of the faces in the room turned towards her and the bodies rose from their chairs. She folded her hands while standing next to the head chair and she began to speak.

"Good evening, all! There is only one announcement before supper this evening, but it is one of which I am sure you are all aware by now. Standing next to me is Matron Kirsi's Collector. Please extend your welcome now."

"Good evening, Collector!" The gathered greeted as I bounced my gaze between each of their faces, stopping on Geir.

"Good evening, all! Thank you for allowing me into your home, which is lovely, and for all of the hospitality given and to be given. I look forward to our future interactions!" I replied, knowing they couldn't have refused my entry should they have wished, though appreciative, nonetheless.

"Matron Kirsi will not be joining us this evening, as she still holds vigil and makes preparations for the Ascension, but she will be present tomorrow to meet with you all. Please ensure that you are prepared, and you are to clear your schedules absolutely for your designated meeting time period. That will be all. Please dig in!"

Milla motioned towards the table as she finished and those gathered took their seats and began reaching for the dishes. Milla motioned for me to sit as well, and I alit gently on the black leather cushion of the chair.

"Attendance seems high this evening, despite the Matron's absence, so that is well, don't you think, Milla?"

The young man seated to my left began in a nasally voice, as he passed a plate of food to me that looked a lot like pizza in the speckled black and brown dots covering its surface, the middle of which had been removed to make space for a bowl containing an orange jam of sorts. I supposed it was a cheese of some kind, and I removed a slice to my plate, without taking any of the jam, and I passed the remainder to Milla.

"Only seven unaccounted for, though our numbers account for two of those. What are Hale and Tim doing? They reflect poorly on us by not attending. Screen preference is more acceptable among the underpercenters, but we are supposed to be modeling better socialization for them." Milla replied, staring at the young man, cocking her head to the right, and widening her eyes as she passed the plate across an empty chair to a girl who had yet to say anything since my entry into the dining room.

"If I may," I joined in, "seven missing is well attended? How many children are at Onniheim, currently?"

"Nineteen, as usual. Launo, by the way." The man inclined his head as he passed me the bread plate, from which I took three discs of the flat bread and a couple pats of butter. "Tim is delivering an oral that is running late for his business ethics course, Hale is probably eating instant again. You know him."

"Pleasure," I replied. "Though, I suppose having this many people gathered at a table is an accomplishment these days."

I looked down the length of the table to see the empty chairs and deduced the number of percenters in each category based on the coloration of the chair cushions, which matched the uniform trim coloration of their designated inhabitants, and the chairs that had remained pushed in for which a table setting had not been laid out. There were, assuming settings were laid out for all of the children in the orphanage: eight 1–percenters, six 2–percenters, and five 3–percenters and up.

"Is it this bad overairs as well?" The girl who had yet to speak asked me, quickly flitting her gaze from my injection gauntlet to my eyes as I forked some kind of sautéed meat over mashed potatoes on to my plate with a louder than intended splat.

"Worse, Miss . . ." I dangled.

"Elli."

"Much worse, Miss Elli. From where I hail, it is all too common to see families and friends eating while taking their present company for granted. Screens of one kind or another abound. If those have been revoked, chances are clandestine ComCom messaging is the next step in the algorithm of alienation. I've started to wonder if some of these people would converse with the person on the other end of the channel if that person happened to walk in and sit at the table at that moment or if they would change links to someone more distant out of discomfort. The more one eats with someone else, the more likely this becomes. Unless an event is scheduled far in advance for a purpose of import to all the parties hoped to be involved, any attempt at a family dinner of old is either a form of suffering from which many would like to escape as soon as possible or an exercise in futility and the invention of excuses. It seems you all have precluded that with the option of allowing some to miss supper?"

I looked down the table again, as I began buttering my bread, to gauge the conversations being had.

"Correct." Milla chimed in. "Attending mealtimes is technically optional, a provision from Matron Kirsi set about six years ago. She didn't want to deal with the children protesting a number of issues surrounding the set times. Although, for some dedicated individuals, it is an allowance that is appreciated. They are allowed to scavenge what is left after we have left from the kitchens if they would like, but it seems Kirsi appreciates a proper supper as well."

"Well said. That is immediately apparent. Would any of you care to educate me on the vittles before me before I devour them?" I asked, looking around the table.

"Elli?" Milla inquired.

Elli waved the suggestion off as she ladled some soup into a bowl.

"I asked because Elli is one of the chefs, but I suppose I'll do."

Milla gestured at her plate initially to the food we had in common. The cheese was known as *leipäjuusto* and it was made from cow's milk. The bread was made from potatoes and it was called *rieska*. It was quite good if a little tough compared to my favorites, but the butter softened it up a bit as it percolated through the layers. The mashed potatoes were obvious and needed no introduction, unlike the meat served over them. This meat was reindeer steak, a first for me, which was sautéed in butter and oil, seasoned with salt and pepper, into which a bit of cream had been added. It was served with a garnish of pickled cucumber, an option I did not relish, and so I left it by the wayside. It was exceptionally delicious, and it defied my expectations to the point that I will miss not being able to eat it regularly. Truly a delicacy. Drinks ranged from water, to juices, to a mulled wine. The soup Elli was drinking was a thick, pea variety into which mustard had been added along with optional thyme. My grimace at the imagined taste of the combination of these ingredients elicited a vigorous roll from Elli's eye that was not hidden by her upturned bowl.

"It's not for everyone," Elli said, as she set her empty bowl down and began reaching for a pancake with jam on it, which was apparently served as a companion to the soup, which befuddled me even further.

"And for dessert, you're in luck. It hasn't been brought out yet, but we have a *pulla*, right, Elli?" Milla confirmed. "That's basically like cinnamon rolls from the States only with almonds and cardamom seeds, but it's bread, so you should enjoy it!"

"Well," I held up more of the reindeer meat, called *poronkäristys*, and shoveled it into my mouth while grinning at Elli, "I have tried everything on my plate and I must say, it has been months since I have been so satisfied with my expectations being so terrifically exceeded. Perhaps, I'll visit for pleasure again one day when you all have this meal. Thank you, Elli."

Were it so easy.

Milla, Launo, and I talked for a while about my trip and I told them what I was allowed as we finished our main course. Elli listened for a time and then she lifted a sleeve and checked her data pad under the table as we began setting our plates aside for dessert. Launo excused himself and headed back up to the rooms on the third floor. The kitchen doors slid open for Elli and one of the 2–percenters I had yet to meet in response to the fobs tucked into their pockets and the two came back out a few minutes later, arms balancing trays laden with piping hot pastries, of varying qualities, which they dropped off at each third of the table. Milla caught the ear of one of the 1–percenters, who was trying to escape to her room, pulla in mouth, and forced her to sit and finish before she departed. I slouched in my chair and tilted my head back to be cradled by the backrest, admiring the faux wood paneling of the vaulted ceiling of the dining hall and its etchings of unique snowflakes, as I waited for my pulla to cool.

"Are you not going to eat it?"

I rolled my neck along the curvature of the chair to gaze upon my ambivalent interrogator, a boy who was playing a game on his data pad.

"Patience is a virtue, young sir, and one that is often practiced by those who would prefer their oral anatomy unseared. When it drops another 20 C, I'll gorge myself sure enough."

"Is that an EinIn Pistol?" The kid gestured at my thigh with his elbow, without taking his eyes off his screen.

"It is, yes."

"Can I shoot it?"

"You may certainly not."

"Why? I've shot one in some of my games before. I wanna see if it's like the real thing."

"Stop pestering me, young one, and run along. Stick to your games. I can see that will not be difficult for you."

"Lame."

The boy walked off, never peeling his eyes from his data pad as he exited the dining hall.

"You have little patience for children?" Milla asked, reseating herself as the last few diners at the 2-percenter table cleared off.

"I have little patience for such impropriety. I detest children whose every moment in analog life is but another manacle, detaining them from their next fix of derivative, digital death dealing."

The angry knot forming in my stomach was not sufficient to deter me from devouring my dessert. I washed my hands of the remaining sugar granules clinging to my fingers over my plate with the assistance of one of the hot towels afforded to the 3-percenters and up, and I felt my ire dissipate somewhat as the warmth from the pulla spread through my torso.

"So live the 1-percenters. His piece of the fortune is much greater than any inheritance his parents left behind. He is one of the unfortunate examples that comes along every now and again, perfectly content with sitting back and nursing his percent without any care for the future when it will be gone." Milla bit the corner of her lower lip as she reflected, the notes of her voice not quite giving up the child as a lost cause.

"Will you attempt to improve him?"

"I have, and I will continue to try." She replied, weary, but not beaten.

"Matron material indeed. I no longer possess the beneficence to while away my time developing one such as him."

"I'm sure that's not true. Thank you, Elli!" Milla offered as Elli set to clearing away the dishes.

I offered to help, but Elli insisted she clean up. Milla informed me that one of the rules of Onniheim is that every child is assigned rotations of housework, related to percenter status so that the orphanage can run smoothly on a self-sustaining model for all involved. Many of the tasks could be accomplished via mechanized systems, but the orphans are taught to work harder in the absence of automated assistance, as a mock price to pay for their fortune percentages. 3–percenters and up are allowed to use Domestidrones for select tasks, given the burdens associated with their elected skills are taxing enough. Though she was a 3–percenter, Elli volunteered for food prep and dining detail, a task normally given to 2–percenters, due to her passion for cooking. My 1–percenter interrogator happened to be in charge of laundering the uniforms for the orphanage. Milla unbuttoned her immaculate left handcuff, unspattered by the various liquid threats of the meal, and checked her data pad as she inspected the area.

"Matron Kirsi should be ready to see you now if you would like to head upstairs," Milla said, handing me one of the silver barrettes that had been restraining her bangs. "This is a guest fob that will get you into any door on the third floor save the Matron's. You'll just have to knock on that one. Her room is all the way down the right hallway. Your room is the one all the way down the left hallway when you are ready to retire for the evening. Feel free to use any of the facilities as you see fit. I'll be milling about for the rest of the evening doing my rounds. Should you need anything," Milla finished by tapping behind her right ear.

I thanked Milla for showing me around for the evening and headed out the hall and up the right-wing staircase to the third floor. The door to the right hallway slid open, and I noticed this wing only had three rooms. The digital placard on the left door on my approach read "Milla—Matron–Prospect," the right door placard was blank. Deciding to test my access, I moved to this door and tapped the entry pad, and the faux wood door swung open on its hinges with the sounds of displacing air. Then, I heard a whirring rapidly approaching my position from inside as well. I checked around the door and was disappointed to see that the room was entirely empty except for a vac disc that was finishing up its job. I watched it position in front of its entry gate, and I followed it through the wall and back out into the hallway as I tapped the entry pad to the empty room for the door to close behind me. The vac disc continued on its path across the hall towards Milla's room, and I thought about affixing a camera dot to its housing, but I retracted my hand at the last second. Milla had been open enough with me throughout my time at Onniheim so far. She deserved her privacy. I adhered the dot back to my belt and strolled down the hall to Matron Kirsi's room, trying to make the sounds of my footsteps identical in my mind by shifting my weight to my left hip a bit, and failing.

I looked around Kirsi's doorframe and knocked twice, and then I looked back down the hallway while I waited to notice that Kirsi either had the best surveillance setup I had ever not seen, or she had no equipment on this floor at all. The door swung open, much like the door to the empty room, though the sounds emanating from behind it were of the trickling of what I inferred was water. I swept around the door to find myself in a darkened room, illuminated here and there by lamps casting red and purple lights on to various plants. Data pad scans revealed that they were all of the botanical family Bromeliaceae. There was little else in the room except for a desk, a few chairs, a couple of tables, and a four-poster bed covered in a heap of blankets.

"I'll be with you in two secs! If this damn thing . . ." A tired voice mumbled from a corner of the room.

I walked down one of the planned pathways of the room between two rows of planters, the left of which contained pots from which bloomed magenta flowers that looked like quills, and the right of which contained pots with plants that looked wounded in the way the crimson pigment in the center of the leaves gradually decreased in concentration the further out you looked over the green and white base towards their tips, much like the blood from Milla's bit lip, furtively smeared across a towel when no one should have been looking. Stopping in front of the bay windows and two of the same chairs as those that were in front of the fireplace on the first floor, facing out across the fells, away from the city proper, I was treated to an extraordinary sight of emerald auroral ribbons, undulating their electromagnetic brilliance in the firmament.

"Finally." Matron Kirsi groaned, as her spray bottle began working again.

I walked over to see what she was doing after reveling in the resplendence of the north for quite a bit longer than "two secs." Kirsi was gently spraying three pots that couldn't have been much wider than ten centimeters in diameter, in which a few prosaic green plants with leaves possessing tiny teeth on their edges were planted. I looked over the climate–controlled chamber in which these pots were stored, which firmly locked into a rolling cart, and I wondered why these plants that looked only slightly more attractive than a typical weed were deserving of such a home. I scanned the plant as I approached, and I did not turn up any reliable hits.

"*Encholirium biflorum,*" Kirsi recited, demonstrating her impressive peripheral vision. "You won't find much on that data pad of yours about it, I bet."

"You are right. Unusual. May I ask how you knew that?" I replied, amused.

"The last one of these was supposed to have died off about twenty-two years ago. Extinct. Data pads wouldn't be able to turn up anything by scan, because no one had scanned it into a database before." Kirsi closed the door to the chamber and punched in a few settings on the cart as she wheeled it back into the corner.

"Fascinating. So you have taken it upon yourself to keep the species alive? Do others know?"

"It's just another burden I decided to take over from Eevi, though taking care of these kids can be easier than taking care of those pieces of work. Restoring the population to the wild is unlikely, but I'll have someone tell people if things pick up." She sat down in the left chair in front of the windows and gestured for me to sit in the right one. "The last populations were in a rocky area of Nueva Amazonia that had been privately owned. The owners didn't care at all about the plants. Who would?"

"They aren't particularly attractive, I must say." I inserted.

"Right. And conservation is just another popularity contest. If it isn't pretty or large, think the polar bear for animals, which is just barely getting along, who cares? How will you get the money to save it? No one would notice if this plant disappeared from the world entirely." Kirsi sighed.

"You would notice. I suppose, now, I would as well."

"Is that enough?"

"No, but it makes a difference. Your children are much the same in a way, though I hope they give voice to their appreciation."

"Are you allowed to admit that as a Collector?" Kirsi asked, surprised.

"Admit what? Fact? The Bureau is a conservation organization in essence, and it works on the same principles you have identified, though with much greater funding. They try to conserve beauty from the threat of excess; given our species will most likely not become extinct any time soon. Your children might have faded from existence unceremoniously without the Bureau's intervention here, or maybe some, like Milla, would have blossomed without it. In fact, this entire edifice was built as a conservation effort, if only to conserve the Bureau's reputation. The Bureau provided the home for these children, but you, as a concerned Matron, are the one who makes a real difference."

"What a treat. The Collector that facilitated my Ascension was a bloodthirsty pig of a woman. I'm glad Milla won't have the same experience. Honestly, I don't care much for your kind. I'm surprised I've talked with you this long as it is. I just wanted to check in to see that everything was proceeding as planned and to ask about how Milla is doing with all of this."

"Well, she had a bit of a meltdown upon initially speaking with me. There is a lot of pressure on her, after all."

"Hold on. Sorry. A meltdown?" Kirsi asked, in disbelief, while adjusting her black, wool sweater and turning towards me. "That's not like her at all—"

"I'm sure she only allowed herself to do so because I am an outsider. She seems the stoic type, and her sense of duty would not allow her to break down in front of you all. She would not want to alarm any of you. That said, she is perfectly fine now, and I think it helped her steel herself for what is to come. Onniheim is in good hands. Rest assured." I smiled as I watched Kirsi dangle a slipper off her toes, just like Milla had done before.

"I never forced Milla to accept her role, you know. I'm afraid I did everything but that, but it's not an absolute requirement. I only saw what Eevi saw in me, so I chose her. She could still technically back out if she wants. Will you tell her that?" Kirsi asked, regretfully.

"She knows. She's horribly, beautifully altruistic, like you, in a way that I could never be. It must be difficult to have someone take notice of you in a way that dooms you for the benefits you might bring to a community. I would have felt cornered by your choice were it me being asked to don such a mantle, and I think she felt that in the beginning, but she has really chosen of her own volition in the end, or you are the greatest indoctrinator I have met. You must realize how powerful an influence you are in her life." I weighted my words.

"I've struggled with that every night since I made the suggestion and much more, recently." She replied, the circles under her eyes corroborating her response. "Though, it is the Bureau that mandates she pay for this with her life, as they did with mine."

"It does seem excessive, doesn't it? Though, I suppose the Bureau doesn't want people feeling like they have lost control. The life for the fortune is their primary tenet. Why did you choose Milla?"

"The underlying reason was her sense of responsibility, as it was when Eevi chose me. It manifested early, was demonstrated often, and was shirked only in rare instances, but there's always a crystallizing moment that brings out the question. Eevi chose me when I took an interest in those insufferable plants after listening to her sob story all those years ago," Kirsi reminisced, as she brushed some dirt off of her black slacks on to the ground for the vac disc. "I chose Milla when I caught her trying to bring some of her dinner to one of our boys, who I made go without dinner as a punishment because he punched Milla out of frustration during a game. She said she felt bad that he had to go hungry because his favorite dish was being served that night and it wouldn't be served for another two weeks."

"Funny. I've seen her punishing kids all day, but you make her seem as though she is averse to punishment."

"No," Kirsi responded, chuckling. "She just felt that she should be the one to punish the kid. She didn't like my punishment, so she took it upon herself to correct the boy's behavior. She brought him his favorite dish, and only that dish, set it down in front of him, and then she slapped him clean across the face. An eye for an eye was how she saw punishment back then."

"Hahaha! It's hard to imagine her doing that with how prim and proper she has become."

"She has matured a lot since then. She was nine at the time, and she will be eighteen tomorrow. She has come a long way."

"Do you think she is ready to take over Onniheim?"

"Oh yes. I think she could have done so two years ago and done a passable job, but, from what you have been confirming, I think she'll be the best Matron yet. She said something the other day that resonated with the reason I initially took on the role, something I had forgotten over the years."

"What was it?" I asked, watching the Matron scratch at her scalp between her brown braids.

"On second thought, ask her about it when I'm gone. I don't know if I'd do it justice anymore," Kirsi said with a doleful frown.

"I'll be sure to do that. It is an onerous task for me to consign Milla to the fate of a Matron after seeing you so downtrodden. I wonder if it wouldn't be worth allowing this place to fall into disrepair in order for her to be spared."

"I wonder if you'll feel the same way after your tour tomorrow. Seeing what the orphans are accomplishing might change your mind. The average orphan here gets ten years of a better life than they would have had otherwise. The question you need ask is how many good years for others is one good year of yours worth. Consider the other orphans Milla will mentor in her time as Matron each get ten years of a great life before ever having to make a choice to seek a fortune or not and that adds up to a total of around one hundred and eighty years of benefits paid for by the sacrifice of Milla's sixty or so years she might have to live if she were not collected. That's a 300 percent return on the Matron's investment."

"Assuming all of their lives average out to be worth the same, that is. I've always found it difficult to quantify lives with such figures."

"Your Bureau doesn't."

"True enough."

"Well, Collector, I believe I have gotten the measure of you, and I am glad to hear of Milla's determination, but I believe I am growing weary. Perhaps my last night's rest will be a good night's rest. I will be making arrangements for the Ascension Ritual tomorrow and meeting with the children one last time."

Kirsi got up from the chair and shuffled over to a closet and paused as the door opened before her.

"Do we have your permission to conduct the Ritual as planned?" She asked, turning her head slightly to better hear my response.

"You do. Good evening, Matron."

I keyed the entry door to Kirsi's room open and walked out into the hallway, yawning. Walking into the left wing, I saw two older boys, presumably Tim and Hale, talking in the hallway. They were discussing some coding issues one was having with a gift he was working on for Kirsi. I wondered what kind of gift one would give someone about to die that would have any value as they moved aside to let me pass. Arriving in front of the door to my quarters, I looked over my shoulder to check on the two boys, who were moving into Hale's room to discuss their problem further. I waited for the door to close, and then I began my safeguard procedure.

I adhered a camera dot to the upper left corner of the door and synced it to my data pad, swiping over and suspending the dot I had adhered to the fireplace mantel earlier, as the fire had extinguished appropriately. I also slapped a holo bar over the blank placard and set it to scroll "No Entry" followed by the Bureau's flipping three-sided coin logo. I watched it flip from the three shooting stars, to the parchment and quill, to the draining hourglass and back again. I tapped the keypad to enter and adhered a mag strip connection pairing across the seam of the door on the inside trim of the door-frame and on the inside face of the door itself at about eye level. I pulled one of my auto-turrets out of my pack and positioned it on the ground about a meter from the door at a forty-five-degree angle from the point of entry, elevating its conical head to fire at about the average chest height of the orphans I had seen. I paired the strip, an alert pulse in my suit, and the turret and calibrated my alert to go off and the turret to fire stun round bursts once every second upon a twenty-centimeter separation of the mag strip leads. I followed all of the procedures. Such a good little Collector.

ComCom: Send Milla: "I'm retiring for the evening. If you could send out a message to everyone barring entry to my quarters, that would be appreciated." PendCom

I turned around to see my room had identical furnishings to Kirsi's, save the planters. Remembering one other point of entry, I wheeled around and brought up the vac disc settings on the door keypad and ensured that its route excepted my room for the time being and toggled its access to the entry gate off.

"Done. I can conduct your tour starting at nine tomorrow morning if you'd like."

ComCom: Send: "Only if you feel up to it. Rest well." EndCom

I set an alarm for 8:00 a.m. on my data pad, shrugged my pack off, unclasped my belt, unanchored my EinIn and set it on the bedside table, rolled on to the bed, kicked the sheets away, and hummed a lullaby in my mind until I fell asleep.

I awoke a few minutes before my alarm and decided to get up. I provided a status update to my handler and then decided to read through the dossiers of Milla and Kirsi again while I waited for the

breakfast chime that would sound at 8:30. When it did, I tidied up the
sheets on the bed and thought about requesting access to update the
dossiers, which were devoid of personality for the women, in order to
cast them in a more humanizing light. But the last time I had done
so for a target I was summarily rejected. I deactivated and stowed
my security measures, keyed the door to the room open, grabbed my
camera dot and holo bar, and strolled down the sumptuous hallway
carpet that I surmised was commissioned for Onniheim, given its
pattern was diamonded in red, white, and black, like the uniforms.
This carpet was another privilege for the 3–percenters and up, as I
did not see any of the like on the second floor when I tested my guest
fob again to find it granted me entry to both wings of that floor as
well. The 2–percenters were allowed doormats at least, a convenience
the lowly 1–percenters had to go without. I doubled back to the hallway leading to the dining room, and I found Milla in the dining hall
eating a lemon poppy seed muffin and drinking coffee in what must
have been her seat, at least for the rest of the day.

"May I sit here?" I asked, standing behind my chair from the previous evening.

"Of course!" Milla replied, setting her mug down on the table.
"We don't actually have mandatory seating during breakfast. It allows
all of us to mingle with the other percenters a bit more, though most
don't eat breakfast anyway, so it's made to order."

"Your muffins are larger than the other girls'," I said, immediately
regretting not adding more descriptors to the sentence.

"Excuse me?!" Milla asked, appalled, raising her free arm over
her chest and turning a bit as I waved my hand and turned my head
left, wincing.

"Apologies. I meant your lemon poppy muffin," I indicated with
an open hand at the untouched muffin on her plate, "is considerably
larger than theirs."

I finished, mentally cursing the omnipresence of slang for seizing yet another word from my lexicon and dragging it through the gutter while pointing down the long table at a few of the girls at the end, one of whom was still eating my comparison point while the other was folding the liner of hers into an indistinct animal shape.

"Ah." Milla breathed a sigh of relief, for both of us, while returning to ease. "How indecorous of me. Yes. Another aspect of the per-center class system set forth by Eevi. It even extends to food quality and quantity, as you can see, though I hope not for much longer."

"You mean to say you are thinking of changing it? Where do I fall in if I would like a muffin?"

"Would you?"

"Change your class structure or like a muffin? I would like a muffin, and I'll hear your thoughts on the class structure, as I have noted its material manifestations, but I am ignorant of its rationalization."

Milla held her right index finger up, as she often did when communicating by ComCom. Then, she took another sip of coffee.

"Did you want coffee as well or anything to drink?" She asked, the perfect host as ever.

"Hot chocolate?"

Finger up.

"On its way. Matron Eevi enacted the class system initially because of a suggestion made to her by the Bureau of Fortune. They told her that it would help keep order, and it has. However, she cited in her transcripts she left to Kirsi that it seemed to drive the children further and further apart and felt that it fostered a sense of community that was closed off to others and it became jarring for a number of orphans when they left to integrate into society."

"As intended. The Bureau doesn't see socialization as particularly beneficial. Society has evolved to a highly individualized norm where we interact with these," I held up my data pad, "more than those." I pointed to the same girls from before. "We crave control, even to the point of conversation, and the data pad will conform with greater facility to my desire for self-indulgence and validation than will you. Right? Why should we even be speaking right now?" I finished with a mordant mouthful of my muffin, which Elli had so kindly dropped off without a word.

"We do need them, though, right?" Milla asked, glancing at her own data pad. "They are useful tools."

"I think we have greater need of this," I pointed between us, "to ensure that we don't become consumed by the tools we have fashioned, but enough of my acrimony. You were saying?"

I caught Elli's eye as she whisked by and tipped my mug in appreciation before taking a sip of the liquid luxury contained within it.

"Well, when Kirsi ascended, she didn't give the class system a second thought until I asked her about it a few years ago. She said that it worked, and she was accustomed to it, so why change it? You know how she is." Milla began curling her fingers through her bangs as she finished her breakfast.

"Ha. Barely, though her pragmatism is apparent."

"When I asked her why she was okay with the stringency of the system and why it was fine that I was allowed access to so much more than some of the other orphans, she told me that it was a good model for what we would experience once they left the safety of the orphanage. She asked me why I thought people sought fortunes, and I told her that I thought it was because they were greedy. I remember her telling me that that was the case for some, but an underlying cause for many was feeling they had no recourse."

"That most likely would have been my reason, were I not afforded... other opportunities," I replied, recollecting the feelings I had before an angel descended upon me.

"The children admitted here are taken in through a lottery system run by the city and overseen by the Bureau of Fortune where individuals who are below the poverty line or can make a strong case for themselves, in rare instances, are drawn from a database and asked if they would like to enroll. You must be between six years and fifteen years of age in order to be considered eligible for enrollment. Once enrolled, you enter a variable trial period based on your age to examine aptitude for a number of community outreach opportunities we have available to pursue or to demonstrate a skill of your own and then a committee of the Matron, the Matron–Prospect, and a percenter from each category place you in your percent category and assign you your fortune sub account. These sub accounts total up to a maximum of forty percent of the Matron's assigned fortune through the Bureau. The Matron is supposed to spend the other sixty percent on orphanage asset development or something unrelated to the orphanage itself, all of which is tracked and approved by the Bureau."

Milla paused briefly to answer a question for the 2–percenter boy who worked with Elli in the kitchens.

"So what's his role?" I asked as the boy left. "Why did he deserve 2 percent?"

"Yng? He is a mascot artist. You know the mascot from the Senergy Soda Company?"

"'Electrolyte needs your help to save you from exhaustion at the hands of the nefarious Electrodark. Drink up to power up!'" I mimicked the commercial. "Scientifically ridiculous, but I hear kids say it all the time, usually before smashing their cans together."

"He designed, animated, and provided the voice over for the commercials."

"Interesting. Does he profit from that?"

"Not quite. That falls under another regulation from the Bureau in our contract. Any credits that are made by the orphans are either diverted into the general fund for the orphanage, which is run by the Matron, or relinquished to the Bureau through taxation. The Bureau also seizes any remaining funds held from the Matron's initial fortune upon Collection, before assigning a new fortune to the new Matron. The rationale for that is that the orphans are profiting enough through the development of the skills associated with their work, which will make them competitive prospects for companies when they exit at age eighteen. To give credit, the Bureau did wrangle about 80 percent of the community outreach and remote internship programs that work with our orphans, and children like Yng will almost certainly be hired as soon as they turn in their fobs, but it's hard not to feel like the Bureau is taking the lion's share."

"They always do."

"Oh! Not that I am unappreciative of what they have done for me! I was homeless before my number was called . . ." Milla squeezed her left forearm and looked down at the table.

"Back to Kirsi's rationalization for the class system you have here?" I circled back, popping the last moist morsel of my muffin that I had forgotten during my analysis into my mouth.

"'It's simple,'" Milla mimicked Kirsi's trite voice. "'If the children make something of themselves during their time here, they won't feel compelled to seek a fortune as they leave. In fact, I don't even want the thought to cross their minds. This system teaches them that complacency is ill rewarded in the world.'"

"People will inevitably stagnate if they don't have a goal towards which to aspire. A common rationale, but oft proven true as I have seen. But you don't agree? Aren't you worried that more of the children will end up like the kid from last night? I never even got his name!" I gestured to the right of my chair where the boy who asked me about my armament stood the night prior. "What reform would you bring?"

"I think I would still keep the merit-based stratification of the percent allocation of the fortunes intact as is, but I might reform a few discrepancies in things like the varying food qualities and quantities and leave allocation." Milla tapped her fingers on the table as she thought more on the subject. "What are your thoughts?"

"You are far more experienced than I when it comes to running things here. The only advice I would give would be that, were you inclined to change things, watch closely for changes in inter-percenter interactions. Kirsi has kept things mostly as they were from Eevi for a reason, though she did change the mandatory dining you had set before. If you notice changes you don't condone, you can always change back, but the masses will learn that they can ply you with further suggestions. The others seem to like you a lot, and you have strong leadership qualities, but you are kind, so taking a hard-line approach may be difficult. When they exit here, those considered of lesser merit to society will almost certainly not earn enough to enjoy the larger, moister muffins of every scenario. Social stratification is inevitable out there and mechanical capital is often appreciated more than human, so people that don't work diligently to develop marketable skills to be able to enjoy the muffins of their labor won't be able to outcompete a machine that can do what they can without being motivated by muffins of any kind. The child whose number might have been called in place of yours may have never seen a muffin, never mind a small one, real or analogical."

"So, what I'm getting from your analogy is to not change the food, because it might eliminate one more aspect that makes the children strive to do their best? Or are you just obsessed with muffins?" Milla asked, raising and lowering the uneaten half of her second muffin while watching me stalk it with my eyes.

"Both might be true. It's up to you to make the decision on the former, given the intimate knowledge you have of your orphans, and lemon poppy happens to be my favorite. Just some food for thought."

"Here's some for yours. I'm full." Milla slid the muffin half and its plate over to me.

"I should expound more often for rewards as handsome as this! I've thought of a new nickname for you, for your plethora of kindnesses as opposed to pinkies. Milla the Magnanimous." I knighted her at a distance with the muffin before two-biting it.

"Because of half a muffin? You are obsessed." Milla re-crossed her legs as she sat back in her chair and finished her coffee.

"Modesty is a quality above, but you could do with a little less," I avouched.

Incoming transmission from Orbit 9–9, receive?

"Pardon me, Magnanimous Milla," I supplicated. She waved me off, rolling her eyes and curling her lips into a smile.

ComCom: receive last

"Collector. I am aware you are technically on leave currently, but you are reminded that you are slightly more than two days out from your yearly relicensure date. You are still required to submit pertinent material by 0900 NER for review unless you wish to file for an extension. That leaves you until 1600 today, your time, or a delinquency charge will be assigned. Course of action?"

ComCom: Send: "I will submit pertinent information today by the requested time." Endcom

I sighed.

"Bad news?" Milla asked.

"Bureaucracy. I will be indisposed for a few hours later today due to my procrastination, well worth it, but I should complete the task assigned. I have been off the clock since last night."

"Do you still want to go meet some more of the orphans?" Milla asked, flattening her skirt as she rose from her chair. "It's almost nine, and I have an hour free."

"You could take that hour and do something for yourself instead if you'd like. Don't feel obligated to wait on me. I'm sure you have other prepossessions that would be more worthwhile," I replied, feeling a bit of guilt at monopolizing so much of her time.

"You'd be doing me a favor, actually. I'd like to keep myself distracted from tonight as much as possible, and the others are best at doing that. Plus, I see this as a marketing opportunity to impress the Bureau." Milla walked around the table and tapped a few times on her data pad before looking at me to see if I would be following.

"I'd bet that I'll be impressed, but you're mistaken if you think the Bureau scans my reports for anything more than time and method of my Collection."

"Maybe one day you'll climb high enough to make a change and you'll remember us?" Milla supposed.

"In that, you and I are different," I extinguished.

Milla ended up taking more than the hour she had originally allotted in introducing me to the orphans. They were certainly remarkable. Each one had carved out a niche related to the skills they were developing, and their rooms were ecosystems that they could shape with their fortunes. Very few of them felt the need to speak with me during their tour, as they were all busying themselves during one of the day's "Productive Periods," as Milla called them, and so I was relegated to mere observation outside of asking a few questions every now and again to clarify Milla's tour.

The rude 1–percenter boy from dinner, who was mid-game when we stopped by, was a promising pro gamer on the FDFPVR shooter circuit. Other 1–percenters I met were a hypermodern poet who was working on developing her AI to intuit the next great epic, and a cyclohop musician who would probably suffer from tinnitus for the rest of his life from the blaring rhythms that assaulted Milla and me as we breached the soundproofing to his studio. Milla had a few words for him before we moved along, of course. There was Geir, who was an aspiring mechanist, a boy who maintained a cell line for a research lab in Helsinki that was running a long–term study on ComCom effects on synaptic plasticity, and Sanna, who spent her time absorbing various posts on psychology as it pertains to mechanization. The final two were Aina and a boy who, accord-ing to Milla—who still cares for them despite their indolence—were content to "piss their fortunes away." I was surprised at Milla's choice of verb as well.

2–percenters included a sixteen-year-old girl, who was responsible for teaching math to the rest of the orphanage; a fifteen-year-old girl, who wrote and installed most of the e-security for some of the city's notable restaurants as well as Onniheim with Bureau oversight; and an impressively fit eighteen-year-old boy, who was allowed to stay at the orphanage until the following day due to a bylaw concerning Matron turnover and orphan turnover syncing, and would be second in command for a local gymnasium chain in a few weeks. He oversaw Onniheim's gym and its maintenance as one of his household duties. I almost shot another of Geir's teddy bears as it was sneaking up on us when I spotted it on my HUD as we entered the room of a fourteen-year-old fashion design aspirant, who was upgraded to 2–percent status when Yelka Swarovski took notice of one of his LCD–weave dresses and wore it to the Global Gravball Games two years ago. I tossed him the bear, which had cyberpunk-themed augmentations including a spiked head of antennae, with Milla's approval, and the young man put it on a shelf next to a scuba-themed version. Next, we stopped by Yngvar's room, and he showed us a sneak peek at the next mascot he was designing, which was an animated rock that was supposed to court donations to a certain company, that I know would wish to remain anonymous, for the ongoing snafu the terraforming of Mars has become. I was unable to meet with the final 2–percenter because she was holding her last meeting with Matron Kirsi at the time, a disappointment to which I responded with a vehement plea to move on to the wonders of the third floor before Kirsi got to them, mostly to distract Milla so I wouldn't have to see her lower lip tremble any further.

Elli was leaning on the banister just to the right of where the two spiral staircases to the third floor converged at the landing with her head in her hands, waiting for her meeting with Kirsi. She perked up a bit when Milla and I arrived, and she said she didn't want to go into her room at the moment, but she would be happy to talk about her skills. Elli was found on the day of her ticket–calling in the residence of a famous local architect. She liked watching him wave and tug and pinch his creations into existence in the prototyping phases of his projects, but she initially took interest in him from the drawings he would do on paper. She had never seen someone use paper and pencil before, and the man allowed her to come around every so often because she showed a rare appreciation for his design methods. She tried to mimic his work frequently, and I had never seen her as happy as when she was describing how he complimented one of her drawings of a gate she had made once, the structure of which sounded quite similar to that of the gate I entered through the previous evening. After his designs fell out of favor and he fell further and further into the clutches of dementia, the man spent most of the credits he had earned through his career designing and building shanties for displaced children, like Elli, in various parts of the world. Elli said she almost turned her offer to join Onniheim down because she had never heard about it before and thought it was a scam, but the man, in a moment of clarity, told her that he had applied for her after the first week she had spent with him because he wanted to take any chance he could to lessen the need for his work. The man died from an aneurysm eight months after Elli entered the orphanage, but she said that his will to build for the people that need it most has survived within her.

Tim, who spent an estimated 92 percent of his time in his room, according to Milla, was up next, and we only had about four minutes with him, as he was in the middle of tracking the progress of one of the newer companies he had added to his investment portfolio in the wake of their declaration to cut back on mechanization in the workplace. He forgot to untether the leads for his cursors and tabs on his right hand as he pounded it on his desk in frustration, scattering the containers of his previous instas everywhere, and he slapped his closely shaved head a few times and screamed a bit after he realized that he probably just lost an additional 2 GCs in broken parts. Milla thought it was a good time to leave at this point, and she assured me that Tim wasn't always so irascible.

Launo was practicing a speech as he came to usher us into his room, eager for an audience that was semi-willing to listen, and we were treated to an opinionated and haphazardly researched stance on how people who practiced fad diets were often shown to raise children who would overeat. When I critiqued his view with a few points to which he had not yet thought up counterpoints, he waved me off and said that good speeches are more about passion than getting the facts right. I flippantly told him that he would be a great politician. He asked me how I guessed that's what he was going for. I walked out of the room, without waiting for Milla.

We walked across the hallway to Hale's room to round out the tour after Milla caught up, and he practically bowled her over when he walked through the doorway as Milla reached out to the keypad to signal our presence. He flung his arms out to catch his gadget while mine shot out to steady Milla, who, serendipitously, happened to be the exact person he had been going to find. He was wondering if Milla could let him into the Matron's room since Kirsi was conducting her meetings in a sitting room on the first floor so that he could calibrate his gift for her. Hale had been illegally tampering with a domestic Agridrone model in his free time, outside of his engineering coursework, in order to reprogram it to take care of Kirsi's various plants. Milla let him in without any further questions after he told her that, were it to work correctly, she wouldn't have to take care of any of the plants in the room for the foreseeable future, though his plans seemed to have forgotten to account for the *Encholirium* specimens, which I mentioned to Milla. She said that was fine since Kirsi wouldn't want anyone but her to look after them anyway and that it would be a small way she could give back to her predecessors. Hale set to work while Milla stood in the doorway and I stood lookout over the staircases. He exited the room around twelve minutes later, cradling his creation, and he proceeded down to the first floor with the enthusiastic grin of a procrastinator that finished with seconds to spare, a young man after my own heart.

"I know you Collector types aren't usually keen on taking tours in the flesh, so you have my gratitude for helping to distract me. It's not often that I miss a deadline," Milla said, cracking her knuckles out over the balustrade as she leaned over it next to me.

"I figured you had noticed, but I wouldn't deign to pull you out of your element. I can tell you have found your purpose here after seeing how you interact with the others. Was the deadline important?" I asked, checking my data pad to see how much time Kirsi had until her deadline.

"Not anymore, I think," Milla replied, waving to Elli with a smile on her face as the girl wound up the stairs. "I was going to take some time to think about what I want to say to Kirsi when I wait with her until you are ready, but I don't want to script it. I want it to come naturally or if there is naturally nothing at all, that would be fine too."

"That is how it should be. I'll leave you to it. I'll come around again at 3:40 to ensure that it will all be over by 4:00. I'll leave the choice to have the children sequestered to their rooms or not to you, but, due to the circumstances, the cleanup crew and the appointed auditor will arrive promptly, as the Bureau does not account for grief, for which I am sorry."

"Very well. Until then," Milla managed, as I left her in tenuous peace to return to my room.

I spent the rest of the interim time submitting records to the Bureau via my data pad while chatting with Daria, who decided to reenact the Collection she had just completed from the PsOV of all involved. Her target was a former worker of a deep-sea mining operation for rare battery metals who decided to spend most of each day for the rest of his days starting the week before his thirty-sixth birthday in a submersible, thinking that it might help him avoid Collection.

Daria screened into my data pad to show me her imitation of the triumphant look on his face when he finally surfaced in front of Daria's team's skimmer drones, and then sent me a pic of his crestfallen expression after she told him this was the first day of his Collection window. He was thirty-seven years and five days old. She doubled over laughing and almost split her head on the toilet when she slipped on the shower terrace while getting out as she sent me a clip of Gis' new avatar in a VRMMO she was playing, whose sinewy barbarian was rendered with state of the art, photorealistic graphics, except for its head, which was replaced by a cropped image of this poor target's head that had become slightly pixelated in the compression and transfer. I didn't stop laughing until my image of her cabinets automatically opening and shutting stayed in-frame for forty seconds and I thought I should summon paras, but I heard a few more *snrks* and then she patched herself up. I told her that she might be in for some trouble if the image went full meme, and she said she tagged the initial release, so she'll know who releases it if it gets out of the Bureau and that person would be in for the worst of it. She allowed me to return to my submissions after that, and I was able to finish with enough time to scroll through the rest of the eight-sec files she had sent me of "Cocky Collectee" and "Crestfallen Collectee" before checking my gear on my way to the Matrons.

I walked across the third floor while updating my handler, the cleanup crew, and the auditor of my plan. Then, I ComComed Milla that I was on my way. I walked through the Matron's door, hijacked the inside keypad and placed the room in lockdown while illuminating the overhead panels.

"Good evening, Matron Ki —"

"Good evening, Collector," Kirsi cut in. "I heard from Milla about your generous allotment of twenty minutes, but I'd just like to get this over with if you don't mind."

I looked first at Kirsi, who looked remarkably similar to how she had the previous evening, sitting in the same chair, looking out the same window, same hairstyle, wearing the same shoes and sweater, same terse affect, but she had on burgundy sweatpants. Then, I looked at Milla to gauge her mood. She was standing next to Kirsi; hand on her matron's shoulder, Kirsi's hand over hers. She nodded with an easy smile.

"We're ready." She determined.

"Say only one thing more, then! Milla, please come here."

I gestured in front of me and Milla stood in her place. I activated one of my collar cameras and then I raised my injection gauntlet, spun up a new syringe, and dislodged it.

"Due to the special regulation of Onniheim Orphanage pursuant to article 57–b of your contract with The Bureau of Fortune, I, Collector H 66K28, authorize you, Milla Jokela, Matron–Prospect, to collect the life of Matron Kirsi Halko, through lethal injection, as my proxy. Should you accept and commit actions warranting reasonable suspicion of dereliction of duty, your life may be forfeit to my immediate Collection. Do you accept this charge? Answer yes or no."

"Yes," Milla responded, with confidence.

I held the syringe in front of the camera and indicated how Milla should hold it. Then, I set it down on the edge of one of the planters and backed away. Kirsi rolled her right sleeve up in preparation, and then she resumed looking out the windows in silence. Milla retrieved the syringe, holding it appropriately, and I unanchored my EinIn while following her over to Kirsi. She bent down to embrace her mentor, her hero, one last time, and they whispered something into each other's ears. Milla administered the injection, and I walked over and retrieved the spent syringe, turning it over in front of the camera, and then I cut off the camera feed. I stepped in front of Kirsi to confirm her passing and sent my CC ping. I studied Milla's face and admired her conviction. She spoke first.

"You want to know what we said, don't you?"

"I don't. That is for you two to know. There should still be some privacy in this world. You can have the next sixteen minutes to yourself. The team can wait that long on my account."

Milla sat down in the free chair, beside her mentor, staring out at the snow.

"Will you come for me at the end of my time?" She asked, tears beginning to roll down her cheeks.

"I would say that is unlikely, given any requests to that effect would raise suspicion. Would you prefer me to come?" I asked, turning to leave and returning the security of the room to normal.

"I would. You understand how these things should be. You might also be the only one who would be able to attest to whether or not I have fulfilled my goals," the Matron replied, wicking the last of her tears with her blouse cuffs.

"I have every confidence in you, as did Kirsi," I bolstered, looking back at the *Encholirium*.

"What if I told them that? That you would be the best one from a data collection standpoint?" she said, looking to check off one more box.

"Hmmm. Now there's an idea. Ask to put it in the contract you are about to sign," I proposed, having difficulty detaching.

I keyed the door open, and then I looked back.

"One more thing I feel compelled to ask, if you would honor me with a response. When I spoke with Kirsi, she told me about the moment she knew she wanted you to become the next Matron and she told me to ask you about it. Apparently, you gave voice to something that resonated with why she initially took on the role. Do you remember what it was?"

Milla thought for a moment and then she got up from the chair and looked at Kirsi, around the room, and then at me.

"It was about why this place exists and why I want it to still exist."

She looked back out at the skies and raised her arms and her voice.

"One life, unwillingly taken, set the foundation for all of this. I wonder . . . what can one life, willingly given, do?"

6

2355 – The Friend

I was walking under the tracks of a mag train on my way to the factory when I was accosted by some slummies who were surprisingly bold in their approach of a Collector. It turns out they were looking for an audience as opposed to trouble. They fancied themselves performers, and they were wondering if I would be willing to pay to hear a few songs. I asked them why they didn't upload if they thought they were good enough to make money and they shook their wrists to show they didn't possess data pads, which was not surprising given the rest of their ratty attire. One of them had decided shorts and just the hood and tassels of a hoodie was an outfit worth wearing. They boasted that they could beatbox any song I could request, and they would dance too, even though one of their crew had clearly been hobbling along as they hounded me on my way. Despite my telling them I didn't have any cash on me and they didn't have any CFOBs, given the lack of data pads, they still wanted to sing for me so that maybe I would spread their name where I go and more people would come and see them. They followed me most of the way, belting their raps as I filtered through the crowds of Joburg in the early morning. After their maimed buddy hollered in pain as a suit pushed him to the ground and out of his way without so much as a blink, I turned around and tossed them a few bags of enriched candies I had pulled out of my pack after telling them to call it quits for the day and they seemed appreciative. They had little, but they had each other.

I walked past the chipped sign standing in a courtyard out in front of my target building, the face of which had been tagged with graffiti too many times to fulfill its purpose anymore, and I rapped on the reinforced rolling door after verifying that the biometric entry methods had been vandalized as well. After three minutes passed with no answer, I stepped back out in front of the decrepit building and began surveying for an alternate mode of ingress. Some of the windows closer to the roof had been shattered, so I flicked up the controls to one of my sniper drones on my data pad and steered it in through the breach, down to the factory floor, to the other side of the door, and directed it to slam the barrel of its rifle into the manual release for the door security a few times until I heard a buzz and a clunk. I rolled the door open slightly, shimmied in, closed the door and relocked it, calling my other sniper drone to me via a follow command executed on its twin's line before releasing them both to roam within the dank confines of the premises.

This factory was one of two major facilities in the area that used to produce the world's lines of Betje Bot, an early service bot model that would eventually be outcompeted and rendered obsolete by Domestidrones. The appeal of the Betje Bot models was that they were tailor-made, customizable, and were developed with exceptional abilities to develop familiarity with a large range of interlocutors and tailor interactions to individual users, though they would begin to degrade after a few years of continued use. The models had initially impressed early adopters to sell well enough to merit further development, but the company had focused too much on personality engineering and not enough on adaptive service functions to be able to compete with the Domestidrone line that launched nine months later. People were more interested in domestic mechanical laborers or sexual servants than domestic mechanical conversation partners, and Domestidrones could perform the tasks of the former roles with aplomb and the tasks of the latter horrendously for my standards but good enough for the general populace, who often found it grueling to muster much more than a simple greeting for a stranger, electronic or otherwise. The company behind the Betje Bots went bankrupt around fifteen years ago and they ceased production, closing their two factories. This factory, the smaller of the two, was purchased almost immediately after it closed and has been reactivated four times since the date it was ostensibly decommissioned.

I clicked on one of the flashlights embedded in my chest plate and began to follow one of the assembly tracks further into the building, ducking under a few of the massive mechanical arms positioned along them that were used to piece the bots together. Suddenly, one of my sniper drones pinged my pad to warn of a movement within my threat radius that I couldn't quite see as I heard a scraping sound in the darkness off to my right under a walkway. I pulled my EinIn, clicked its flashlight on, and covered behind one of the assembly arms, feeling my heart pounding in my throat. As I listened to more scraping and the sound of metal parts colliding, I flicked up the NV feed from the drone that detected the disruption to see that the threat was armed with . . . arms. Vaulting over a conveyor, I disengaged the sniper drone and approached the Betje Bot that was dressed in a baker's hat and an apron that was dangling from its neck without being tied in the back. It was picking up parts of discombobulated bots from a scrap heap.

"Betje Bot? What is your name?" I called out.

"Shopper . . . is my . . . name." The bot replied in a fragmented voice.

"Hello, Shopper. My name is Collector. What are you doing?"

"I had tOOOooooo visit the bakery. Would you like to come aLOng?"

"Where is the bakery?"

"Well, we are already at *specify location*."

"Where will you go next?"

"My next desTInaTIOn is the club . . . house. I need two more loaves before I LEEEave."

"Can you show me the clubhouse?"

"YEsss. More friends are allllways welcome!"

I picked up another of the tarnished arms that Shopper seemed to be collecting, whose shoulder joint had been cracked and from which a few fingers had gone missing.

"OhhhHHH. Collector. You found another loaf! It's a little burnt. You are so *adjective missing*! Can you carry it to the clubhouse with me?"

"Yes, I can."

"Can you ffinnnnd one more first? Then we will have theee five loaves I need."

I looked around the back of the pile for another intact bot arm and tossed a hand over to the other side as I rummaged through it.

"Collector. ThhhAT is a biscuit. Harvey asked for French bread this morning. Can you find FREench bread?"

"Will this do?" I asked Shopper, showing it an arm I had retrieved from the center of the pile that seemed to be in decent shape.

"That is a great loaf, Collector? Let's go back to the clubhouse! Harvey will bEEEe pleased."

Shopper turned its roughly 1.8–meter–tall frame around and began trundling along down the factory floor and I followed it for a time, shining my lights on the few remaining mechanized assembly stations that had not been sold off for repurposing before the factory was reacquired.

"Shopper? May I fix your apron for you?" I asked as I watched one of its tassels brush over a set of gears, almost getting stuck.

"I don't know what *missing queried subject* is, but I could use soOOme fixing. It has been two hundred and thirty-six days since my last maintenance."

We turned down a hallway, and Shopper circumvented the remains of a light fixture that had crashed to the floor.

"SOOOo, Collector? Where are you from?"

I had never interacted with a Betje Bot before, as they had become collector's items as soon as their production stopped. This one had degraded considerably but had not become rampant by any means. It still seemed to carry out functions well, and this attempt at small talk was impressive. If not for the occasional inappropriate intonation and volume changes in its speech and monotonous error and update messages, I might have forgotten I was conversing with a bot at all in the darkness.

"I'm from the NER. Do you know where that is?"

"Yes. Harvey is also from the NER! What AAAAaa coincidence!"

"How do you know Harvey, Shopper?"

"I am Harvey's oOOoldest buddy."

We approached a door that was cracked open, and I saw light coming from inside and heard voices conversing.

"Shopper? Is the clubhouse through this door?"

"Yes. I will introduce you to Harvey. Come in!"

"No. You go on ahead, and I will meet with you two later. Can you keep me a secret from Harvey? I want to surprise him!"

"Okay. Bye, Collector. *User profile archived.*"

Shopper entered the room and returned the door to its previous cracked position and I spent some time observing my target through the windowpane set in it.

Harvey Brackson was one of the many mentally-challenged individuals that are often displaced to the margins of our resource-challenged society. The times in which we live already make it exceedingly difficult for the average, cognitively-normal person to acquire the resources he or she may seek without difficulty. In the competitive milieu that governs this everyday struggle for the poor of wealth, the poor of wit or those who may not be able to make ends meet on their own have been all but forgotten. Gone are the days that would have once afforded social supports for such individuals of ignoble status.

Now, they are outcompeted in essentially every domain including the workplace, the homestead, companionship, and the social graces of others. Many of them linger on the fringes of society, eking out an existence in solitude and dying out of the public's eye after a while. The typical person doesn't devote too much time to thinking about such social pariahs and, from what I have heard a few times in passing conversations, they could care less about how these forgotten souls end up.

"It's their parents' faults, really. Why not prescreen and abort the bad ones?"

"They are just one more mouth to feed, and those idiots couldn't even feed themselves anyway. They're better off dying than me."

Birth rates of these mentally-inferior individuals have decreased with the increase in awareness and employment of the socially conscious pre-fert screening methods developed by medical science and lauded by governments, but every now and again one such as Harvey is unlucky enough to be born without the cognitive capacity to comprehend his existence as the scourge the untouched would claim him to be.

The Bureau of Fortune has accommodated for the existence of these beings, as they would not be so crassly prejudiced as to exclude them from their attentions, unlike much of the public. Ever the shining beacon of equality. On pad, this is a testament to the all-encompassing declaration of their mission statement, but behind closed doors in the cross-departmental conversations with Pop–Reg it's simply another means to shorten the life spans of another demographic.

The restriction on receiving a fortune for a mentally-challenged individual is based on whether or not said party can understand what the process entails, which is subjectively assessed by the Bureau at the eligibility medical examination. Those who can understand the process without assistance would likely be capable of living a fuller life, in terms of years lived, on their own anyway, so why not offer them a fortune to trim that time? If they transgress, they can be collected early and there is no leniency on transgressions, regardless of mental faculty. Those who might be unable to understand the process without assistance occasionally curry increased attention from one of the most despicable societal predators to evolve within these times.

This predator, known as a "scrounger," by those in the business, has taken to scouting out potential candidates that might need a bit of interpretation work, cozying up to them under false pretenses of friendship, kinship, or the like, and suggesting that they submit for a fortune in order that they may pursue whatever simple passion may govern their innocent minds after educating them in the basics of a fortune contract, all so that the predator can benefit from the monetary consideration received in the acquisition. Stories about such parasitized candidates acquiring fortunes and never utilizing them abound. Of course, the Bureau repossesses all unused funds at a Collectee's time of death, so it's a win–win where the Bureau is concerned. Harvey's underdeveloped mind would have, in my opinion, placed him safely within the category of those who could not understand the details governing a fortune even with assistance. However, I am not the one proofing the Bureau's decisions in this domain. In the end, Harvey did spend his fortune about as wisely as one could have hoped, considering his state.

Harvey possessed the wherewithal to attend to his basic needs for most of his life. His developmental deficits manifested in a manner that perpetually arrested this thirty-six-year-old man in a state of cognition that would normally be likened to that of an

average six-year-old boy with little to no formal education. When
his debt-ridden, alcoholic, single father ended up perishing in a traffic accident, Harvey was deprived of the last human presence with
which he associated at the age of twenty-one.

A few days after he was evicted from his unit, a scrounger in an
alley found him with the only possessions he thought to bring with
him: a box of cereal, a coat, a blanket, his data pad, a hairbrush, and
a Betje Bot with which he would sing. The scrounger deactivated the
Betje Bot and sold it for parts after convincing Harvey that the bot
was going away on a vacation for some time. He spent a few days
preying on Harvey's trusting nature and growing loneliness before
convincing him that he could go on the same vacation as his bot if he
would let his new pal take care of everything. Harvey had lived a protracted childhood with little to offer in the way of tribute for the often
obtuse rituals associated with the social competitions governing the
pursuit of companionship. So, when the scrounger concocted a story
about the factories that were responsible for producing Harvey's only
playmate, Harvey signed where he was told, hoping that he might be
able to have some more fun. He acquired the factory, the services of
a helper for a few months to produce a few more bots and set him up
in a secure and sustainable living state, and a scheduled drop of food,
meds, and water on which he might subsist.

After watching Harvey at play for a while, I could see he was
happy. His four companions and he had spent the first seven minutes
I had spent in study playing house. Shopper had unloaded the "bread"
it had been carrying, and Harvey pretended to eat it after comment-
ing on the quality of each "loaf." Harvey pretended to break off and
offer pieces of the bread to his other Betje Bots as well, even the one
he had commanded to suffer a time-out in the corner. Whenever
he told a specific bot that it was "nap time," the bot would enter a
standby mode. The engineering behind the bots prohibits them from
prompting each other into conversation, so they would only ever

engage with Harvey as opposed to conversing amongst themselves, though Harvey never seemed to notice or mind this sub-human constraint. As long as he was the center of attention, he was thrilled, and he seemed to interact with all of the bots regularly so I could not tell if he had a favorite. He had a wonderfully inclusive personality, despite being excluded most of his life.

Later, Harvey squirmed into a puffy floor chair, pulled a tattered blanket over his pajamas and decided that he wanted to tell a series of stories. The whimsical nature of each of the tales, which he recited from memory to the group before asking a different bot for its opinion upon the conclusion of each, stirred a latent longing within me for the days when I used to ingurgitate such tales, fervently entrusting my youthful hopes to their blithe affiances of structured accessibility to a sanguine future. Oh, to be a child again, protected by the dearth of skepticism consanguine with the undeveloped mind. I envied Harvey in that moment, so full of promise, so terrifically content in his back room to reality that appeared to me as a grungy, thirty-six-square-meter prison, but must have appeared to him as a sprawling plain, or a roaring ocean, or a bower safeguarded from the threats of situational awareness.

Harvey only told one story for each bot, and I wondered if he only ever told four stories each day for every day that he had lived in his clubhouse, if he only ever played house and told stories, if I was just witnessing a routine with which only someone of his mentally-deficient classification could be content repeating day in and day out. Truly, I wanted more for us. I pushed through the door.

Harvey looked up, in what I surmised to be surprise, as his typical expression was somewhat spacey, and he welcomed me.

"H–Hullo!" he said, eagerly, seemingly without a care in the world that a stranger just burst into his kingdom.

"Hello! What's your name?" It had been so long since I had tried to do this.

"I'm Harvey! Ummm   what's your name?"

"My name is Jackandjill." I lied, though I figured this would help in my attempt to fetch a pail of solace. "You are good at telling stories!"

"Thanks!" Harvey giggled. "You're nice!"

"Thanks!" I mirror giggled. "Could you tell me another one?"

"Sure!" Harvey yelled, throwing his hands above his head.

I sat down on a foam pad in between Shopper and another bot.

"You should meet my . . . friends first."

Harvey screwed up his face as he inflected with what I sensed to be embarrassment related to his fabricated friends as if their presence might lessen the impression I might have of him.

"They look really apt!" I covered, slinging some slang into my speech.

"Really?! Yes!" Harvey exclaimed, jumping up and returning to excitement.

Harvey used the next few minutes to introduce me to each Betje Bot, and I complimented each in turn.

Skip was dressed in a t-shirt and had no bottoms on, and I told it that I really liked the red, pink, and blue splotched design on its shirt, to which it replied that Harvey had made it for it and it really liked it too.

Ramp had a baseball cap that was taped to its head in order that it may remain on during locomotion, a gravball jersey pulled over a turtleneck that must have restrained its arm range of motion, and a shoe buckle on a string that was wound around its torso to make a belt. The brim of the hat looked like it had been chewed up a bit, but I said I liked its iridescent purple coloration. I asked Ramp what its favorite baseball team was, to which it replied that it was the Durban Dinos, which was not the team supported by the oak tree logo on its cap, and I emphatically and fallaciously yelled that that was my favorite team too, though I have really never cared to spectate that stagnating sport.

Mason was wearing one of those red, X-shaped vests that were popular a decade ago along with some swim trunks, and it looked and smelled like it had some sunblock lotion smeared over its soft, white cheeks and knobby, gray shoulders. I told it that I liked the beach and asked it if it did too. Mason replied that it did like the beach and surfing, but it was scared to go swimming because of the sharks that were around sometimes. It adopted a pose as if it were riding a board while talking to me as well.

Finally, I was introduced to Shopper, who began a new profile to associate with my adopted name, and I told it that it seemed like it liked to work hard. It replied that it enjoyed work, but its favorite thing to do was to play with its best bud, Harvey.

"So how about telling me a story now? Do you have a favorite one? How about one that your friends haven't heard before?" I asked, looking to test Harvey's range.

"Hmmmm." Harvey covered his face with his blanket, taking some time to think. "Yeah! That one! I know a story about a worm! You want to hear it?"

I didn't remember a worm being mentioned in any of the stories on which I had been eavesdropping, which was a good sign.

"Yeah! Tell me that one! Worms are gross, huh?" I switched to lying on my stomach in order to demonstrate that I was ready to listen.

"I don't think they're thaaaat gross," Harvey said. "Just different!"

"Maybe."

Harvey made himself comfortable on his stomach as well, and he inched closer to me so that our faces were less than a meter apart before he began.

"There was once a worm named Tim. Tim was a little slower than all of the rest of the worms, so he was always late to everything! He was late to school. He was late for dinner. And he was late to get to bed too! Since Tim was so slow, he would neeeever get to eat any of the good dirt in the tunnels because every other worm got there first. Tim would try to slide around with the other worms, but the other worms never wanted to wait for Tim, so Tim was sad. One day, Tim was trying to follow aaaaaaaaaall of the other worms up to the surface to play, but he was late again, so he didn't get there until nighttime! When he finally got to the surface, he didn't find any other worms except some that were skinnier and harder than normal that were asleep and a weird one that looked bigger but was not like Tim. This weird worm was a little different. It was black and it had a pattern on it, and it moved funny, but Tim and it were able to be buddies! Tim liked being buddies with the new worm and his other buddies so much that he never wanted to go back into the ground! Tim played all night and the funny worms waited for him every time he wanted to go somewhere. But worms can't stay above ground! Tim's buddies stayed with him as the moon dropped and the sun went way up in the sky and Tim became sleepy, just like all the other worms that had stayed above ground. When Tim finally closed his eyes to sleep, he was happy because he had found some buddies. The end!"

"What a melanch—I mean that was a sad story!" I laughed at Harvey.

"No, it's not! Didn't you listen? Tim the worm got some buddies! That's happy!" he replied, throwing his blanket up in the air.

"Yeah! You're right!"

"You want to know a secret? Tim always wanted buddies. He really wanted other normal worm buddies, but the big weird worm buddies were pretty good!"

"Apt! Do you want to play some more?" I asked, finding that I enjoyed spending time with Harvey, as his perpetually innocent, yet earnest mind allowed me to fantasize about what it would have been like to remain a child, irresponsible for and oblivious of the inevitable burdens that beset the mature. We played for another half an hour or so, idling away in a purgatory filled with bouncy balls, and funny faces, and silly games, and racing cars. Harvey's inextirpable smile during our time at play together made me feel as though I might enjoy an eternity in his world, expiating on behalf of the "cognitive-ly-untouched" for the neglect they had shown this wondrous worm. Alas, like a bolt from the blue, my ComCom sounded the clarion call that would drag me back to the festering earth, that I might do the bidding of my master at an inconveniently accelerated time and, unlike Tim, that tardy invertebrate who demonstrated his spine more than I ever might, I was rarely so unpunctual.

"Hey, Harvey! Do you like to play house?" I asked, tilting my head and kicking my feet up and down in excitement.

"Oh yeah! I already played some today! Ramp likes to play too and Shopper!"

"Yeah. I think playing house is pretty apt, but have you ever played doctor? It's really fun!"

"No! But I went to the doctor a few times . . . I think!"

"Nice! So if we play doctor, you could be the patient! Do you want to try?"

"Yes!" Harvey yelled, rolling around a bit before settling down again.

"Great. I'll be the doctor. But you know one thing about doctors? They usually see their patients alone, so can you make sure that your buddies give you some privacy? I can examine them after you if you want!"

"Okay!"

Harvey told all of his buddies to take a nap as I prepared my tools. I tested Harvey's reflexes with the grip of my EinIn, pretended to draw some blood and analyze it with my data pad, making ridiculous noises as I did so, checked his vision, and asked him to stand up on his floor chair so I could take his weight. As my data pad glowed with the ETA of my ride at two minutes, I delivered my assessment.

"Harvey," I ordered in my extra-low doctor voice, "your profile shows me that you are going to need a few shots."

Harvey giggled, as I patted his bed in the corner so that he could hop up on to it, and I unbuttoned his pajama top and exposed his shoulder.

"Hey, Jackandjill? I mean, Doctor Jackandjill? Are we friends?" Harvey wondered, kicking his feet back and forth and looking at me with an impeccant and auspicial fervor as I spun up a syringe.

"Yes!" I yelled, in the same way Harvey would, as I applied his treatment.

"Yes! This is so . . . fun . . ."

Foreign tears streamed down my friend's grinning face as I laid him down to nap.

7
2712 – The Rogue

My transport drone peeled off its line, and its engines barked as it whipped around on a new heading while a route update on my data pad bounced me out of what would have been a record run on Quiche Commander. I tried to swipe back in to reconnect so I could complete my dailies before the reset, only to find that it was a hard bounce from Bureau–side, and I groaned while I awaited the inevitable.

Incoming transmission from Shepherd 5–5, tagged urgent RASAP, receive?

ComCom: receive last

"Collector, your transport has rerouted to pursue an HVT. You are to abandon your previous target. No new dossier will be forwarded as the information is classified need-to-know at your level. All information you seek will be vetted and provided through this contact. ETA is three minutes twelve seconds. Target will go to ground before your arrival. Essentials will follow. Confirm active reception."

ComCom: Send: "Ready for Essentials." PendCom

"*Your target is Daemun Thompson, a former Collector who went rogue three months ago. We had not detected him since his dereliction day until this morning through reports from an informant in the Lewiston slums. Identifier's initial suspicion arose through sighting of a unique scarring pattern attributed to Thompson posted on a watch site and a positive ID was made through a citizen's watch ranged STR DNA probing transfer. The radio tag embedded in the probe was squelched at your current insertion coordinates. Target has been diagnosed as a paranoid schizophrenic through the Office of Mental Well-Being. An image taken from an entry pad cam across from his current location has been forwarded to your data pad for sight ID along with a thirty-two-parse voiceprint and the aforementioned scarring pattern on his left shoulder. You may select weaponry from the forwarded log to be spot-dropped to your LZ, and you are to discard all Bureau resources with sensitive information upon touchdown. Cloudshift backup to your secondary of choice and a tertiary, if you wish. Sensitive Bureau resources will be fried thirty seconds after touchdown. You may retain your combat skin. Target is designated TOS. Repeat: Target is designated TOS. Disposal will be handled upon your exit. Repeat essentials?*"

ComCom: Send: "No repeat necessary." PendCom

My handler cut the Com, and I brought up the requisitions list and made my selections, electing to retain my EinIn R–45 and my injection gauntlet. I scanned the image of my new target and embedded it in my mind while I waited for confirmation on my cloudshift of my hardware data to my secondaries in my residential unit, which came about fifteen seconds later. I played selections of the voiceprint files I had been sent and mimicked them a few times while wondering how useful they would be when I was ordered to terminate on sight, as opposed to sound.

The hold flashed orange, and I locked into my drop port. Looking through the small, telescopic window, I could see a bit of the ocean between the surrounding buildings as the transport drone dove. The shoreline was peppered with desalination plants and the no-fly lights atop an offshore nuclear waste transmutation installation caught my eye before a terraced high-rise impeded my vision. Dialing back to 1x, I saw my delivery drone swoop by before I was ejected and had to accommodate my landing so as not to hit the cases it had discharged after warning the people below it. I touched down and informed the crowd of miscreants that had not obeyed the flashing text of the evacuate scrolls on the surrounding buildings and overridden advertisement drones to make themselves scarce before detaching my data pad, dropping my belt with all of its surveillance equipment, stripping my visor, and emptying most of the contents of my pack for the recovery drones to police.

Poking the combinations I had been given into two of the cases that had been dropped yielded me my exiguous selection of equipment. Thinking it was laughable that a Collector still had to abide by the three-mode execution limitation during a TOS mission, I inspected my new mode, one that I had selected for devastation. I ran my hands over the bullpup frame of the stripped-down version of an EinIn SMG 4SB that was lacking any authentication security by design. The modified weapon is technically not street legal, and the manufacturers would deny its existence, but certain investors can pay a premium in order to commission one, at the risk of forty year's imprisonment for possession. Collectors could get them fitted for det rounds as well, and this one happened to be. I did not have time to waste on calibration, or tampering, or my target shrugging off a shot.

I grabbed a flip clip from the smallest case and loaded the weapon, toggled the fire rate to semi-auto, flipped up the sights, and clasped the belt with my three backup clips around my waist. I compacted and anchored the SMG to my lumbar polarity pad, drew my R–45 pistol, and hefted the final case in my left hand before following the bread crumb trail that had been painted by a seeker drone to a door beneath one of the dilapidated, concrete skeletons of a parking ramp. The door from a bygone age had no entry pad, so the seeker drone painted red squiggles where one should have been installed. I popped the third case open and traced the pathway of the laser cutter around the padlock of the door, zapped it and listened, kicked the case closed, pulled the padlock out towards me, extricated the deadbolt, swung the door open, and proceeded inside.

The air in the tunnel was damp and stale. The only illumination came from flickering lamps every twenty meters or so, about which not a single insect was fluttering. I traced a finger along the wall further in and the coarse concrete was covered in a fine coat of dust. No one had inhabited this place in some time. I jerked my head around the left-hand turn after the third light and jerked it back into cover even faster as I heard a snap in front of me. I waited for a few seconds, cursing my lack of visual uplinks until the hot pain of the tendon I pulled in the back of my neck dissipated, and I popped back out in a crouch. No threat. The snap sound came from a piece of paper taped to the wall a little in front of me. I scanned down the next leg of the tunnel from my position, stood when I was satisfied, and I snatched the paper from its anchorage, tearing it at the top a bit. From the construction of the tunnel so far, I bet that it was going to lead either to a dead end or to an access point that the Bureau hopefully had covered from the other end. If I were incorrect in these assumptions, I believed the Bureau would consider it understandable, given the dearth of information provided in my briefing, and my hunt would become protracted. I couldn't help myself. I took a look at the paper. It read:

acking

rget 10: Age 45

Target 11: Age 41

Target 12: Age 40

Target 13: Age 42

Target 14: Age 38

...

Target 216: Age 38

Target 217: Age 36

Target 218: Age 36

Target 219: Age 39

Target 220: Age 41

...

Target 2059: Age 36

Target 2060: Age 36

Target 2061 C*: Age 34

Target 2062: Age 29

Target 2063 C*: Age 33

There was nothing on the back of the list, and it had been written in pen, a few letters of which were smeared recently. I stuffed it in an open pocket and removed my boots at this point, sacrificing stun ability for stealth. I padded down the hall to the next left-hand corner, the light for which had burnt out. I checked the corner, turned around it, clicked on the flashlight attachment on my pistol, and slid my left arm along the left wall to retrieve another note, which had been crinkled a bit, peeling the tape off with it this time. This one read:

Target 2059: Sheila. Age 36. Fortune spent on drugs. In a stupor, begged me to let her try the drugs in my "apt glove thing." She injected herself. That was easy.

Target 2060: Sammy. Age 36. Fortune spent on luxury. Penthouse. Drones. Cars. Food. Prostitutes. I slit his throat while he filled up at a petrol stop. Old car. Blood was the same color as the coupe it spilled on.

Target 2061: Collector ID: I can't remember. Age 34. Fortune classified. Reason for Collection: Diagnosed PTSD. Declared unfit for duty and in breach of contract. Assigned as her partner during a fake recon Collection staged by BoF. Shot her in her sleep out in the Gulf, destroyed the skimmer drone.

Target 2062: Axel. Age 29. Fortune spent founding a program for special needs individuals. IPL violation cited. Informed him of the violation. Repossessed the Fortune. Shot him at his desk. Center closed down as reimbursement.

Target 2063: Collector ID: D30 something. Age 33. Fortune classified. Reason for Collection: Diagnosed Psychosis. Sabotaged IFF and anti-missile defense security on his transport drone. Dreadbore missile blew it apart.

I crammed the note into my pocket, clicked off the pistol flash-light, pressed the clips on my left hip close to my thigh in order to dampen their clacking, and half-limped down the hallway. I stopped and crouched about three-quarters down the hallway, and my breath caught in my chest as I thought I heard a peeling sound from up ahead around the next corner. Feeling the tingle in my shoulders as adrenaline began coursing through me, I strained my ears to pick up any sounds. A second later, a tear ripped through the silence and the scrape of a shifting boot provided me some cover as I moved up. Then, the sound of a rock cast across the floor by my sinister, sinistral foot betrayed my presence. I heard a *click–click* as something fell to the floor ahead of me and a head peered out from around the corner along with a finger tapping furiously on a shoulder-mounted data pad. I had sighted my target.

Thompson ducked around the corner and broke into a sprint. I sprang after him, leveled my pistol, which had a strange, pink light emanating from the grip, at his head from about eight meters, and pulled the trigger. Nothing. *Pink No Link.* I remembered too late. Throwing the locked pistol away, I unanchored and uncollapsed my 4SB into my shoulder, crouched, and fired three rounds at my quarry, whose superhuman, cybernetically enhanced legs had carried him down the length quicker than anticipated. Thompson's left shoulder dipped, and he stumbled a bit and careened through the doorway to a room, slamming the door shut, and a *cachunk* accompanying a sliding bar informed me of an auto-lock engaging behind him. A red light winked on in the distance as I darted down the hallway, almost slipping on a pen underfoot, and then the light flashed purple. I began clicking the primary detonator on the 4SB, and I heard the notes of two rounds going off on the ground next to the room, though no notes of pain accompanied them. When I reached the purple light, I understood why.

The word impressed next to the purple light on the lock bar was

"Anechoic." Thompson had ensconced himself within a panic room. The door was completely locked down, and I didn't have anything on me with which to penetrate its armor. I began searching around the area for a weakness, finding the chamber to be impregnable, and I noticed a camera, which must have been closed-circuit, following me around from one of the corners of the room. As I looked at it, it nodded twice, and I stopped moving. Then, it looked past me and nodded. I turned around to see a space in the wall open up to reveal a keyboard and monitor. I walked over to it and examined the setup, noticing that a few coils of FO cabling flowed seamlessly into the chamber from the devices. I looked at the camera and noticed it was the same. Thompson had me at a stalemate. I looked at the flashing teal cursor on the black screen, awaiting his next move. Then, text appeared.

"Did you see the notes I left for you? Type and hit return to respond." Thompson typed.

"Two of the three, yes." I returned.

"Notice a pattern?"

"Several. To which one do you refer?"

"The Bureau is cleaning house. 'At least thirty-six years old' is starting to become 'At most thirty-six years old.'"

"Thirty-six satisfies them both. The age limitation language is very specific in the contracts. Were I to have taken a fortune as an individual not employed by the Bureau, I would have expected to die at 12:00 a.m. on my thirty-sixth birthday. What's your point?"

"Did you notice the Bureau employees, then? The Collectors?"

"Of course. Both deemed unfit for duty through mental health evaluations, much like yourself. Our contracts clearly state: 'If a Collector is unable to remain mentally stable under the BoF DSM until exit after forty-six years of service, said Collector may be subjected to consequences including but not limited to fine, detention, and/or Collection.' Those two happened to be subjected to the latter and you were their subjector, as I am yours. I also happened to notice that you appear erudite in electronic security measures, given your modes of dispatch, your tampering with my R–45 biometrics, and your current abode. Does your chamber block out the voices in your head as well as those without, I wonder?" I pressed, with a sneer.

"Voices? What are you talking about? I built this place with my fortune to ensure that I could get away from the Bureau's constant monitoring. I wish they would be so kind as to speak to me. What did they tell you about me?"

"Not much. Daemun Thompson. Rogue three months ago. Paranoid Schizo. ID info."

"Schizophrenic! Do I seem schizophrenic to you?"

"I find that difficult to tell conclusively, what with the panic room, not seeing your expressions, not hearing you speak, not knowing if you have AI running these responses."

"They silenced me and then they called me crazy! Target 2061. Remember her? PTSD? She didn't show a single symptom when I went out on mission with her. She even seemed excited to get back out into the field. The OMWB told me that she had been sedated before being released so her symptoms wouldn't be apparent. I checked. I was a phlebotomist before entering the Bureau. I ran blood before destroying the skimmer as cover-up. No known sedatives. I didn't like the idea of killing one of my own, so I started asking questions. I asked too many questions and now you're here."

He could be spinning these stories in order to lower my guard. The camera is still watching.

I leaned back from the monitor and looked contemplative, then indecisive, adding a few nervous strokes of my cheek, then inquisitive, never looking towards the camera.

"So, what do we do now?" I typed. "Did you lead me in here to tell me that the Bureau is killing off Collectors under false pretenses? Why would they do that? Seems like paranoid ramblings without a reason."

"I couldn't get that far before they sent you after me. I tried."

"Convenient."

A Rogue Collector is the most dangerous target you may have to Collect. They are adept at physical, electronic, and psychological modes of warfare. As such, they are often labeled TOS. This means Terminate on Sight.

My training from the Bureau surfaced as I waited for Thompson's response. Nothing came, so I probed.

"Thompson? Are you still alive? I know I hit you once. Are you bleeding out?"

"No. Bullet is still in, and I've applied staunching foam around it, but it is getting painful to type this long. I can see you don't have any comms gear except for probably a ComCom. I'd come out to talk, but you would have to drop your three modes."

"Whyever would I do that? You have me at a sight disadvantage."

"Once you have this information, you'll be able to avoid the Bureau better when they decide to diagnose you with something ridiculous. I've compiled files on this hard drive of my research. You are my best opportunity to continue it, now that we are at this impasse."

"Show me a feed of your room on the monitor, so I know I can trust you. And show me three fingers, wiggle your elbow, and draw a circle above your head with an arm, all with your primary arm for real-time confirmation."

"Hold on."

The feed flicked up a few seconds later, and I could see Thompson accomplishing the tasks I had assigned, all with his left arm, despite the wound in its shoulder, wincing from the pain but managing. The room was padded in a lumpy, gray material and largely empty except for his computer equipment on and around a table, some boxes of food and water, a reclining chair, and some books. Thompson was spinning around slowly, in his t-shirt and sweatpants, showing me his hard drive in between his left fingers. I could see the wound in his shoulder, patched up as he said. There were only a few, small, blind spots in the room. The monitor reverted.

"Satisfied?"

I did want to know more about what Thompson had uncovered. While handlers during missions were generally abrupt, the handler I was assigned this time was particularly forbid in a way that disquieted my mind. I thought that was expected, given my first rogue Collection, but that hard drive would sate my yearning for understanding. A seed of doubt had been planted.

"Mostly. You rendered my first mode incompliant via your blanket hack. Well done, by the way. Re-calibrating to a new model will be tedious. My second mode is my injection gauntlet and my third mode is an EinIn 4SB. Watch the camera."

I walked over to the camera and unclasped my extra clips, held them up, walked over to the hallway, and dropped them, seemingly by accident, just out of reach. I sighed, and walked further into the hallway, out of the sweep angle of the camera and slid the secondary detonator for the det rounds off of the 4SB and into my pocket before retrieving the belt, showing it to the camera once again and throwing it clear down the hallway. Then, I held up my injection gauntlet, unfastened it from my wrist, showed the camera the intact safety, folded the pads underneath it and slid it down the hallway. Finally, I uncollapsed and showed the side of the 4SB with the fire mode dial on it, opposite the primary detonator, to the camera, dialed to safety. Then, I lowered it and tossed it into the hallway before walking back to the monitor.

"Good." Scrolled across the screen.

"At your leisure. I'll wait here." I typed, sarcastically waving to the camera after hitting return.

"Coming out."

I saw the auto-lock bar slide back and the purple light changed to red, then to green. As the door swung out, I leaned back, with practiced nonchalance, against the wall and clasped my hands in front of my chest, positioning my right forearm next to the pocket with the notes and the detonator. Thompson still had not come out.

"You know one thing about us Collectors?" I heard Thompson say, echoing voice track seventeen from his file, with all its malevolent surety, as the sound from his second step rang out of the chamber. I finished replaying the track in my mind before his third, and I squeezed my forearms to my ribs as if in a bid to break them.

We'll do anything to live another second.

The prodigal det round sounded a fragmented melody that was a sweeter music to my ears than any I had heard in some time, but I hadn't a moment to spare in relief. I bolted around the corner and slammed into Thompson with all of the force I could muster, sending him sprawling into the chamber. His fall was cushioned by the padded floor, but the recoil of his body was sufficient to send his weapon, a late 1900s pistol with tape still clinging to it, flying safely out of reach. I leapt on top of him and drove my elbows into his chest, a precursor to my primal, fourth mode of execution, then scrambled to clasp my hands around his throat. Thoughts related to tightening my grip barraged my mind as Thompson struggled to speak.

"They'll . . ." I let go slightly, reflexively, "silence you . . . too . . ."

I tightened my grip further as my hands slid along Thompson's neck courtesy of the blood sprayed there from his gaping shoulder wound, feeling the pulses of his carotid slow, and I headbutted him in the face twice out of desperation. He kicked a few times, helplessly, and the image of a goldfish flopping on a table swam into the foreground of my consciousness as his mechanical legs scrabbled for purchase on the ground and found none. His eyes rolled back, and I felt the amplitude of his chest expansions dwindle and then flatten. I looked away from his face, and I must have held on to his neck for five more minutes after his breathing ceased before looking back up. I had to be sure. His eyes seemed to have swelled, their widened pupils

weren't quite centered, and turning his head produced no oculoce-
phalic reflex.

I jumped up from the corpse and catapulted my cognition
towards covering up my blunder. I retrieved the hard drive from the
floor of the chamber and moved to Thompson's computer setup, from
which smoke was rising, to check if camera feeds had been running
during my assault, and breathed a sigh of relief to see he had already
destroyed everything but the monitors himself. I sprinted back out
of the chamber and scraped my 4SB off the floor of the hallway while
looking down its length to ensure no one else had entered the area.
Then, I sprinted back to the corpse, stood over it, dialed to single
shot, shouldered and fired two det rounds into its neck, walked out
of the chamber, and tapped the primary detonator. Proceeding back
into the chamber, I surveyed the corpse to find any exterior signs
of strangulation had been blown away as Thompson's head, which
was recognizable only from the lifeless eyes up, had severed entirely
and was resting a meter from the corpse's mangled upper torso, with
little sign of cervical spine and attending tissues to be found between
them.

I recovered and reattached the rest of my weaponry on my way
out, stopping only to snag Thompson's final note he had abandoned
in his flight from the ground. It read:

We should talk so you don't have to be led as a sheep any further.

I'll pay you for your time. Something is not right in the Bureau.

You can spread the information when you leave here. We need more people.

I was not convinced, but I was alarmed. An asset like Thompson with aberrant thought processes is considered supremely dangerous in the Bureau and, though I had not felt mentally tainted by his diatribes, I was not going to risk the possibility of any of his scribbles compromising my imminent dress-down psych eval. Before turning the corner, I pulled out the other notes, memorized their contents using a few different mnemonics, carefully ripped each one into manageable, though not particularly palatable, fragments, wet them in the palm of my hand with some water from my pack, and swallowed them in a few handfuls. I turned the corner, put my boots back on, and walked out of the tunnel.

After emerging from the tunnel, I sent a CC ping while shading my eyes to allow them to adjust to the sunlight sifting through the cracks of the buildings, and I waited less than thirty seconds for a sniper drone to whir over to me with a message from my handler to remain where I was for a psych team to arrive, as expected. I spent the next six minutes sitting with my back against the wall of the parking ramp, scrounging for pebbles in the dirt to loft at my mechanical monitor, my spirits raising with each successful *plink* resounding from its housing. The white Bureau coin insignia holos projecting from the side of the descending transport drone indicated my ride had arrived, and the sniper drone whirred off to embed itself in its dock in the starboard hull of the beetle-shaped craft as the stern of its mother flapped open to receive me. I maintained my peripheral vision on the blue chevrons rippling across the length of the sniper drone's rifle, indicating stun priming, as it swiveled to keep me in its sights until I stepped into the rear of its mother to an unceremonious welcome.

I had yet to experience a dress-down psych exam in the field, though I had heard a bit about them in training. That said, I was still surprised at the literality of the term. The drone lifted off to return to the NER Bureau, and my attendants assured me that we would be finished by the time we arrived. I surrendered my EinIn weaponry to the first attendant, a quiet human male in a lab coat with a black and blue chevron tie to match the drone rifles, who waddled them over to a polarity strip and anchored them, locking them down and coding the release to prevent any unauthorized reclamation attempts. The second attendant, a bot imitating a female, prompted me in a voice programmed to soothe to relieve myself of my injection gauntlet and to place it on one of the burnished steel shelves extending from the wall to its left, one arm raised to beckon me over and one poised in defense, as if the contents of the syringes contained within could contaminate its electrical circulatory system. Next, I shrugged off my pack, emptied my pockets, kicked off my boots, and unclasped my combat skin, peeling it off slowly from the collar down to my ankles. Thinking I was finished, shivering in my undergarments with only Thompson's hard drive clutched in my fingers, I moved over to the examination slab and hopped on to it. I surrendered the hard drive as a sign of good faith to my human examiner, who then walked it over to the bot, which attempted pairing to access the information. I had to surrender my undergarments as well, but the human was able to take care of those on his own. He swiped and tapped on a data pad a few times before approaching me.

"Drive's encrypted. We'll take it back to da lab fer analysis." My cockney doc said, extending a few probes and a monitor from the wall while spinning his downturned wrist around in order to get my body to do the same. I obliged. "All you need ta do is answer da prompts on da screen n' we'll take care o' da rest. Wait firty seconds fer background n' den well begin. If we land low, you'll be in good shape. If not, well . . ."

My robotic attendant moved back into my plane of vision and squatted down, resting a hand on its knee, staring directly at my face while the human one slapped a pulse strip across my wrist.

"Sorry. He is not very good at this. Just relax. Please answer the questions." The bot soothed with decently appropriate inflections.

"The old curmudgeonly shrink, smooth shrink, eh? Trust me. I'm quite at ease." I bantered, settling in to watch the questions flash across the screen.

I am more or less as able to work as I ever was: Yes.

I work under an appreciable amount of stress: Yes.

I have difficulty keeping my mind on a task or a job: No.

I am open with information concerning my coworkers: Yes. Addtl: Hard Drive

I recently had a peculiar experience: No

My sleep is disturbed frequently: No

I have lived an ideal life: No

I sometimes continue on something until others lose their patience: Yes

I have often had to take orders from someone who knows less than me: Yes

It would be better if most laws were abandoned: No

I have a strong sense of duty: Yes

I enjoy the rewards of my labor: Yes

I feel comfortable in this moment: Yes

Do you wish to alter any of your previous responses: No

Background Information Recorded

"Now on to more meaningful questions, I suppose," I shot at the bot, which was ambulating over to sit behind me across the walkway of the hold.

"'At's good fer background. Go ahead an' spin round there and we'll ask what we been forwarded from yer handler," the aged man croaked.

"You must be close to retiring, old-timer," I plied, pressing my hands on the slab and lifting while rotating in order to decrease the friction applied to my legs. "How many more years of this for you?"

"Welp. Dey keep us support on fer seven more years 'an you, and I got 'bout free more years ta go. You do da math."

He pressed two fingers to his jowls as he studied his data pad, remembered the information for which he was searching, and brought it up.

"And do you 'enjoy the rewards of' your labor?" I could read the answer in his scowl before he worded it.

"Wot labor? Firty years from now dey'll've cut me out entirely. Ya know wot I'm doin' right now? Feedin' da questions to Stacey, da super psych over there. She can ask da questions in an impartial manner. Bots've made da work so easy it's not even worf doin' 'cept it's all I done fer years. Pays the bills, I guess." He sighed.

"You still have final approval though, I'm sure, similar to how humans are required to pull the trigger in the field, correct?" I feigned nervousness.

"Yeah, I got dat. You'll be fine. Dey're mainly lookin' for corruption and traumatization and, dough Stacey," he tilted his head at the bot, "might not be able to encode it yet, I don't see any o' dat 'bout you. I still have ta get frough the questions, dough. Look at her directly and we'll get it over wiff 'n all."

I gazed at the plastiform face of the bot and watched it blink regularly a few times and then it began to execute its line of questioning

while adopting a posture with a straight back and its hands resting
flat on its knees.

Incoming transmission from D, receive?

*ComCom: Decline last, Send: Comback ping for approximately
fifteen minutes*

"We only have two questions we need to ask you from Shepherd
5–5." Stacey began in a monotonous recitation. "First question: Did
Collector Daemun Thompson seem to communicate anything to
you that you felt was notably exceptional compared to your typical
Collections?"

I paused an amount of time I thought sufficient to suggest genuine contemplation before answering with a prepared statement for a
question of this ilk.

"Thompson fled to an anechoic chamber he had constructed,
which was the reason his DNA probe radio tag went silent, and he
attempted to communicate with me about his former targets, as
Collectors often do, but it came off as the inane babble of someone
who was mentally unstable, as was suggested in my pre-drop briefing.
The mode of communication was a two-way computer interface on
a closed network. I bluffed to indicate a perimeter had been established in the area and he could be collected by me or he could wait in
there for an O–strike, given the Bureau might resort to that in this
breach of contract scenario. After communicating this, he seemed
to become desperate, and he bartered with me to try to save some
data he thought were important. I informed him that an O–strike
would leave little chance for that. He unsealed the anechoic chamber, a struggle ensued, and I dispatched him with my 4SB. I didn't
know where the 'important data' were, but Thompson dropped the
drive I gave you all earlier, so I brought that with me. Perhaps you
could consult with the cleanup crew for more information," I finished, yawning.

"Transferring . . ." Stacey updated, its head tilting down slightly, then back up a few moments later. "Shepherd 5–5 wishes to inform you that the drive in question was blank."

"Seems to check out with the schizo diagnosis," I returned, unsurprised.

"Transferring . . . Shepherd 5–5 wishes to inform you that the cleanup crew found no other information of note. The computer interface was scoured but user data had been sabotaged."

Lovely. I shrugged my shoulders and tossed my hands up.

"Would I be allowed to ask a question of Shepherd 5–5? Out of curiosity?" I niggled, desiring one last piece of information at the risk of besmirching my performance.

"Transferring . . . Submit question."

"When was Thompson diagnosed with schizophrenia? I was unable to ask him during the Collection." I conformed my emotions to mild indifference throughout the question and concentrated on maintaining them through the answer.

"Shepherd 5–5 wishes to inform you that that information is irrelevant to this debrief, and its records are released on the purview of the OMWB to necessary parties only."

"Okay."

"Transferring . . . Question 2: Given the operation had only two sources authorized for information tap, the CC camera and the computer interface previously discussed, which were tampered with by the Collectee, and your sources were decommissioned for safety purposes, this Collection will be processed as NoSurv, initiated by the NER Bureau of Fortune. You have been awarded a temporary clean bill, but you will be expected to comply with any further inquiry on this Collection, NER BoF CID: Y*54–77, for the next sixty days. A copy of these examinations will be forwarded to you, and you will be notified of proceedings via data pad. Are you accepting of these statements?"

"I am accepting," I replied, allowing an appropriate amount of relief to skip across my synapses.

"Transferring . . . This concludes the examination. The Bureau appreciates your participation," Stacey concluded before standing up and moving to the intersection of its slab and the forward bulkhead to sit back down in a casual standby setting, raising its knees to its chin and clasping its hands around them in order to stow itself away neatly.

"See? Nuttin' ta worry 'bout. We'll be landin', second floor pad, 'at's as low as low gets fer this baby." The old-timer knocked on the wall before throwing me my clothes. "We'll be landin' in about fir-teen minutes and we got a nice, new C–skin for ya'. Go ahead an' put 'er on. We'll be confiscatin' da rest of yer stuff as well unless you want'a submit for any valuables."

"I'll be fine without. Can you just ensure that the Bureau replaces all of the items one for one except the 4SB? I can report for calibra-tion tomorrow."

"Bureau's givin' ya' a day off tomorrow as compensation fer da whiparound op. I'll tell 'em ta have it all waitin' for ya' on Tuesday."

"Sounds fine."

"Welp, if'n dat'll be all, I'm off fer a wink. Wake me up if ya' need summat. Stacey'll keep an eye on ya'. Don't do anyfin' stupid."

"Wouldn't dream of it, sir."

The old-timer double-checked that all his tools had been stowed appropriately and then he headed across the hold to a reclining seat just off the near lip of Stacey's slab, keyed the straps to remain off, plopped down into it and closed his eyes.

I allowed my mind to dwell only on sexual fantasies for the rest of the flight, the prurience of which should have been unassuming enough to convince any other probes that might have been occurring that I was thinking normal thoughts. The drone landed in NYC on time, and I was able to walk free without any sniper drone tracking.

I ComComed Daria a bit late and calmed her down before spending the next half hour requisitioning materials and queuing a Bureau car to drop me off at my residential unit.

As I climbed into my bed, I reverted to my typical mindset and began processing the psych eval in relative security. In the choice of wording Shepherd 5–5 had used in denying me the information I sought on Thompson's diagnosis, she had nurtured the seed Thompson had planted in my mind, and I knew I was not going to glean its fruit of knowledge from the Bureau's withholding orchard. A transplant was in order and there was one fertile source of information about which I had heard whispers in my work that could have yielded a bountiful cultivar from the germinating grain. I finished planning my day off with the help of some '030s jazz hop rhythms from my data pad and then hit the sheets.

I snoozed my alarm a few times before getting out of bed to get dressed. Walking over to the wall bureau, I swiped on my data pad to bring up the arrangements I had made for a lift drone to see that the price of my day trip had gone up 0.6 GC. There was a bit of rain trickling down outside the window on the April morning, which was always good for drone business. I tapped to summon the drone and a sixteen-minute ETA popped up on my screen. I keyed open one of the drawers to grab a collared shirt and some shorts and put them on, bypassing my typical shower routine, as I would be cleansing later. Then, I sat down by the lowest of the drawers, authenticated to the biometric lock using my right index and middle fingers, slid it completely open, reached around the back of it, and pulled out one of the smaller bags of gold I had stored in a hole cut into the floor of the fifty-eight-square-meter unit and stuffed it into my pack along with some water. As I stood back up, my hand hesitated over my combat skin lying on the floor next to the bed. I would be going out weaponless. Then again, that helped to cement my happy-go-lucky image of

the day. I found the flip flops I had received as a gag gift from Daria
before our desert operation in the shoe drawer next to the entry door
and was glad that I had another rare occasion to use them. I flipped
and flopped out the door, watching my data pad for the lock confirmation icon to flash up, took the stairs down four floors past a couple
of kids who had paused on their ascent to comment on a stream one
of them had going, and I waited behind an old lady just inside of the
taxi exit and excused myself as my ETA wound up earlier than hers.

The doors to the lift drone were open almost level with the
awning protruding from the building so that only a few drops of rain
were able to wind their way into my fabrics before I ducked into the
vehicle. My somniferous lift companion had the cabin lights turned
down and the windows tinted, and I checked the text in the panel
above his seat, which informed me his destination was Plattsburgh.
Celebrating my luck in passengers for my bargain booking price on a
form of semi-public transportation with a couple nods, I tapped the
depart command next to the doorway and took my seat as the door
hissed closed.

Sifting through the digitized stacks of the NYPL, I settled on a
brief period piece and whiled away the rest of my ride reading about
a man named Gatsby and his struggles to make a dream few have in
this country anymore a reality, to amass new money to court old love,
and to prevaricate his persona in pursuit of a chronological impossi-
bility that would never come to pass. Consulting literary sources estimated that he died at thirty-two without achieving his goal. These
days, we're offering a bargain price: 12.5 percent more years than
Gatsby got for you to try your luck. Step right up! As the door hissed
open to let in the crisp mountain air of my destination, there was one
lesson on which I perseverated due to that great man's plight: I would
abnegate my entire fortune in order to pluck my Daisy from a bed of
weeds. At the time, I thought this little more than a romantic whim.

Aogami Onsen was a popular No Surveillance, or NoSurv, retreat carved into the side of Mount Ellen owned by the third son of the Com[3]. It was once a private resort that catered to the super-rich in need of pampering, for the most part. The resort itself is sourced from a number of artificially-drilled geothermal springs and its sukiya-style architecture is gorgeously traditional in its simplicity. However, other clients sought passage through its walls not for respite within its comforting waters but for a particular service they provided via illegal taps to ComCom devices: information. Confirming a spouse's suspected infidelity, the ideal time to trade stock before a company higher-up is collected, specifications of weaponry being developed by the military, all of these things and more could have been yours at the price of acquiring and furnishing a form of payment that was electronically untraceable.

The NER government raided Aogami around nine months after my visit on suspicion of exactly what was occurring there due to a leak that had sprung related to some scandal or another. The Bureau was thought to be involved as well somehow. The dome that had been erected to ward the patrons from prying eyes, whether digital or visceral, has been torn down since then, but the inn still operates today much the same as it did then, just without the resource I utilized.

My ankles were aching by the time I ascended to the entrance since my class of lift drone was only allowed to disembark passengers at the foot of the mountain, and I was looking forward to bathing almost as much as receiving my answer. An attendant bowed in greeting as I approached, and I slowly placed my pack in the dirt in front of me, backed away, and waited for him to search it. His face remained expressionless as he rifled through the pockets.

"Thank you, prospective guest. I have a 6/10 tatami room available for you if that will suffice. Open air." The man waited for a response as he returned my pack.

"6/10 is rather large, is it not? How about something with a garden view?" I returned, inserting the code phrase I had learned.

"Of course. However, it will still be 6/10. They all are."

"That will be fine."

The man signaled for the dome door to open and led me inside. As I removed my clothing and checked my belongings, including my data pad, in behind a counter, the man checked me over for any surveillance forms and grunted when he was satisfied. I received a bathrobe and a pair of geta clogs in return. Then, another attendant escorted me to my room. I dangled my clogs from my fingers as I padded down the polished wood floors behind my escort. She knelt and slid the door to my room open before informing me that I would be able to bathe in either of the baths closest to my room starting in fifteen minutes and any other needs could be taken care of by ringing a bell that was sitting on a pad on the glossy black table in the center of the six–tatami room. I bowed in thanks before wandering across the sparsely furnished room, between the sliding doors on the opposite side that had been left open in welcome and on to a large boulder fashioned into a step just under the terraced porch that looked out into a garden that led to the pools, where I deposited my clogs. Then, I retreated back into the room and began checking its perimeter, partially out of habit and partially to find menus, knowing it would be garish to misplace my upcoming order.

A seeker of information at the Aogami of old became ensorcelled in an elaborate dance of duplicity from the moment of identification of payment. Compared to other patrons, the information I sought was singular and direct. I only needed to consult a single information broker, so a waltz during the dining sequence would suffice, though I had only practiced the steps learned from my civilian instructor in my mind. I picked the bell up from the cushion on the table and jangled it to summon an attendant, who arrived with startling haste, sliding my room door open to receive my request. I communicated my desire to order lunch, and that I would like to begin with a water and a carafe of umeshu, or plum wine. The attendant left and returned almost immediately with a napkin, chopsticks, and a chop-stick rest, with which he set the table in front of the squat, zaisu chair I had pulled out before excusing himself to return with the water and wine on a tray moments later, giving me just enough time to flip the orientation of the chopsticks on the stand. He knelt at the table and poured the first cup of the wine before taking my kaiseki order.

The next three hours played host to the most heinous act of food wasting I am like to ever commit in my life, though karmic justice was almost immediately served in the repugnant stimuli coursing from my papillae courtesy of a number of foods I choked down from the ten-course meal to clarify my purpose. After plucking the calyces from the strawberries of my final dish and aggregating them along-side some pickles in the corner of their plate, which was accented by a rough line drawing of a crane, I re-deciphered the code written in the leftovers I abandoned from each course to ensure no information filter had gone awry. Untouched plum wine, one topic. Kaiseki three, governmental. Wasabi, population regulation. Sushi, Bureau of Fortune. Soup, Office of Mental Well-Being. Bonito sashimi, patient records. Pickles, mental health history.

The attendant returned around half an hour later with a tab and a pen. The total came out to be around nine GCs. I signed, trying to spell Daemun as it sounded, and I flourished the n at the end of Thompson before adding an 80 percent tip, as 80 percent or 24 per-cent would amount to nothing either way. The attendant nodded and smirked as his eyes scanned the paper, which he folded and tucked away in his pocket, and he gestured to the garden with a bow before he left the room on his way to the incinerator. I got up from my chair, slid the doors to the garden open, slid into my clogs, slid the doors closed, and ambled off to the mixed baths.

The steam rising from the private bath allowed my sinuses to open wider than they had in some time as I disrobed, hanging the blue garment on one of the offshoots of a bamboo culm growing next to the larger of the two baths. The scent of cypress wood suffused my nostrils as I sat on the edge of the rectangularly bound spring, first looking around at the rods of dried bamboo forming the perimeter wall of the enclosure, then up at the dome, which was built almost high enough to stay out of your field of vision. I tossed my clogs over towards the bamboo stand and daintily lowered myself into the spring, catching sight of the grisly scar I had gained in a youthful game of hide and seek courtesy of some barbed wire, winding up my right thigh. I couldn't quite immerse myself up past my shoulders while retaining a comfortable reclining position at first, so I took to rocking back and forth for a while before finding that to be tedious. I settled into a corner and rested my back against a rising pillar as I watched one of the doors set in the bamboo wall for my broker, who arrived later than I expected.

"Sorry I'm late! Sorry! My last appointment went long! Some people just can't get enough, you know?"

The slender man called out, waving his hand dismissively above his head as he closed the door I had been watching behind him, dropping his robe on the ground at its base. He was covered ankle to neck in an interwoven tapestry of tattoos, presumably inspired by Japanese folklore, though I didn't have a data pad to scan it in. I locked eyes with the blue demon on his chest and admired the detail paid to its furrowed brow, bloodshot eyes, and baleful glower, wondering how much of his earnings the broker injected into his dermis, as the waves inked on his left leg cascaded into the gentle waters of the bath, plunging the fishing boat on his knee into a watery grave.

"Perhaps you will be early to the next one, then. I aim to be alacritous."

"You seem to know your stuff from your food! Thanks for playing along with that. We like to see you all can follow directions. Great! Great! So, what'll it be?" the man asked, in a voice loud enough for me to wonder if the NoSurv status of the resort was to prevent him from being heard from space.

"I would like to know the exact latest date former Collector Daemon Thompson was under OMWB record without a diagnosis of paranoid schizophrenia. The official date of diagnosis would help as well, but the last date free of any e-trail related to that update, if possible, would be ideal."

"Tricky!" The man's enthusiasm remained in his voice, but he did lower it to a volume appropriate for discretion. "Taps we ran got a communiqué between his handler on the date of his last active duty Collection and Director Mint of the OMWB. That was four months ago to the day. Another conversation between two secretaries of the OMWB, no doubt unauthorized, had one of them telling the other that she was 'changing Thompson's status to reflect his recent diagnosis of paranoid schizophrenia.' That was about a day and a half after that. If you need up-to-the-minute, I'd have to run back and check that. Memory's not perfect. We can't pull file information because the only stuff we've got on the Bureau is audio. I think that's all I got on that. Hold on . . ."

The man poked his nose a few times while he pondered the rest of his information.

"Do you know when Thompson went rogue? Snippet synthesis seems to point to most conversations saying it was just under three months ago. March 5th, if I had to guess. Did I answer your question well enough?"

"That should suffice. The Bu—" I replied, thinking I would elaborate on what the Bureau had officially communicated to me, but I backed off. "Never mind."

"Nice! Nice! Next question?" He asked, eager to please, as the brokers could earn commission percentages from satisfied customers.

"There isn't one. That was it," I stated, cupping water in my hands and pouring it out as the broker flopped backwards, submerging

himself in surprise. He resurfaced moments later, his back and the
kappa painted on it facing me, and he jittered around.

"You dropped like a k in bulli on this! You indicated one topic,
but one question? Are you sure? You could get like," he started counting on his fingers before he decided he would run out of appendages,
"at least fifteen more questions or something! You're some kinda big
spender! Where'd you get all that gold anyway?"

Back when Daria and I had visited the UAE, I had negotiated a
trade of 44 percent of my fortune to a sheik for gold bullion at an 87.5
percent exchange rate after the Bureau took off 2 percent, though I
didn't feel the need to disclose that to Aogami.

"I'll chip you a 3 percent commission off of it, and you can consider 10 percent of it to stand against any of my information being
released. The remainder is for the establishment. You accommodate
that request, correct?"

"Defs! You can be insured for probably about twenty something
years if someone asks about you. Otherwise, we don't leak unless
asked!" he said, climbing out of the bath.

I retreated back to my corner, thinking I could take refuge from the
red faces of yet more demons grimacing at me from the broker's lower
cheeks and my thought resonated with the makings of one other question I had been weighing since I cornered Thompson. I took a chance.

"Broker. I seem to have spoken hastily. I have thought of another
question, possibly three, though I am unsure if you will have answers,"
I admitted.

"Shoot!" The man turned and shot from the hip with a couple of
finger guns.

"First, are you a Bureau information specialist?"

"You betchya! One of two here."

"Thompson was killed in an anechoic chamber after being cornered, and I have come to understand that his Collector wanted to
ask him why he didn't flee further from the Bureau. Have you ever

intercepted communications related to Collectors or Collectees fleeing to a non-Bureau-affiliated country successfully?"

"Oh! General Bureau trends! I also handle these!" He walked back
over and lowered his voice. "From what I have put together, there
have been a lot of these throughout history. I deal mostly with stateside Bureaus, but it has been happening internationally since the
original Bureau founding in the East. I know of at least four successful flights and hundreds of unsuccessful. There's got to be way more
that succeed that the Bureau is covering up, though. That's why the
Bureaus try to fast track their best agents into counter-flight units.
Attempted flights have decreased for the most part over the years and
they are currently at their lowest ever, estimated at one per every five
thousand-ish contracts. The Bureau doesn't have much of an issue
there, though, cuz they're damn good at killing the ones that try, and
they just get their money back. Scavenger countries are mad, though."

"Scavenger countries?"

"Oh. I figured you'd know this! Some of the B-UA countries stim-
ulate their economy through funding gained from people fleeing into
their country. It really helps some of the ones who haven't had as
much mechanization. They try to poach the remainder of the fortune and even saddle those that successfully gain asylum with debt.
Canada has been doing this for years."

"You said you figured I would know this. Why?" I asked, adding
another question.

"You're here to prepare for your counter-flight rotation, right? I
think we heard you would be rotated in starting in a few weeks," the
broker replied, melding his finger guns into a rifle and scoping in on
my face.

"Hmm. Very good. That will be all. Certainly, this time. I'll up
that commission to 5 percent." I dismissed the broker, who grooved
over to his robe and sprang out the door.

I melted back into the bath, incensed at learning about the time of my final rotation placement before the Bureau would allow me the choice to return to general Collection from a source other than the Bureau itself. I didn't move from the bath for the next three hours, which I had originally planned on enjoying in tepid relaxation. Stomping back through the hallways and dressing in the entrance availed me of a breeze that cooled off every part of my body save for the part under my collar, which smoldered for quite some time.

8

3367 – The Biologist

The pitter-patter of un-forecasted precipitation off of the foliage overhead was the only sound to keep me company on my composure walk. I was on my break and, at its outset, I had decided to head back to the assault drone convoy in order to play a game of cards with the drone net monitor team members, as we had only had a few strikes from the roving scarab drones in the last six hours and all of them had been confirmed as various non-human mammals, which could cross the NER–Canadian border unfettered. Working in the counter-flight rotation was excruciatingly boring. For many on the squad, this was due to a lack of killing, for me it was a lack of stimulating conversation. At least it was almost over.

I had played my hands well and a few strokes of luck allowed me to win the first few games, and I felt comfortable enough in my play to converse freely with the crew. One could say I lost the conversation. Once we had proceeded through the customary inanities regarding significant others and minor work gripes, the topic had settled on the Bureau, its checks and balances system, and how it should evolve to become a full branch of the government as opposed to the twig it is, a proposition put forth by a particularly gung ho employee and one with which I disagreed.

This day happened to mark my fourth anniversary of joining the

Bureau and a little over three years since my first Collection. As my data pad had reminded me so early in the morning, I had spent most of the fourteenish hours between my awakening and this rude awakening excogitating about a few of the changes in Bureau policy that had taken effect over my tenure and the discordance they brought to my once-harmonious vision of why I joined in the first place. In my pithy dissension to the topic, I had found myself outnumbered six to one in our conversation, then argument, then lambasting, and I saw fit to alienate myself, as I had no desire to remain in their insular, incontrovertible, and self-aggrandizing world and, in a careless demonstration of my ire, I stormed off into the rain without reattaching my chest plate or helmet, which were lying face down on the ground, cameras–down, as was the custom for breaks during which Collectors might be engaging in approved camaraderie building, so much for that, and I began my walk.

I was leaning against the trunk of a willow tree about four kilos out from the convoy and as far away from the data pad dots denoting the drones of my haranguers as possible. Availing myself of the cover its drooping eaves offered from a particularly forceful shower, I chuckled at the idea that the species was a perfect analogy for my employer. Above ground and visible to all, the branch of the willow seems submissive and not nearly as ostentatious as the heaving bough of, let us say, an executive branch, yet, beneath the surface, its insidious roots wind their way through any crack in the governmental pipeline, looking to take hold.

I turned towards the bole of my protector, my employer, my umbrella cane I had initially held up for its shield against the downpour of doubt raining on my naïve parade of angst held for a world irreverent and devoid of promise, and I hefted an imaginary axe in my hands. I poised to cleave it in twain and my upstart resolution faltered. I let the axe slide from my palms and back into the aether whence it came. I wasn't ready. I still required its aegis. I was weak

and uncertain. Four years and little had changed except for the sour-
ing of my idealistic expectations for my profession.

Turning back around and stretching my arm out to sweep away
the curtain of leaves that had obscured my antics from the possibility of unregistered, prying lenses, I locked my ankles and froze
as I caught a glimpse of an aberration through the wisps of green.
I dropped to a crouch as silently as possible and moved my arm
around behind my back at an agonizingly slow pace to unanchor
my SorFab Switchshot AR without ever diverting my gaze from the
apparition. Under a copse of elm trees around a quarter kilo away,
I saw a lumpy object that looked like a stump of a tree over which
grass had grown, which, were it not shuffling slightly, would have
looked perfectly at home in the landscape. Its surface seemed to be
shimmering ever so slightly as rain slicked down it. I scrutinized it
further for a few minutes with my rifle resting across my knee, and
then half of the stump moved again, and I tapped to switch the rifle's
40/20 mag from lethal to stun and waited the advised half a second
as the barrel shifted conformation to accommodate before scoping
in on the target, nudging the barrel of the rifle through the leaves.
Toggling the scope from the NV filter, since I didn't have my helmet
to sync, to IR, I noticed that the object had no thermal signature, so
I toggled to clear filter and fired two rounds at the center of its mass.
The stump seemed to deflate on one side as the pronged leads of the
rounds punched through its surface.

"Mom!!!"

The stump keened and my heart sank into my stomach as I fired
another two rounds into the remainder, which had already readopted
its previous image, only in a smaller scale, and the entirety of the
stump crumpled.

I scanned the area for a few seconds for any other abnormal-
ities, knowing that the stun state would last for minutes, before
shouldering through the willow curtain to slink through the verdant

undergrowth to uncover the mystery. An arm and a couple of legs were convulsing on the ground slightly under what appeared to be a sheet-like material as I approached, silencing any playful suspicions of the supernatural stemming from my sleep-deprived state. I swept the parts of the sheet that were not pinned to my quarry by the stun rounds off to reveal a bald woman and a young boy, both dressed in black cloth jumpers up to their necks, writhing on the ground beneath the tree. I drew out an exhausted sigh to the exhalative capacity of my lungs and began running through some algorithms in my mind. Settling on one to which a pinch of rebellion had been sprinkled, perhaps due to my mood, I bent down and kicked away a device of some kind from the woman's hand before delicately clench-ing her head between my boots and I ran an iris scan through my data pad, figuring my break was over, as it returned:

Name: Schehera Jones
Sex: Female
Age: 34
Blood Type: AB –
Occupation: Current: Unemployed
Former 1: Research Endocrinologist
Former 2: IVF Technician
Residence: Thompson Ward, MN, NER
Pop–Reg Status: Mandated BC*, Default Count 1
BoF Status: Contracted, Awarded for Business Endeavor, No Collection Window
Collateral Cosigner: Wilbit Hocksley 16/17, Capped at 20

I acted as though I were tapping on my data pad then pointed the barrel of my rifle at her forehead, despite finding the act distasteful, in order to drive home my point.

"Listen very carefully, Schehera. You are in breach of your

contract. Your status has been updated. You will be collected pursuant to Article 77 Clause 3 concerning Flight Under Contract." I shot another stun round into her presumed-child's leg. "When you are able, and, should you wish to remain compliant, I will discuss the possibility of not collecting your son as a violation of your MBC. Nod if you wish to comply when your stun state ends."

I waited another minute or so for Schehera to return to her senses, and she began nodding furiously as she tried to get up. I looked once more over the area and checked my data pad to confirm the positions of the scarab drones on the ground relative to ours and scanned the skies as well. Airspace was tightly regulated this close to the border around most B-UA countries, so we shouldn't have had too many small-scale aerial drones in the area and none of the assault drones had taken wing either based on my readings except for one that was forty kilos to our southwest.

"I want to . . . erghh . . ." Schehera tried to speak.

"You'll be completely recovered soon. Don't push yourself," I replied, scrabbling in the mud for the device and finding that it could anchor to my left thigh polarity pad.

"When your son's stun state ends, I want you to carry him over to that gulch."

I pointed a little past the copse at the scar carved in the land that wound for a few kilometers northwest while prying out her stun rounds and dropping them into a hermetically sealed bag I had retrieved from my pack.

"We'll have a bit more cover there. I'm sure you have a lot of emotions welling up inside right now, but, if you want any chance at saving your son, you are going to have to follow my orders perfectly. Though it seems cliché to say, if either of you makes any false moves . . ." I locked eyes with the son as he began to recover, "I will collect both of you instantly."

I tapped to switch the Switchshot back to lethal.

"Do you understand?"

"Y–yes," the woman quailed, resignation beginning to creep into her expression.

"He's ready." I began.

I carefully grabbed the stun rounds that I had fired into her son and put them in another bag. Schehera picked up her son, I grabbed their sheet, and we walked over to the gulch and hopped in. We moved along its length to the deepest point that was also wide enough to accommodate sitting, and I instructed them to do so while kneeling in front of them.

"First," I began to whisper, taking extra precautions despite the sounds of the storm most likely being of a sufficient decibel to drown out our discussion, "speak only in a low whisper, and I don't want your son speaking, if at all possible. Nod or shake no if I ask for understanding. Do you understand?"

She nodded.

"How old is your son?"

"Eight and a half." Tears began flowing at this point and she found it hard to whisper as her sorrow caused her voice to become guttural.

"So, he should be able to understand enough to stay quiet?"

I looked at him and his eyes grew wide, but he nodded.

"Do you understand what a Collector is?" I addressed the child.

He held his hands up to indicate uncertainty. I grumbled.

"You're going to have to find that out some other time. Sorry. Are you working with a guide?" I turned back to his mom, and she began kissing the top of the boy's head repeatedly.

"Yes."

"Do you know where he or she is right now?"

She pointed at the controller on my hip.

I brought it up and tapped the screen and it was passcode locked. I looked at her, waiting.

"9812 . . ." She began hyperventilating, "4."

I entered the passcode and a map with a glowing, red line stretching from our current position northeast across the border, which was only about 1.8 kilos away, popped up. They were so close.

"Does your son know how to use this?"

"Yes. He's good with it."

"Okay. Here's what I'll do." I showed her my data pad. "I can control the positioning of our drones in this area based on when I clock back in. They fan out based on our IFFs. The only reason this will work is because you caught me on my break. Thank whatever deity you choose for that. When I do that, it will clear a path for your son. He will have to follow this map on his own at a run. Understand? A run. During that time, you will answer the remainder of my questions. If I sense a lie, and please know I am exceptional at this, I will reroute our fastest drones to his position and he won't stand a chance. Understand?"

She nodded and her son looked up at her, trembling.

"I have about . . . two and a half minutes before I have to clock back in. Go ahead and say your goodbyes."

Schehera looked at her boy and lifted up his data pad, swiped over to the camera and composed herself before beginning a recording as I copied information on their guide from the device to my data pad for later. I didn't understand why she thought this was necessary at the time, as I doubt the last words of a mother would be something anyone would ever forget, but, as I would learn later on in my career, this type of self-styled epitaph would be added to a digital cemetery now that gravestones were rarely fashioned anymore. It was not the dirge I had expected. Throughout bearing witness to it, though none of it was intended for me, of course, I learned quite a lot. It even ended with her son laughing a bit at one of their most cherished memories. I confess I don't remember most of the middle, as I was swept off to a plane of possibility that I had been seeking for some time. A plane posed possible by a certain Collector's small amount of attention paid at a pivotal point. A plane where I might be able to contribute to the rise of a life protected and paid for with the deaths of so many others.

Schehera let the data pad fall after stopping the recording, and I returned from my reverie as she embraced her possibility-made-reality tightly, one last time, giving him her love as she hoisted him out of the gulch and onto its lip. I clocked back in after entrusting the boy with the device. I slipped his bag of stun rounds, into which I had deposited a camera dot, into a pocket in the back of his jumpsuit and told him to dispose of them when he crossed and he would be safe. I watched the arrows indicating the scarabs POV directions fan out away from my location. The boy took a deep breath and began running. I turned my attention back to Schehera.

"Can you show me your MBC implant? I have a record that says you defaulted once." I anchored my SorFab and unanchored my EinIn, freeing up a hand for palpation.

She lifted her arm up and pointed at the area of her underarm in which it had been implanted, and I felt the nodule.

"It's a fake, though." She told me, cocking her head a bit and sniffling.

"Really? But that can't be the reason for your default. They would have rendered you infertile on that offense." I returned my hand to my side.

"No. My default was due to not making my appointed inspection on time. I had booked a vacation about nine years ago, when I was more rebellious, and I forgot to check the dates. It's something I worked on during my research. The implant is the same timed-release device used for standard MBC, but the hormones have been replaced with inerts. Street and other scanners are fooled by it, because I removed their initial implant and used the same housing, complete with embedded radio tag."

"The procedure for that must have cost—"

"A fortune?" Schehera said, flashing the wry, manic smile of a vid super villain amidst the revelation of a plot before returning to a glum frown. "Not quite. I was so close."

"I'm impressed. Birth control is readily available as well, so you must have used pill forms around the times of your checkups to disguise your tampering. Careful, or I may not regret collecting you quite so much. You resided in a ward that I believe is of sufficient population density for the government to instate blanket MBC, but you have an asterisk appended to your status. Why were you on the list and why did you resist?"

"Where MBC is normally allotted randomly, and I do think it is truly random for most of it, I'm sure you know of the exception."

"You were assigned due to a possible lethal genotype that the government is trying to snuff out. Which one? It can't be one that shortens your life span, or you wouldn't have been awarded a fortune."

"DMD."

"And the boy?"

"Unaffected. He was an IVF screened via PGD before I carried him. My job made it easy."

"It was quite the risk bringing him here, though I suppose you didn't have much choice with the Sins of the Father Clause."

"Isn't that a shitty little thing?" Schehera spat. "The kid didn't even have a real father! Where does the BoF get off thinking they can take someone like him?"

"That was initially conceived by Pop–Reg within the regular government, actually. The Bureau only gets involved when it concerns a contracted parent, such as yourself, though the government is thrilled when we enforce it because it makes us look like the villains-in-chief. There is a high correlation between MBC listees and fortune seeking, you see. The Bureau agreed in order to get a better seat at the negotiating table for Pop–Reg legislation. Mech'd pharma companies line our coffers as well because the policy wouldn't be working nearly as well without our enforcement keeping cross-listees on the straight and narrow, MBC is subsidized, but it's not free, after all. In fact, my abhorrence of this and other issues like it had a hand in inadvertently putting me on my path to stumbling across you two this evening, and my allowing your child a chance at escape is, in part, a validation of my viewpoint."

"Well aren't you an angel," Schehera said, with no small amount of scorn.

"Samael at best," I replied.

"No. Sorry. I really do appreciate that. I thought he was dead the moment I got buzzed." A bit of relief slipped into her tone as a flash of lightning illuminated our surroundings, drawing my gaze to her baffle sheet.

"I suppose the only technical questions I have left are regarding how this works." I wrinkled the sheet in my left hand to test its durability. "I have yet to see its kind employed, and I'm sure the Bureau will ask after its function. Would you be so kind?"

"I don't know exactly how it works, but it's a micro–LCD weave that projects imagery recorded on the thing you let Victor run away with. Our guide was able to get it to us, so that's your source. The sheet shows whatever recordings you scan into the pad on top of it, and it can change the scale to fit what it's covering. We had pre-loaded images of grass, trees, bushes, dirt, even river water, all seemingly recorded from this region."

"Fascinating." I hung the sheet from a root growing out of the side of the gulch.

"It is a neat little trick."

Schehera cracked her knuckles as I prepared to change subjects.

"Why, if I may ask, have the child in the first place, knowing that this encounter would be a likely result?"

She required little time to reply.

"I'm a biologist. I have studied life for most of my life and, when it all comes down to it, life exists simply to reproduce. I was pulled to the field after hearing how some male mantises go willingly to their death in order to give rise to the next generation. I wanted to know why. I thought it was a privilege that we humans were not hormonally compelled to do the same. I had always dreamt of having a kid or two if only to fulfill my biological responsibility to continue my line. I was never too interested in the romantic entanglements involved in a relationship whose ultimate purpose is procreation. I was never very good at that part. Lucky for me, we have developed a scientific workaround for that barrier. And now, here we are. I get to die in a ditch as opposed to being decapitated."

"I could arrange for both, should you wish an emulation?"

"Ha. You're too much." Schehera laughed, mirthlessly, leaning against the wall and sliding a bit backwards before steadying herself.

"Do you find that sentiment irresponsible, knowing your child will struggle to get by without your guidance?"

"As do many organisms in life."

"You are likening yourself to little more than a bacterium if reproduction is all you find important. I have been at a loss for my purpose in life for quite some time, but it must be more than just that. Surely you understand we have evolved to be different than many of those organisms."

"We have evolved to become," Schehera looked up and down my person, "something monstrous."

"I was abandoned by a parent like you. It certainly didn't do me any favors."

"Was your parent able to have you freely? Was your parent's basic biological right seized from her due to genetic prejudice?" Schehera asked, closing her eyes with excessive force, seeming tired of hearing the same questions she must have asked herself over and over in her rationalization exercises. "You know, if I defaulted one more time, they would have rendered me irreparably infertile. What kind of creature does that to their own? Actually . . . some ants do to main-tain their social structures . . . huh."

"I am unsure. It seems my parent used me for little more than a lot in genetic experimentation." I widened my eyes in front of Schehera and tilted my head upwards to allow a few forks of lightning to illu-minate my irises, waiting for her to look into them. "I keep thinking that I might see him or her again one day, as the only reason I feel I am alive is as a result of a longitudinal study, or perhaps a passing mercy, though almost twenty-two plus years seems like too long a time to pass without taking any data. Maybe I've stood face to face with him or her and never knew. I know of two other children that were raised to term from the first gen. The three of us were unloaded at an orphanage that solely admitted children possessing certain genetic markers for success. Lucky us. One was irreparably blinded to ward off cancer that was developing as a consequence of the oper-ation. One had glittering rubies set in her scleras, and she killed her-self by shooting a bullet right through one of them. The blood wasn't nearly so lustrous."

These words seemed to tear through Schehera more than any physical projectiles I could propel at her person.

"That is . . . sad." Schehera conceded, smearing her cheek with mud as she rubbed it on the walls in her effort to turn away from my gaze.

"Indeed. I have never had the urge to seek out my creator either. Why care about someone who obviously cared little for me? But, hey, that's the progress you get with science in this day and age. You can have a relatively risk–free augmentation done for a hefty 1500 GC transfer on top of the lives lost in R&D. Lives for which I can't even properly account."

My whispers sizzled the air between us, and Schehera withdrew further from me, still averting her eyes. I realized I was being too harsh, as the onus of my abandonment was not hers to bear. My temper evanesced as the transient moonlight twinkling down from above was occluded by more rain clouds.

"You obviously care for your son more than your disposition would suggest. Your fortune was awarded for research. I wonder . . . what did you sacrifice in the name of science? I suppose most of the embryos with which you worked were discarded. Potential for life lost. There is yet another life you may have endangered in your flight this evening. Do you feel its responsibility? Can you call the person to mind?"

Schehera thought for some time, scratching an ear all the while.

"Yours? That's the only one I can come up with."

"Now that you mention it, I suppose that is true, though that comes with the job. I appreciate your consideration. No. The life of which I was speaking is that of your collateral cosigner on your fortune, the man who counted on you to obey your contract. If he cannot pay for your expenditures, he will die. Does that unsettle you at all?"

"Not in the slightest. I know that might seem callous, but have you ever met one of those preening vultures? He must have cosigned seven or eight other contracts by the time I got to him. He lives like a king off of those 1 percent considerations. Eight contracts like mine would net him . . . something like 2100 GC. I don't mind keeping him on his toes. You should have seen him saunter into the Bureau to greet me in his livery."

"Very interesting. One of the ways I have been passing my time in the wilderness has been surveying on that question. Most don't recall that someone else was liable for their actions, but they do feel remorseful for it when they learn as such. However, most also have someone within their family cosign." I swiped a few times on my data pad to add another tally to my survey results, and I checked on the boy's blip on my map from the radio tag embedded in the camera dot he was carrying.

"Your boy is almost across," I swiveled my wrist to show Schehera my data pad screen, and she rocked back and forth with her hands around her knees, "so I'll ask my final questions."

I unsealed her bag of stun rounds and dropped them into the mud in front of me and knelt on them to press them into the slurry increasing in volume around us.

"Do you feel like your life was worth living, taking up a space in this overcrowded world, full of lives struggling for meaning, space that could have been filled by someone with grander designs than you, if all to which it amounted was the propagation of your genetic legacy?"

"I do. You never know what someone will amount to until they are given a chance. I wanted to birth a life and give it a chance as opposed to not provide the opportunity at all. I'd have felt like a waste of a life if I didn't give rise to one in return. That's just my opinion."

"It seems a popular risk, as it is one of the seminal causes of our current predicament as a species. I, for one, have thought about contributing to this issue myself, but I never quite felt deserving. The world is too unstable a place for me to take a chance like that right now."

"Haven't you killed off enough competitors to make room for your child? That is what you are going for, isn't it? It's nothing new, biologically speaking. You're like a walking, talking lion." Schehera folded her arms in front of her chest, matter-of-factly.

"Without the pride. Good conjecture. That is one of the reasons I do what I do, if you'll excuse the tautology. I am unsure, but I feel the average overall quality of a life is starting to creep back up. What do you think?"

"You should go for it. It's clear that you have been trying to rationalize this for a while, but you don't have to. It's your birthright as an organism." Schehera readjusted and stretched her legs out across the span of the gulch, flexing against the resistant wall, which gave slightly under her efforts to allow just a centimeter more room.

"Would you want more for your son? More than living to reproduce?"

"No." Schehera blinked, twitched her shoulder, and flared her nostrils.

A lie, and one of the most consoling I had ever seen.

"He made it," I spoke at my normal volume, and I allowed a few seconds for tranquility to register in Schehera's mien before firing two rounds through her pate. Mentally decrying the Bureau for its execrable decision in not allowing me a more irenic mode of execution to lay the triumphant progenitor low was the only eulogy I could offer at the time.

I ComComed my superiors and a scarab drone over and fed them exactly what they wanted to hear, holding aloft the baffle sheet as a trophy. I was awarded a special commendation for my work in uncovering this "novel, high-tech mode of deception available to the public," when my rotation ended three days later and any vestiges of my ages-old, low-tech mode of deception had been washed away in the muck. I felt the endorphin rush associated with the notion of "getting away with murder" for the first time that day. I found it both ironic, in that it arose from sparing a life, and humorous, in how killing people for the Bureau never elicited that response.

9

Interlude – D–Day

"Submit docking code."

A voice prompted from the drop-down screen extending from the ceiling of the lift drone, bathing my face in an orange glow as it awaited my authentication. I tapped in the alphanumeric enclosed in the reservation Daria had sent to my data pad and the light flashed green before asking me questions pertinent to my plans for the purpose of further advertisement. I swiped most of them away before commanding the screen to switch to a mirror function so that I might check my appearance once more.

It was not often that I had occasion or motivation to dress in such opulent attire as the outfit I had selected for the evening, but the destination dress code demanded lavish linens, and I found the possibility of outdressing my lady-in-waiting a tantalizing prospect. Daria had included the words "red to match" at the end of the invite, which limited my options severely. I chose a glossy black, androgynous suit accented with candy apple red cuffs on the jacket, a tie to match the cuffs, and onyx cufflinks and lapel ornaments in the shapes of crescent moons, the latter of which I was currently checking to ensure they dangled at equivalent heights from their triangular lapel clasps.

Everything seemed to be in order as the lift drone jostled to a halt on one of the docking leaflets that unfolded from underneath the bulk of the pleasure liner to receive me. I tapped the doors to swing open, my CFOB vibrated to confirm payment, and my shoes clanked on to the metal pad, which folded back in to deliver me to the port-side entrance of the dirigible airship. As I entered through the doors, a nostalgic voice greeted me.

"Good evening, guest, and welcome to The Mercurial above New York. My name is Alyona. Have you dined with us before?"

A telepresence of a gorgeous, twenty-something-year-old woman in a '050s, magenta stewardess uniform bowed slightly at the shoulders as she heralded me with a lingering Russian accent.

"Hello again, Alyona. Four years have passed since the last time I dined here, and you don't look a day older. What's your secret?!" I asked, astounded.

"Oh, you," she capered, before shifting to monotony. "I have many secrets stored in my database. Military. Political. Other. Your selection, please . . . Just kidding!"

I'll admit I was taken a bit off guard this time, as I could not recall this exchange occurring the last time Daria had brought me, though we arrived together. I chortled as Alyona's joke registered.

"That's quite amusing! How many of those do you have left in your arsenal?"

"I suppose you'll have to come back to find out!" Alyona winked. "I see you have a reservation for this evening. The other member of your party was seated three minutes and forty-two seconds ago. If you would follow me?"

"Of course!"

Alyona walked out from behind the fixed, aluminum podium that was her base of contact with customers and out in front of me. Speakers in the floors of the 3DLCD hallway matched the sounds of high heels clomping with Alyona's smooth walking animation, which included stochastic "wind" interactions with her pencil skirt and ruffled blouse. I even thought I saw a lock of her blonde hair

worm its way free from under her newsboy cap. She was a magnificent feat of preservative holo engineering.

As we entered the reserved dining room, the theme of which was
an extended composition of the 3DLCD flooring with aluminum
furniture that seemed to project from its smooth surface, almost
like stars protruding from the vacuum of space, I knew my favorite part was fast arriving. Alyona skipped over to my chair, synced
her hands with it and slid it back for me while invisible automated
microllers on the bottoms of its legs matched speed with her arm
animations. Standing back proudly, hazel eyes glittering, she ush-
ered me to sit with the warmest smile I had ever seen from an inor-
ganic construct.

"Please enjoy your meal, you two." Alyona offered, spreading her
arms over the sleek, black, touch screen tabletop as if to set it with
menus. "And if there is anything you feel I can assist you with further,
please don't hesitate to call on me!"

I couldn't stop myself from turning around after taking my seat
as Alyona took her leave, and I was treated to an animation I had
not seen before. She waved with both hands as if she were saying
goodbye to someone she held dear. For those who knew the story of
her origin, it was a simultaneously heart-warming and heart-rend-
ing adieu. Alyona was constructed to preserve the memory of the
deceased daughter of the Mercurial's captain, and he opened the
restaurant portion of the airship to allow the public to experience her
effervescence, as she always enjoyed meeting new people more than
anything else in life.

"Helooooo . . . helOOOooo! Apple of your eye calling! If you two
would like to be alone together, I guess I could just leave!"

"Hello, Daria, darling. You told me red to match, but you seem to
be coming off a little green . . . with envy?" I replied as I began to turn
around. "You know I don't like Granny Smiths . . . oh my."

"Mmmhmm. Good thing I went with Red Delicious," Daria

crooned, leaning back in her chair to allow me to take in the fruit of her labor.

I have had the privilege to bear witness to Daria's lithe form in civilian clothes numerous times, but this was something else entirely. For once, I did not mind being speechless.

Her dress was of the skin-tight variety, halter top, sweetheart neckline, and it tapered down to a mini skirt that flared out ever so slightly with a cutoff just below a lascivious person's line of decency. Think what you like about turn-of-the-twenty-first-century fashion, this marvel couldn't have been made without it. The color faded from a moderately bright red, to venous, to black as you glanced down, which contrasted drastically, miraculously, with the fifth of a meter of pearly thigh exposed between its hem and the black, bowed ribbons securing her thigh-high stockings just above the knees.

She had dyed her hair again, this time to match the outfit with a raven base and crimson-raven swirls taking over her bangs and the curled ponytail she had tied off with a bow to match her stockings. It was a look for which she was well suited with her angular features. I awarded her bonus points for bringing to mind a taste of Old–world ice cream cones. She was smoldering good looks epitomized.

"Well, aren't you going to say anything?!" Daria kicked just above my ankle with a flat, and I heard a couple joints crack. "O–Owww."

"Hahaha! You win! You look positively stunning. I'm just glad you aren't wearing your boots, or the sensation would be taking on a connotation much more real."

I smiled as I said this, but Daria's wavered for a moment at the mention of our work footwear before restabilizing less than a second later. I didn't pay this flag much more mind than I typically would at the time, as Daria had already launched into her typical, upbeat, stimulating slate of conversational topics, but, now that I go over it again, this is the one time when I should have tuned those out. It wasn't an egregious error, just another inefficiency I would have liked to eschew. While Daria had rarely ever seemed more at ease than that evening, and that was just it, she was seeming, there was something amiss in her demeanor. She was uncertain of something, and I had never really known Daria to be uncertain.

"So? You gonna get the steak again? You said it was really good last time!"

Daria wondered while she tapped the M in the center of the table to expand the menu lists across the flat screen surface, swiping various visualizations of the Michelin three-star entrees to the left before stopping on a Cornish game hen that had a pat of butter slithering down it's steaming surface, speckled with herbs.

"Absolutely! I haven't dined everywhere on this speck in the cosmos, but I'll say one would be hard-pressed to beat New York's best New York strip! There it is!" I screeched as Daria scrolled to it. "The rendering doesn't even do it justice!"

"Open wide!" Daria yelled as she jiggled the image on the table.

I flattened my cheek against the flat of the table as Daria tried to slide the rendering into my mouth.

"Smash, smash, smash!" Daria squealed as she leapt up from her chair and sprawled over the table in her effort to really drive the meal down my gullet as I gnashed my teeth together and a ballad of borborygmus bellowed from the pit of my intestines.

The kitchen door to our dining room slid open at this moment, and Daria yelped and rolled off of the table out of instinct as our waiter doubtlessly got a full look at her undercarriage. She couldn't stop laughing as she attempted to return to a dignified, seated posture.

"Hahahahahaha! Could you imagine how embarrassing that would have been thirty years ago! Ahahahaha! Whew!" She snorted into her hands as she waved an umpire's safe in an effort to collect herself, before giving up and cracking up again as our Domestidrone servitor delivered our drinks without a word.

"A blessing in one way. Though, a proper steakhouse from the Old–world would have spat on service like this." I gestured at the chic drone that was gliding away with little more than an almost imperceptible whir. "I understand the facility it brings for the routes this kind of liner travels every now and again, but I still think that mechanization has overreached in this regard."

"Oh, pish posh, dahhhling!" Daria frittered my concern away with a languid wave. "Let's enjoy ourselves!"

We clinked our flutes, which were blown into the shapes of oyster drill shells, one with cola and one with true champagne, and Daria wriggled her free hand across the table and meshed her fingers with mine as we plumbed the depths of each other's eyes, an act that would have been terrifically uncomfortable for me with anyone else. Her hands were clammier than usual.

Let it be. Let it be.

"I'm surprised they were able to hold your reservation for you, given the change! You had originally scheduled for us to celebrate your twenty-ninth, but that's not for another nine days. How did you swing that? You said that this place is usually booked eight months out the last time."

"I was able to pay a surcharge to convince someone to vacate for us. Money well spent!" Daria ramped up to exclaim as our meals arrived.

Must have been a pretty convincing sum. Stop prying! She doesn't deserve this!

"I don't know! This Cornish game hen looks pretty amazing! It might be better than yours! You might have buyer's remorse! Wait. I might have buyer's remorse!" Daria teased, musically.

"Cornish game hen Pornish . . . I'm going to desist there."

"No, no! I want to see where this is going!" Daria pointed her knife at me, egging me on.

"Hahahaha! Nope! Also, there is such a low likelihood that you will feel buyer's remorse, but you could have let me cover this to reduce that further."

"Nonsense. I don't need the money."

"Fair enough. I certainly appreciate it."

I beamed as I raised the first medium rare cut to my lips, and we spent some time savoring in silence. Daria was always interesting to watch as she ate. We had dined in circumstances with others where she could convince you that she was raised sipping soup out of a silver spoon, and that she could out-prim any fair lady. However, when she and I dined alone, she felt comfortable enough to unleash the voracious beast she sequestered from the public, a beast I lovingly dubbed *Dichotomous rex*. She scraped the last morsels of meat from one of the bones of her hen as I looked on, recalling the stories she had told me about her homeless upbringing and the leftover bones she would crunch for the marrow left outside the back of a butchery for the dogs across the street from her hovel.

"Hey! What's wrong?" She puppy dogged. "Everything okay?"

She was always worrying about me. Even at a time like this.

"This taste is very nostalgic. Nostalgia abounds this evening, apparently."

"Well, you can't fill up on nostalgia. Go on! Keep eating! You hate cold steak!"

I did. I do.

"Daria? Why did you choose me?"

The moment felt right to ask a question of which I had frequently seemed to lose track in my career. Daria had given me a glimpse of purpose, and I suppose I just ran with it because it felt right. I trusted her.

"Because of your eyes," she said, before biting the tip off of a piece of asparagus.

"Seriously."

"Seriously. Well, that's the reason you initially caught my attention when I was scouting for preliminary candidates. I thought you were really cute! I scouted you and two others. You made it."

"Score one for Tampertech. Holdings. I never thought I'd be praising a GAC."

"Right! You know third gen and onwards just don't shine the same way yours do. But you know the main reason I chose you? What's my ID number?"

"H 24K06."

"What was my hair color on the day you met me?"

"Your typical raven with green splotches. I thought it looked almost like jigsaw puzzle pieces."

"What perfume was I wearing on the day you accepted the offer?"

"Like I'll be able to name it! You don't wear perfume often. It . . . you're wearing it again right now! It smells like fresh apples! Olfactory memory. My memory is the reason you chose me. No wonder I have been dwelling so much on the past this evening."

"I kind of wanted to cause that. Maybe just a teeeeensy bit." Daria winked as she extended the wishbone from her hen across the table at me, which snapped in her favor.

"Why? And you cheated."

"Why not use all the wiles I can to win your affection? And offering you the inferior lever is strategy, not cheating."

"You almost always win. And you won my affection a long time ago."

"Enduring?"

"Enduring. And I find you more than endearing."

"Awwww. I'm smitten."

I finished the last of my steak, which was just as delectable as the last time, thanks to the consistency of the plasma searing preparation method, and Daria fiddled with the table to project our view of the NER capital skyline on the sloping wall of the room.

"Ehhh. I don't think the resolution is quite as good as the real thing." She niggled.

"It's startlingly close."

"Ehhh. I wanna feel the wind on my face."

I cued a fan function, of a surprising force, from a sub-menu in the table to oblige.

"Ptheh ptheh." Daria spat some of the hairs from one of the fang-shaped tresses framing her face out. "I want to be escorted on to the observation deck by a beautiful young suitor."

I summoned our waiter back to the table.

"By a suitor in the flesh."

"Say no more!" I offered her my arm.

"Oh, really! Say no more! Actually, now that I think about it . . . that mechanical maître d' is prettier than you." Daria looked back over her shoulder and blew a kiss.

"Uh huh."

I tapped the door to the observation deck open, and we strolled out into the sultry summer night. We walked up and down the length of the portside observation deck for some time as Daria tried to pick out particularly effulgent stars in the heavens above through the almost impermeable curtain of light pollution maintained by the LED-plastered buildings below, whose every free meter seemed to be dedicated to one form of advertisement or another.

I was telling Daria about how I had always been fascinated by the estimated margins one of these advertisements might accrue, and the tracking process behind it all, and how it must no longer be a very profitable industry since most people spend most of their day looking down at their wrists. I felt the only entity in the business that might make a fat transfer would be the chiropractor whose sign happened to meet one's gaze at a time concurrent with the pain response elicited from one's anterior scalene as it cried out transmitters of protest from the first neck crane of the day.

But I had been digressing. Daria rarely allowed me time for introspection in her unrelenting assault on my senses, as the wavelengths of light I most adored came reflected courtesy of her natural, opalescent, emerald eyes, now downturned, and the wavelengths of sound that formed my favorite song were filtered through her full, pert, amaranthine lips, now concaved in . . . anxiety? Daria's taciturn expression allowed the sentiment I had been struggling to drown for most of the evening in the shallow waters of my humors to resurface to a breath of vindication: I was right. Something was wrong.

I bent my head down to catch her eye, a ploy she had taught me in the countless times she had done the same to cheer me up, hoping that it would convince her to cut to the chase.

Is this it? Is it over? Have I done something wrong? *Is the Bureau finally going to bring me in on recalcitrance? Daria's going to collect me. I'm weaponless. That's irrelevant. I wouldn't kill her anyway. Well played, Bureau. Take my king with my own queen, will you? Smart. No. No. Trust her. I trust her. If I can't trust her, then this has all been for nothing.*

The ploy worked. Daria tugged me over to the balcony, and we looked along her outstretched arm into the void above, as she nuzzled into the crook of my neck.

"I wonder if we can see Pluto from here?" Daria whispered in my ear.

All of my previous neuroses imploded and coalesced into one throbbing concern as I snapped my data pad up and ordered an express lift drone to Daria's leisure apartment ninety-eight kilos away, paying no heed to the cost. We walked, arm in arm, a pair of flightless lovebirds to the lenses, back through the liner to find our mechanized wings awaiting us. Daria quivered a bit as she cavorted in the seat next to mine, putting on an impeccable performance during the ride back to the safe house that put most of my societal stage appearances to shame. To her credit, she was able to keep up the charade until her unit door slid shut, and we collapsed on her couch. Only then did she break character. The rest of her broke down soon after.

When Daria and I had begun to grow closer than colleagues should, she proposed putting into place a code phrase that should only be used in the direst of circumstances by one of us to inform the other of a life-threatening situation related to the Bureau. After looking up into the sky that night, the same way we did on this night, she asked the dumbest question I have ever heard escape her lips.

"I wonder if we can see Pluto from here?"

Assuming she implied via the naked eye, I explained that any light reflected from its surface would be of insufficient magnitude to perceive with the unaided eye. She was impressed for a moment before I began to tease her by using the same inflection pattern to ask other ridiculous questions. Considering Pluto had long since lost its planetary status and with it any significant probability of being mentioned in laymen's conversations, I settled on that as our code phrase, as I doubted Daria would ever be willing to risk that kind of mockery again by mentioning the dwarf planet in passing. I also told her that Pluto was the Roman god of not only the underworld but also wealth, due to prized minerals that were found in the depths of the earth, and that resonated with the Bureau's societal capacity. She had recovered from my lampooning during this time, which I had spent pontificating by the side of the placid pool outside the motel we had reserved in a cavalier splurging of my newly awarded fortune, and she took revenge by slapping me into its frigid waters. She knew I despised being wet. She was cackling to herself as I spluttered at the surface. When I caught enough breath to ask what was so funny, she replied with, "Are you sure you don't want to change the phrase to be about Neptune? I don't think you'll forget your time as god of the pool!" I climbed out and told her that was minorly clever, but, on that day, I had fallen majorly in love.

On this day, Daria declared to me her decision to desert.

When a Bureau prospect agrees to become a Collector, she signs away her life in service until the standard retirement age marked by forty-six years of service from the first Collection. In return, she is granted access to a fortune and placed on an indefinite No Kill list. As long as she adheres to the contract, performs her duties admirably, and does not incur any atrocious infractions, she can retire in peace with a guarantee to remain on said No Kill list for one hundred and fifty years.

There is not a single documented case of the Bureau ever reneging on this agreement, and it is backed by all branches of the government in all Bureau–affiliated countries. In fact, particularly ravenous Collectors can trim down the age of retirement via bonuses awarded for collecting above and beyond the call of duty, as it were. One such Collector, who shall remain anonymous in name but not in deed, is currently looking at the possibility of retiring at the ripe old age of forty-seven. After the mandatory year of BoF training, he started at nineteen and has averaged a little more than twelve Collections per day, compared to my 3.8, with the typical average being set for 3.2, and he takes Saturdays off.

When I queued up behind him at the lunch bar at the NER Bureau one day, he complimented my T Acq. scores, which, along with many other scores, are posted in common rooms to encourage competition. While I tended to bounce within the top three of my leader board, his number had never budged from the pinnacle of his. I asked him how his typical Collection played out. He replied, "fly, hi, bang, bye, fly." What a life. One of the few who enjoys the killing, but not enough to be flagged for psych monitoring, which was the very practice Daria was currently trying to avoid as well.

Daria had submitted for six personal days that morning, which is two under the consecutive maximum allowable, in order to avoid suspicion. These days, whether you are grieving at a funeral or surfing the coast, there are always a few people you could collect hanging around your corner of the globe, and the Bureau would see that you take a break from any elongated personal time requests in order to take them down.

She spent the first forty-five minutes on the couch in preparation, recounting the events leading up to the calamitous Collection that left her in this state, and I advised her to take a break, as reliving even those moments was taking a toll on her delicate state of mind. I asked if she wanted to sleep, as it was well past midnight, and she replied that she didn't feel as though she could and that she was determined to recount the tragedy. She told me she needed me to know, and she needed to know something from me.

Daria had been rotated out of her recon appointment for a few days, because Gis had broken an ankle during an operation in a freak accident. They were able to complete the operation, but the Bureau decided it would be more efficient for the members to split and handle solo ops during the recovery window, as they were not in a scheduled window for a sub to rotate into their recon team. Daria had not given the decision a second thought. On her second Collection of the third day of her window, she had been pursuing a target through the very same streets in which she had grown up, the streets she joined the Bureau in order to leave behind forever.

Daria reached over me at this point in the story and rifled through a drawer to bring out a data pad on which she popped up a vid file as words were beginning to fail her again. The fact that she had access to this file meant that the Bureau had conducted an official review of the Collection. I watched the footage a couple of times.

The target had run into a landfill, the layout to which he clearly knew, and Daria pursued, despite her sniper drone wing having been decommissioned by potshots fired by some intoxicated locals, who were unceremoniously executed post-mission. She had finally drawn a bead on the target in a rare straightaway between the rubbish heaps from forty meters out and she leveled her rifle. In the moment between the curling of her finger and the impact to target, a second figure had burst from behind one of the heaps, startled by someone else running through the refuse, and she collided with the target as Daria's burst hit home. Both figures collapsed and a scream of anguish rent the air, scattering the crows of the area that Daria had once told me she used to have to fight off with a stick to pick through the piles for scraps. Daria, ever a diligent director of her surveillance cinematography, captured the entire shoot on her shoulder cam.

The Bureau evaluated the aftermath at real time plus two minutes with Daria standing over one corpse and one thirty-year-old female spurting blood from her shoulder on a trajectory to Daria's face, which did not seem to move out of the way. The camera was shaking, and Daria had gasped for breath twice before dropping to her knees. Ballistic analysis revealed one of the bullets Daria had fired had ricocheted off of the woman's scapula and into the target's brain, killing him instantly. One had shattered part of said scapula. One had severed the woman's right subclavian artery. Daria was in the process of reaching for hemostat and biofoam when the Bureau advised her to wait. The woman had been caught handing the rifle that was used to decomm Daria's drones to the ones who shot them down. She was complicit in the act and was to be terminated. Daria was the proximate agent. It was her responsibility. The scrape of Daria's kneepads was interrupted by something that sounded like a hiccup. Daria panned the camera up the ragged, crusty shift the impecunious woman had been wearing, which seemed to be more dirt than polyester, to settle on a face wracked with pain, petrified in fear, and devoid of understanding. The woman's head rocked slightly as the final burst tore through it and the frame froze, as did Daria until the Bureau's acknowledgement came through and the camera clicked to black.

I heard that hiccup sound for the first time that night before the vid and more frequently during and after it. That noise was the irrepressible harbinger of Daria's misery. The resolution she displayed to suppress the tears and sobs that would usually come after it on camera was timely and incredible. The woman, who the Bureau had labeled a destitute drifter with designs to disrupt a Collection, was named Sade, and she was Daria's most cherished childhood friend.

Sade was torn when Daria elected to join the Bureau, as they had supported each other since they were young girls, but she didn't try to stop her friend from leaving the slums behind. Daria was scouted for her marksmanship one day when a Collector in the area saw her throwing rocks at a distant sign with incredible precision. It was an old stop sign on the side of a building that had lost its top screw and had turned upside down. He bet her that she couldn't hit the hole in the O three times in a row. It turned out that she could, with very little effort, and then she hit the hole in the center of the P for good measure. The Collector brought her to a firing range to judge her talent further and the rest is history. Dazzled by the opportunity dangled before her, Daria enrolled into the Collector training program and was able to start active Collections on her eighteenth birthday at the minimum legal age, leaving Sade, and her childhood innocence, behind in the dust. She hadn't returned to those squalid streets since, and she had never planned to either.

Sade was an optimistic child. She was a little older than Daria and, at the time Daria had been scouted, Sade had been eligible to seek a fortune for at least a year and a half, by Daria's imperfect reckoning. She never did. She told Daria that she didn't think her life was all that terrible. She had lost her left hand early in life due to a car collapsing on it in the junkyard. She couldn't find work because of being outcompeted due to her lack of marketable skills and her obvious frailty. She didn't have any real aspirations in life. She didn't feel she had any special qualities at all. Still, that was all okay, because she had Daria. Plus, she was one of the few who would rather have a shot at living ninety or so years of life, hoping that something might change along the way than to guarantee death at thirty-six.

Of course, said average life expectancy was based on an upper-middle-class person, possessed of little to no risk-taking behaviors

and the means to retire with financial securities, but I was not present to tell Sade that none of these descriptors matched her indigent
existence. That said, from the way Daria described her to me that
evening, I am not confident it would have changed her perspective
if I had been. The development of Daria's bubbly personality that I
adored so much was due, in part, to this remarkable young woman.
The moment Daria killed Sade, she killed a bit of herself in the process, along with all of her motivation to remain a Collector, but she
had yet to experience the full gravity of the situation.

In our training, Collectors are exposed to a regimen of system-
atic psychological compartmentalization that conditions us to lock
away feelings of remorse associated with killing in order to increase
our durability as tools of destruction. Daria had withdrawn into
a comfort coping mechanism learned in this system that involves
us engaging in activities we enjoy greatly in order to inundate our
psyches with a deluge of pleasurable stimuli to better drown out
any sentiments of sorrow. The true perfidy of this system comes to
light when you realize most of the habits that are encouraged in the
training involve spending copious amounts of credits, such as the
evening to which Daria had treated me, thus thinning our fortunes
while simultaneously providing an indirect positive reward for further killing. These practices are so well ingrained into our processing
that almost all of the emotions Daria displayed during our date were
genuinely affected. What was so incredible was that the implication
Daria had sent to any Bureau sources of information that might have
been surveilling for inklings of contractual infidelity through her
actions, and they always are, would have been one of an evening of
carnal consolation to punctuate her return to form.

Daria went into a mild state of shock when she finally dropped
the act and had the time to realize that she killed her incorrigibly
optimistic friend, who could have had a much better life with a fortune, given the same ending, at the tender age of about thirty-one. I

stroked her cheek in silence until she finally recovered the ability to speak around two hours later, and I knew what she would ask first.

"Will you come with me when I go?"

She asked this fateful question, trembling as she looked into my eyes for a semblance of the support she had offered me in the time we had known each other, an amount of time that had been offered, and was about to be cut short, by the profession that had brought us together.

I am ashamed to say that my reply was not pertinacious and unwavering. I told her that I would go with her while my mind exploded with doubts. The quintessence of my being manifesting in the movement of my duplicitous lips the affirmative option in one of three possible outcomes knew this was the correct answer, the only answer, and still the third option, uncertainty, restrained my conscience.

I told Daria that I had Collections scheduled in a few hours, and I would stay with her until then but ignoring them would jeopardize our chances at escape and the odds were already stacked against us. I told her that I would devise a plan during that time, and that I would take a day off for the following day for us to execute. I told her that I loved her before leaving, and her spirits seemed to lift. What I didn't tell her is that, for the first time in my life, I was utterly terrified. I didn't tell her that I was frozen with doubt. I didn't tell her that the revolting thought of abandoning her to crawl back into the safety that the Bureau offered had crossed the cold, calculating chasms of my mind for momentary consideration. I didn't tell her that I was searching for something and finding nothing.

Fortune is often a fickle goddess, but she found me once again, just in time.

10
4716 – The Devoted

I had been loitering outside a pill bar for a few minutes as I was tracking my second target of the day through his updated route when a couple of cops pointed at me a little too mischievously for my liking before beginning to clop over. I ducked inside the establishment and looked for a seat so I wouldn't have to order in the standing-room-only section, hoping their well-fed frames wouldn't follow me in, as they clearly had access to more than the Pop–Reg-advised daily diet intake. A perfectly panicked young gentleman offered his seat up to me as he was "just about to be leaving anyway," even though his last cuplet was still two pills full. I waved an iris scan in and found him to be perfectly pedestrian as well before handing him his dessert, expressing my appreciation, demanding to pick up his tab, and requesting to have what he was having from the expressly arrived and obsequious keep, who shook out the three-course order with his machines in under fifteen seconds and so adroitly that one would be hard-pressed to find such speedy service ordering over the counter of even a mechanized variant of a medical pharmacy.

"Your add-on had been taking them dry, Collector. Would you like them the same, wet, or with a bottle?"

"Wet will be fine," I decided, looking over the menu scrolling across the bar top. "One dropper per cuplet, 5 mLs per dropper, and I'll take the droppers on the side."

"Very good, Collector."

What a ridiculous concept.

Pill bars were the culmination of a new diet fad of drug-based mental appetite suppression that had gained meteoric popularity over the last three years. The point of impact originated, as many others, in Southern California, and its crater of influence had spread to cover most of the world.

The basic principle behind pill bars involves creating dishes from pills designed to elicit various sensations of, not only taste, but also fulfillment through a cocktail comprised of an unlimited combination of natural flavors, select semaphorins, and a legally regulated leptin load by which all of the competitors licensed to purvey these pills must adhere to within a microgram of specificity, though this chain had a reputation of sneaking in more than a few extra particles per quantum when the auditors weren't around. So, as I knocked back my first tablet doublet of chicken and hot sauce and pressed my tongue to my palate, excoriating the pill surfaces with a counterclockwise wriggle, according to the best practices offered by the screen under my cuplets, I was able to partake of the piquancy of an appetizer of buffalo wings while simultaneously fooling myself further into satiety, despite having not eaten anything calorically significant that day. The only aspect lacking from the flavor profile was the texture of the real thing, though the flavor chemists are working on that at present.

The pills themselves weren't terribly expensive, especially with regards to other weight loss solutions, and people were not finding it difficult to replace a meal or two a day with this alternative, especially since their egos tended to inflate along with their perceived stomachs at the thought of doing their part to lay off of true food so that some malnourished individual somewhere else in the world might be able to gain access to the foodstuffs the customers would have ingested otherwise. Rarely is that the case, of course, but the idea was as fashionable as a slim waistline.

The establishments make a real killing by only providing bottled water, the price of which has remained at an all-time high of .15 GCs per liter for the cheapest of brands for the last eight months. I was about to squirt in my first dropper as the indignant sole of a beat cop boot kicked the pedestal upon which I had perched.

"Hey there, Collie! Don't you know? There are no dogs allowed in these types'a shops, govy or otherwise. Why don't you mosey on outta here! You're bad for business."

The more corpulent of the two cops from whom I had attempted to flee smacked her chops as she finished what certainly had been one of her most brilliant badgerings of her illustrious career, given the busting of her partner's slightly less-gelatinous gut. About half of the patrons of the place had turned around expecting to see trouble, but I had little time to spare, as avoiding an altercation had been the entire point of my purchase and I had immediately grown tired of the torment. I had dealt with police-borne antipathy for Collectors a few times in my career, but the tapestry that is my patience had worn threadbare in the early hours of this morning. I supposed winning over the crowd would expedite my escape, so I stood on my stool.

"Bad for business?!" I yelled. "I should think not! People, if I may tug your ear for but a moment! The Bureau of Fortune appreciates your continued patronage at a venue whose taxation provides us the opportunity to continue paving the roads you follow to your dreams. As such, I would humbly beg you to allow me the courtesy of purchasing your next cuplet of pills as a demonstration of our appreciation! What say you?!"

A roar followed by the clinking of a great many metal cuplets made it clear where the crowd stood, and I took my seat as they rushed the counter.

"Still bad for business?" I whispered, as I leaned toward the portly police officers, who had more than a few pairs of eyes on them now. "I am uncertain as to your quarrel with my person, but I'd be happy to leave it at this if you would leave by that."

I finished by pointing towards the door as I looked back at my data pad.

"You Collectors think you're so great. Getting all the attention. You think you're untouchable." The second surly sow oinked before prodding my vest. "A day will come when you pooches are kicked to the street like the mongrels you are, and we upstanding role models of society will get the attention we deserve for protecting the public again."

"Protecting the public, you say?"

I let off the throttle that had been holding the emotions I had been experiencing from my harrowing personal life in check a smidgeon and bared my lupine canines at the porcine problem barring my passage while showing her the active timer on my data pad.

"I'd say this little piggy joined up solely for attention. I don't find my career particularly glorious, and I don't revel in attention, though I did join the Bureau for equally vain a purpose, or lack thereof, really. At least I am professional in my conduct as opposed to one so indecorous as yourself, who indulges in harassing passersby. For that, I am at least welcomed to gnaw at the bones of the public's meal of excess from my place under its table, but dirty cops like you, content to wallow in the banal pens of insouciant insult that has become the public's prerogative in this hedonistic age of impersonality when you claim to be their paragons . . . ever will the trough be where you are welcome. Now, if you don't mind, I have a job to which I must attend, and I will remind you that interfering with a Collector during an active Collection would ensure that you lose yours."

I brushed past the blubbery blockade and swiped through the street cam views that had been tracking my quarry as I ran out the doors of the swanky storefront into the sweltering heat, ignoring the holo–projected lines and barriers of the crosswalk nearby, to cut across the marred surface of the ruins of a neglected basketball court on my way to the Collectee's complex, minding my footing amidst the pockmarks that would no longer permit any but the deftest of dribblers a legal approach to the hoop-less backboards, skirting the makeshift dwellings some dingy denizens had erected around it.

Alder Rousseau had played the game quite well and better than most. He had been awarded a fortune at the age of twenty-two under the declaration of "Luxury Purchases." He was a salaryman for the first four years of his career at a low-tier insurance company, and he purported that he had "grown weary of the pushing. Pushing keys every day only to be pushed around by his superiors." He had incurred a small amount of debt from his education that he paid off with the first of his fortune and then he purchased a secondhand yacht and membership to a second-rate yacht club in Maryland, ate not quite like a king but sufficiently well for a prince, waited a few years, vacationed in Florida, and got there via a pass to a private transport drone that he used twice, waited a year, all was fine, and then he made a mistake. He peppered in a couple of fine art purchases, got a country club membership, made a donation to a local hospital, and lost a few hundred GCs betting on prize fights.

There is not a single thing you can do with a fortune to court suspicion quicker than to make a donation. Infrequent donations of 60 GCs or under might get through without incurring scrutiny. Anything above that will start turning digital heads. Anything above 200 GCs will start turning fleshier heads. Anything around, let us say, a nice, round 14,000 GCs will bring at least two, if not three separate BoF auditors to the back door of every account you have ever owned, and a Collector to the front door of your residence to lock down your person until a verdict is passed down from accounting. Unlike the typical houseguest, we tend to let ourselves in.

ComCom: Send: Oracle 2–7: "Requesting override for target's unit sec sys. I am approaching the premises." PendCom

I waited on the stoop of the building and screened in my beleaguered target jaywalking across a street, about a little less than three and a half kilos from my position, and watched him accidentally drop his beverage on a curb, which burst open and splattered his trousers. His shoulders heaved as he let out a world-weary sigh, but he didn't tidy himself up as he bent down to retrieve his waste to deposit it in the next appropriate recycling receptacle. He was sleep-deprived as he made his way home from the hospital he had been visiting the previous evening, which was a sister hospital to the one to which his transgression had been donated. The entry door to the complex slid open behind me as the newly transferred passcode notification blinked up on my data pad.

"Done. Target's unit is 503 and that access code has been forwarded as well. Try not to make a scene and wait for auditor confirmation. They are closing in."

ComCom: Send: "Copy." EndCom

I authenticated to Rousseau's door on the fifth floor and walked into the extravagant apartment. The décor was almost full metal except for a few appliances here and there, at least in the main room. I figured it would be untoward to check the bedroom and bathroom without good reason, and this Collection had been shaping up to be open and shut. I slid a chair out from the window bar overlooking the Hagerstown metropolis and pointed it towards the door.

"Irregular footfall pattern detected. Intruder. Images have been recorded. Door lock has been overwritten. Authenticate to terminal designate: Charlie in twenty seconds or local authorities will be notified." A smooth-talking voice from the ceiling warned as a Domestidrone wheeled out of its storage closet to assist in the detention.

A redundant sec sys. I should have figured this a possibility. Only one thing to do.

ComCom: Send: Oracle 2-7: "Emergency request for unhidden retina ID confirmation link to my profile. Active thirty seconds. Trace and erase all accesses on command." Pendcom

"Charlie: Do you have retina scan capability?"

"Affirmative. Eleven seconds remaining for authentication."

"Granted. Working trace and erase."

"Charlie: I am a Collector. I will submit to a retina scan for identification. Upon confirmation, you will disarm, reinstall the previous entry door access code, and surrender yourself to Bureau of Fortune questioning."

"Scanning."

The Domestidrone wheeled over and ran its hand over my eyes.

"ID confirmed. Security system disarmed. Entry code restored. Welcome to the Rousseau and Hanson home. Please make yourself comfortable. Would you care for refreshment?"

"Trace and erase added. Accessing terminals will be decommissioned on run."

A portion of the wall screen in my field of vision illuminated and enumerated the possible drink combinations for which I could ask, complete with pictures dribbling with condensate or puffing with steam, after syncing with the refrigerator.

"I would not but thank you."

I checked the street cam views on my data pad again, and Rousseau was turning on to the street in front of the unit.

"Charlie: How many hours has it been since Hanson's signatures have been recorded in this apartment?"

"38.459 hours."

"Charlie: How many distinct access codes have been recorded accessing this apartment in the last forty-eight hours?"

"Four distinct codes."

"What are the identities of the terminal owners for those accesses?"

"Alder Rousseau. Solara Hanson. Hagerstown Emergency Medical Services Operator T873. Yourself."

Rousseau was entering the building.

"Charlie: This concludes the Bureau of Fortune's questioning. Run forwarded trace and erase protocol."

I scooted my aluminum composite chair away from the dormant Domestidrone and pulled over an additional frame for my imminent guest. I remained standing as I waited for the door to open.

ComCom: Send: Oracle 2–7: "Inform auditors that target cohabitates with one Solara Hanson and have them run a patient search in all local hospitals." PendCom

The entryway door swung in, and Rousseau was speaking with someone on an open line via his data pad, despite being a registered ComCom user. He seemed relieved, and his haggard disposition from before had been replaced with an energetic and inquisitive expression that wouldn't be long for this world.

"That's a bingo. Auditors just confirmed. It's an IPLC infraction. You may proceed with immediate Collection of the target and details on Hanson will be forwarded to your data pad for a follow-up. Do you need to review the standard transplant repossession protocol?"

ComCom: Send: "I do not." EndCom

"Do you feel any pain? I mean, does it hurt a lot? Oh shit!" Rousseau wailed, as he finally noticed my presence.

I pointed at his data pad and then spun the same index finger to signal him to wrap it up.

"What's wrong?!" The disembodied voice of a woman cried in concern.

"Uh. Dearest, something has come up. I . . . I have to go now. I love you so much, and I hope you feel better soon. Uh. I'll talk with you again soon?"

Rousseau looked at me as if to ask me the question. I considered his plea while tilting my head a couple times toward each shoulder in order to receive input from the devil and angel jurors gathered there, and I nodded hesitantly to convey the possibility.

"Okay. I love you! I'll be waiting."

Rousseau cut the feed.

"Good afternoon, Mr. Rousseau. It is apparent you were not expecting me. Care to have a seat?" I gestured at the chair I had pulled over for him.

He took off his jacket and tossed it on to a nearby table.

"Do you uh . . ." He cleared his throat with a nervous twist of his neck. "Do you guys do last meals?"

The gall of this man was incredible, but I still had a few questions I had to ask.

"If you've got instant, I don't mind."

"Really? I was just joking, but I could eat if you'd let me. Is it normal to feel so hungry just before you kick it?" He asked, nervous.

"I have no idea. I have never tracked that trend."

I waved him over to the cabinetry as I pulled my EinIn and set it on the island countertop next to me. He opened one cabinet up that was laden with packets of myriad shapes, sizes, and colors.

"I actually, heh, became a bit of an instant aficionado during my job. It was all I had time to eat." He paused as he tipped on to his tarsals to reach up to the highest shelf. "I could never get off the stuff no matter what I ate, and I've always found cooking for myself to be such a chore. So convenient and life is too short, you know? Especially now. You want one? I've got some pretty rare packages."

"You're oddly hospitable," I accused, as I hearkened to my own resurging hunger.

"I was thinking the same thing about you. Will you actually let me talk to her again?" He asked while rattling a package labeled "Pot au feu" behind his back in my direction as if he were offering a treat to a pet.

I wondered just how many packages I could ransom for one last chat with his chérie before thinking about Daria and rebuking myself for such a churlish thought.

"I could tell solely from the glimpse at your face in a passing moment how much you care about her. That was Solara on the pad, correct?"

"I can't help it. She's everything to me. And the only kind of person in your line of work that would even consider allowing me such a courtesy has to have someone that special as well. So, can I take that as a yes?"

"Sure. I could eat. What would you recommend?"

"There's only one thing for it, though it won't be as good as maman's."

He tore open two packages of the Pot au feu, tossed the contents into bowls, sprayed some water into them from a tap that notified him that he had used 37 percent of his monthly allotment, and slid the bowls into two housings of a three-bowl-capacity bombarder before slamming the door closed and tapping in the cooking protocol. He slid a bowl across the countertop twenty seconds later along with a fork. The stew was warmed perfectly so that we didn't have to wait at all before digging in.

"This is the earliest meal I can remember eating. Not in this bastardization, obviously. It's nice to have it again at the end. Solara hates it, heh."

"How long did she have left without the operation? I know it seems odd to say it, but I hope the problem was immediately life-threatening to warrant your choice." I trailed off as I spun a potato in the broth, thinking about a choice I was going to have to make soon enough.

"Not long. I can't remember exactly. I had put something into place a few months back and when she collapsed . . . I kind of just went. Followed the plan. There was no doubt."

"And now?"

"Not really any doubt. Regret? A bit? I keep thinking about that old saying about being born in the wrong time. Like, if we were born a few centuries ago, we would have been happier. Things would have been easier," Rousseau despaired, idly pushing his bowl, only half-depleted, back and forth in front of him with his fork.

"What if she had a heart condition then as well?"

"That's a good point. Never actually thought of that."

"There was no other way for her to get a heart?"

"Not legally. Artificial would only get her four years. She won't live long enough to make it to her spot on the natural list, and she made me swear not to try black market because she didn't want me to end up dead in a ditch somewhere, not that they would take fortune money anyway."

"So you tried gray market? At least you were able to guarantee the money aspect of your attempt through the Bureau. One less obstacle, I suppose. I haven't heard from the auditors yet exactly how you worked out the deal. Care to illuminate?"

"Not really."

Rousseau walked over and slumped into one of the chairs I had pulled out as I circulated around the island, hand on my pistol, to maintain distance. I took the two bowls and poured his out in the drain before putting both of them into the steamer along with the forks. Then, I took a seat across from him.

"And your motivation?" I plied.

"Simple numbers game. If I did nothing, she would die soon, and I would live on, dragging myself through a life that no longer felt worth living without her. If I went for it and didn't get caught, we would be able to enjoy another ten years or so together, as I would rather have ten more years with her than spend the rest of my life without her. If I went for it and got caught, I would die soon and she would be able to live on, hopefully in a life that might be worth living without me. She's always been a lot stronger than me, so she'll have a better chance at making it without me than I would without her. She has other people that depend on her, that would benefit from her being around. I've always been alone. I haven't touched so many lives. For me, it was only Solara."

The parallels were unbearable and the portents demoralizing.

"I can't allow an active communication with Solara, hence my ambivalence when nodding. It's too messy. However, I can allow you to record a message for her. She may want to replay it anyway. I'll supervise you cueing the function via your data pad, and I'll transfer it when you are gone. On my honor, it will reach her."

"I'll take what I can get." Rousseau straightened up.

"Bring up a video camera function when you are ready."

"Oh! Just one more thing? Could you, uh, plug your ears or something? I'd like it to be for her ears only. It seems more meaningful that way. You understand, right?"

"Completely unlock and hold your data pad up, engage a touch-released app lock function, hit record, and I'll plug. The next time you touch your data pad, you should be finished. I will unplug, you will remove your data pad and place it on the floor, and we'll finish up here. Do you require that to be repeated?"

"No. I'm good."

"Go ahead."

Rousseau followed my instructions perfectly, and I leaned on the island countertop, plugging my ears and quashing the urge to stick out my tongue to complete the juvenile gesture. I thought about how reading lips was significantly more difficult from the profile angle and about how much product Rousseau must have used to keep his sleek, shoulder-length hair flipped up at the tips. I thought about what he had said about his grandest decision, and I started to consolidate the disparate makings of my own. He tapped his screen twice and unfastened his data pad, dropping it after entrusting it with his final message, and I held out before him my pistol in my right hand and my injection gauntlet on my left.

"There's an error in your numbers game for which you did not account," I began.

At that moment, I paused and took stock of what I would want to hear, were I to be in his position, and it had become increasingly likely as of late that I very well might find myself in exactly that in precious little time. I endeavored to empathize. I considered what I would wish my last thoughts to be. Would I still thirst for knowledge of the truth at the very end? Would I be better satisfied with the sweet libations of a lie? Does it make a difference in the end if the end will come just the same? What is the limit of the value of time and how precious are a few seconds? How arrogant a position it was to be able to make this choice and was it better or worse to ponder it? Alas, there I was, and I certainly would not wish a pall of silence to precede my passing.

"You have touched more than one life."

My resolve steadied, I drove the syringe into his deltoid and recovered his data pad, clutching it close to my chest, and I stabilized his lolling head so he could see his message safely entrusted in the end. He passed with a smile. Ignorance is bliss.

Rousseau's error that I had failed to mention concerned his understanding of Solara's estimated lifespan, and it was an error I was ordered to assure, though it would break my metaphorical heart to repossess her literal one. The auditors assigned to his case had found Rousseau guilty of committing an IPLC infraction, that is to say, he violated one or more terms detailed in the Inappropriate Prolongation of Life clause of his contract.

The IPL clause is connected to an ever-updating set of infractions that changes with the times and the novel attempts at treachery they bring. There is very little wiggle room anymore for entrepreneurial efforts of deception in a Bureau contract, and Rousseau's elected method had been encountered and subsequently countered over fifteen years ago. The gist of the clause states that one cannot spend fortune funds on expenses whose primary purpose is to extend the life of the Blank or any other person, existing within or without of Bureau-affiliated countries, in an extraordinary manner. An example that is often given at the time of signing is: buying food for one's children using fortune credits acquired through a declaration of "Luxury" would not constitute an infraction, nor would something such as plastic surgery performed to alter the shape of one's nose, in most cases, but the use of funds to enroll into a radiation program in order to treat a cancer of some kind would be considered inappropriate and constitute an infraction. The IPL clause exists to ensure the furthering of the true goal of the Bureau of Fortune, that is: to cull the population via a method considered somewhat more humane than military genocide. The repercussions appended to these infractions almost always lead to next-to-immediate Collection of the offending Blank, regardless of age, followed by reversal of the effects stemming from the violation or worse.

Rousseau had attempted to negotiate a deal to bypass the transplant list for a new heart for his paramour by submitting an anonymous donation to one hospital within a health network in the area on the terms that a sister hospital would fast-track Solara on their transplant list when the time came. However, the money he could offer alone was not quite enough to sway the decision. He also chose to leak proprietary information on the code and launch plan behind one of the insurance programs being developed at his former place of work, that would be implemented within the local healthcare community over some time in the next five years, to the hospital, which would afford its health group a competitive edge in high-profile patient acquisition. When Solara collapsed, Rousseau ran the promised transfer and, judging by the conversation I had overheard between the two, the operation went well, not that the Bureau was going to interfere with that anyway.

I hopped into the transport drone I had summoned to Our Lady of Preservation Hospital and set to ordering my care package of repo tools from a repository in the heart of the city before reading over Solara Hanson's status report to find the room to which she had been transferred after her operation in the twenty-four story behemoth of a building. I tapped both inbound drones to touch down at one of the eighth-floor leaflets that were targetable on the building model that had popped up on my data pad and stepped off only seconds later.

I spent the next five minutes I would have to wait for my delivery drone looking out over the edge of the leaflet at the circuit of people surrounding the parking lot below receiving Medi–bot treatment for minor injuries and maladies outside the clinic. Cloven finger pad needs stitches? Medi–bot scans insurance data, snags your finger, and you're set to go. Unsure if that sore throat is strep or simply the latest manifestation of the hypochondria you don't have? Medi–bot scans insurance data, swabs, and spits out a diagnosis, all while you watch the next insipid installment of that cooking show that you know you're never really going to try to emulate. Stop by for a vaccine before going out of the country for vacation? Medi–bot scans insurance data, sticks you with a freshly spun-up syringe, and then recommends a slew of other shots in which you might be interested, but you'll have to get back in line first.

My delivery drone dropped my hard-cased repo kit at my feet, and I walked over to the polarized doors leading into the hospital and waited for the scans corroborating the biometric profile I had forwarded to permit me access. I accessed a wall pad and typed in "patient room 7–32–C" and followed my personally generated, fuchsia guidance blip as it traced its way along the strip screens embedded in the walls, winding through hallways filled with the orders and bodies of various people and machines trying to save lives, pausing for me to select my mode of descent at a corner, and then bouncing down a stairwell as I neared my destination.

Upon reaching the cluster of rooms, I deviated from my blip, which forged ever onward towards its terminus, in order to make a stop at the service desk to request manual access to Solara's suite and the presence of her doctor at his or her earliest convenience, while ingratiating myself with a smile, despite the contemptuous countenances one of my occupation inevitably curried in these corridors. Dr. Perales was otherwise engaged and would hopefully be along in about ten minutes. I tapped the furnished code into the entry pad and the doors to the suite slid open.

Solara stirred from her slumber as I set my repo case down on a rolling table in the dimly lit room next to a VR headset and some sensory uplink leads, gently placing Rousseau's data pad on top of the case as a reminder.

"Nngh. Oh!" Solara gasped as I moved to the foot of her bed and tossed some of the sheets she had kicked to the ground over her bare calves. "Are you sure you have the right room, Collector? I've never requested a fortune."

She pulled the covers up further over the sky-blue gown covering her frail frame and elbowed her pillows around to better accommodate her neck. Her speech was still a bit weak, but I could hear one of the reasons Rousseau could be so enamored with this young woman. Her voice was serene and soothing.

"It's certainly the right room. Good afternoon, Ms. Hanson. I've—"

"Please, call me Solara. Also, could you hand me my water over there?" She asked, strands of her auburn hair concealing her face as she looked over towards the top of a set of rolling drawers next to her bleeping monitors. "It's still pretty hard to move after the operation. Got my heart replaced."

I slid the small cup off the surface and extended it towards her, and she drank slowly.

"Thanks. Is there something I can do for you?"

I didn't want to cause her undue stress until the doctor arrived, so I searched for a topic of conversation.

"There will be eventually, but we should wait for Dr. Perales to arrive before we delve into that any further. I see you have a VR setup in here. Is that a good way to pass the time?"

"Oh! It's amazing! They've been around forever, and I've never used one. Alder, that's my SO, he uses them a lot, but he just plays stupid games on them until I get home from work."

"Were you playing less-stupid games on them, then?"

"Nope. VR–Tourism. I've been hiking around this apt rain forest reserve area in Nueva Amazonia. Have you ever been there?"

"A few times for work but not to the rain forest. Tell me more."

"So, VR–Tourism is really big right now, especially in places like hospitals and for people with reduced mobility. You pay a fee to be able to inhabit a Domestidrone that is allowed to move around in a certain area, and you get to see what it sees and feel what it feels. It's gotten so good that I was able to feel a centipede walk across my arm! Ewww. Anyway, yeah, so I was in Old Peru? I think? And I saw all these cool animals like monkeys and these parrots, and I was able to turn off the temperature sensors when it started pouring because who wants to feel that. I think I'll go to the beach somewhere, though, when they let me back in. I have to be here for three more days, and they won't let me use it again until tomorrow. All I've done is sleep, but a couple of people have come to visit me. Mostly from work."

"What do you do for work?" I asked, pulling out a soda from my pack and standing over the trash as I slowly twisted the cap, drawing out the hiss.

"Ooooooh. Hey, can I have some of that? The doctors haven't let me drink anything but water and it's killing me. Just a little?"

I couldn't help but smile as the way she had asked reminded me of Daria, and I couldn't refuse. I poured more than a little of the cola into her cup and gave it to her, which she eagerly glugged down before handing the cup back to me.

"I'm a teacher. I work at a traditional school about thirty kilos from here. We even still use pencils and paper. Can you believe that? I love it, though. It's nice to see kids interacting with each other without screens for a change every now and then."

Solara was one of the flowers of the world, not one who had blossomed among the weeds, but an orchid who had thrived on the wrong tree. Without him, she would wither and die, and I was the one who felled him.

"I wholeheartedly agree. How did you end up choosing that job?"

I continued to procrastinate, trying to work up the courage to get down to business and finding it more laborious than ever.

"I've never had a problem telling other people they're wrong? Haha. No. I've always liked working with kids and leaving school was hard for me, so I went back. I like having a hand in raising them. It gave my short life a purpose."

I attuned to the swishing sound of Solara's ventilator for a time as her downy voice petered off, and she entered a state of reminiscence.

"But now I'll be around a little longer because of a miracle," she whispered, thankfully.

I sighed an empty, mournful sigh. I couldn't bear procrastinating any longer. Continuing to converse in this contrived and coddling manner would only serve to sew greater suffering.

"Listen, Solara, I have something to tell you . . . regarding Alder."

"He's gone. I know," she said, closing her eyes.

"How do you know?"

"This operation was too good to be true. He seemed off at the end of the last time we were speaking. I custom ordered that data pad case for him as well. You showing up with it was the last piece of the puzzle."

"You don't seem all that sad about it."

"I know. Weird, right? You seemed sadder than me when you walked in. I am, though, but I can also see why Alder tried to do this. It's to be expected given how close we are . . . were. I know I would have done the same. I wouldn't expect you to understand. Is killing others the only reason for existence you guys have? If so, you must be lonely. If you had ever grown close enough with someone, like Alder and I had, you would understand."

Solara claimed this as if it were an immutable truth, nodding with a steadfast surety. Her wistful words comprised the last piece of my puzzle, but I still could not discern the fit.

Dr. Perales walked into the room as I struggled with Solara's gospel, and I walked her back out immediately.

"Good afternoon, Doctor. I will explain the procedure I'm going to conduct momentarily, but, before doing so, I have but a single question I must ask you. Think carefully before you respond. Before Solara's operation, how long was she expected to live from your prognosis?" I asked, with as little expression as possible.

"It's hard to tell with these kinds of situations. At most, we'd figure about six weeks. She'd been collapsing often, recently."

"Thank you. I'd appreciate if you would supervise the procedure, just in case complications should arise."

We walked back into the suite, and I spent some time informing the good doctor and Solara about how Solara's new heart had been illegally acquired via a transgression committed by her significant other in breach of his fortune. As such, it would be temporally repossessed by the Bureau of Fortune as collateral. My judgment had determined that she had not been cognizant of the operation in any way, so she would not be collected immediately. In a moment,

I would be injecting a time-released corrosive capsule set for one thousand and eight hours into the septum of Solara's heart with a tag in it that would sync to my data pad, a Bureau database, and another tag that would be affixed to Solara's pelvis. If the distance between the two implant tags were to increase beyond a typical range of motion, suggesting that the heart may have been removed for any purpose, the corrosive capsule would activate early, destroying the heart beyond repair. A Collector would also be routed to Solara's location.

One part that I elected to leave out was that this little barbarism allowed the Bureau to tamper with the potential for one extra life, given that they probably intentionally waited for Alder to enact his scheme and the transplant to finish before sending me. That way, they could heartlessly ensure the waste of a perfectly good heart while tapping it up to "processing time."

I sauntered over to crack the hard case for the procedure and Alder's data pad shifted a little on its stippled surface, beckoning me to honor my word. I picked the device up, in its orange and glittered case, and brought it over to Solara.

"I didn't have the heart to let you two part in so inelegant a fashion, so I allowed Alder to record a private final message for you. Would you like to see it?"

I asked while lying about the confidentiality of the file as I had already scanned it while doing my due diligence to ensure there were no links to other deceptions enclosed within. There was nothing so repugnant, only beauty. Solara reached for the data pad and thanked me with a halfhearted smile.

"You know. I don't even need the six weeks," she asserted, meekly.

"Maybe this will convince you otherwise."

I released the data pad before pointing towards the doors to signal the doctor to give her some time and we walked out. The message was just over two minutes long, and I wondered how one could convey the entirety of someone's significance in so short a time. How could one be so succinct with so sophisticated a message? I had initially thought Alder had been reckless in his script, but, as I watched a somber and scintillating smile radiate across Solara's face, I revised my assessment. Maybe it didn't need to be an all-encompassing recapitulation of the various sentiments they had shared. Maybe it only needed to extol one.

I walked back into the suite, with Dr. Perales lagging behind, as Solara finished and swung the lid of the hard case open and programmed the tagging gun inside. I asked Dr. Perales to open Solara's apron. She did so in silence but with a look that suggested she was reassuring herself of her inculpability in the matter at hand. Solara handed the data pad back to me, and her grip felt stronger than ever.

"Are you sure you don't want to see it again?" I asked, waiting a few beats for the tagger to zero in on the septum of her heart.

"No. It's nice but it's nothing new," she replied, maintaining her smile through the injection of the corrosive capsule and the skin repair that followed it.

I lined up the next site and injected the second tag in silence as Dr. Perales asked Solara for updates on her condition. I walked back over to the hard case and replaced the tagger, checked for the sync between the tags and the Bureau database, slid the case off the table, and made for the door, as my job was complete. I hesitated before leaving and turned back because I still needed to finish the puzzle.

"Solara? If you would humor me once more? About you and Alder. How can you be so sure? How can you believe that you would have done the same for him so intransigently?" My voice inadvertently descended to a whisper, cowering as my own doubts lingered in the forefront of my mind.

"It's simple. We were . . . are in love. Is there a better reason to do anything?"

Solara opened her eyes again with a gentle smile, and I knew I would never be able to convince her otherwise.

She had obliterated my uncertainty.

EPILOGUE
Dissolution and Dissemination

Before I weighed a life in my hands for the first time, a wise woman asked me a simple, yet essential question: "Do you feel satisfied doing what you do?" At the time, I had barely done anything in my capacity as a Collector, and I felt as though I lacked sufficient data to furnish a responsibly contemplated response. The mutant seed of my existence, once discarded in a cave divested of promise, had been recovered and sewn into a soil brimming with untapped potential by a gardener who would lovingly tend it for weal or for woe. Once it had been glutted on that uncommon nutrient of stimulating conversation, rewarding the words of its forerunners with little more than an allelopathic assault, it germinated to find itself not the flower it might have fancied, but a foolish, recalcitrant, and hypocritical weed. And yet, even a weed has a purpose. Even a weed has a possibility.

Throughout my Collections, I have collected more than just lives. I have had the privilege to play spectator to the spectrum spanning the ever-lengthening gap between the very best and the very worst of what humanity has to offer and, though I never knew it at its outset, being able to witness the breadth of human quality has indeed instilled within me a sense of fulfillment, and there are few callings of which I can estimate that would afford a better seat to that opera of opportunity than that of the Collector.

When I think back to the motivations, the driving forces, the reasons for existence, that most of my Collectees, my mentors, possessed, the underlying root nurturing their unique and various blooms was the same. It was love. Love for a bygone world. Love for worlds fantastic that could never truly be. Love for a childhood stolen. Love for what others could become. Love for the notion of friendship. Love for the responsibility of life. Love for another's unwavering love. In the end, and you may rest assured that I am terribly embarrassed that it took me so long to settle upon it, I realized that my motivation, my reason for existence, my purpose, had become exactly the same, and it might meet the same end. The Bureau of Fortune was responsible for bringing my love and me together and the Bureau of Fortune was now threatening to tear us apart.

I had initially conceived this record to assist in the composition of my thoughts on the Bureau of Fortune's progress for presentation at a standard and formal feedback meeting that is scheduled for every Collector after every three-year period of performance, at least, that is what they told me. My gardener, who is preparing herself for an exodus in the next room at present, has assured me that she has attended a few of them. I found it humbling that the Bureau might possibly possess a vested interest in what the expendable digits of its regenerative and extensive arm of the law might have to say regarding its efficacy. Nevertheless, this meeting will inevitably be the one black mark in my record of perfect attendance of Bureau functions.

While the Bureau may have yielded to me the bench in a moment that the puppet might play the judge of this farce purported as an "elective, merciful, and desperately needed alternative population control method"—a method that, along with mandated birth control and other means of suppression, succeeded in herding the NER population below its estimated regional carrying capacity six months ago but will still "remain active in order to continue to oversee population development to ensure we do not make the same mistakes again while offering the same opportunities as always to those with-out means"—I do not consider myself fit to preside. It is, after all, the jury that pulls the strings of fate in a true court of justice, and the lingering voices of my victims have petitioned me to play the plaintiff. And so, I will present instead to you, the masses, via a time-released viral packet that will, hopefully, infect not only the screens to which I am sure you will still submit your senses, but also the minds to which these often-disguised details deserve to be disclosed. It is quite possible that I will not live to see your judgment rendered.

The catharsis from which I emerged only hours before now revealed to me that I had gained the enduring love of another, some-thing I felt I really never had, effortlessly, undeservingly, luckily. This afforded me a significance of self to which I assigned tremendous value. It's all I ever wanted. To feel special. To feel different from the masses in a way that seemed meaningful. To fill in the blank that was my existence. All this time, I had been searching for something that would strike me in its grandiosity, as if the clouds would part, and I would know undeniably that this was my purpose. Reality was mundane. My purpose was to live for the love of another and the possibility of every moment with her.

As I attempt to conclude with a selfish closing statement, in place of a will, I would feel remiss in my blathering if I were not to attempt to atone for one pervasive thought that often plagues people fond of looking back on their predecessors, seeking to cast a blame that will go unheard by those long gone. My slightly younger and much more naïve self used to indulge in disparaging previous generations for their lack of forward thinking about preserving the future for people other than themselves. I would decry them for their iniquity, accuse them for irresponsibly giving birth to the current state of the world, and purport that I would have done better had I been in their shoes. When I had done so, I had very little to lose, very little to risk, and even less to protect.

Human society has evolved to the point that we have to consider our limitations. The superior intelligence with which we are burdened compared to other organisms has gifted us with the foresight to recognize the impending threats to our species, and it has also developed within us an altruistic sense of the other while simultaneously suppressing mechanisms of competition in which other organisms more readily engage. Competition for resources and aspirations is inevitable in the pursuit of idyllic lives, and humans are, at our core, more selfish than we seem. Does the lion feel remorse as a consequence of fatally wounding a competitor for a mate? Hardly. We are not so cold as that, yet, but it is these socially developed sentiments that will continue to force us to make harder and harder decisions as competition for something once plentiful and thoughtlessly taken for granted increases in ferocity. Chief among the motivators that will continue to warrant consideration of the application of the methods behind my employ is another socially developed sentiment: love. A love of possibility. The same love by which I have been struck and the same love I will risk my life to protect.

When I had judged those previous generations, I thought I was different. I thought I would have been different. I didn't have anything that allowed me to understand why we humans had reached this point. I had nothing for which I felt I had to compete. I had not been living in the moment.

Daria came along in one moment.

My best option to increase the likelihood of having the chance to see her again in the competition to keep her in my life was to join the Bureau of Fortune. Now, in this moment, I know I was wrong to judge those that came before so casually. After all, I am poised to engage in the same selfish behaviors because I have happened upon enough meaning to take the risk.

That's all that life really amounts to: a series of risks and the competition involved in taking them. I now understand why we live primarily in the moment and why it is so easy to concert lesser effort towards the future. It is because our loves exist now. In every competition to seek a love, one competitor will be favored the more fortunate, and to gamble on that chance of being so is life's greatest pursuit.

May you be fortunate in yours.

BoF Addendum

"This concludes the case study. Collector H 66K28 has since been captured, convicted of desertion, and executed. Future attempts at desertion will be met with the same end. Let this be a lesson to all of you prospectives. The Bureau always finds out. You cannot escape your commitment. Why would you even desire to? Furthermore, copies of this transcript that have not been approved for internal use at the Bureau are still circulating the public in electronic and, would you believe it, print forms. Any civilians found in possession of this transcript are to be detained and processed Bureau–side, pending approval of our new bylaw."

Welcome to the fold and happy hunting,

Prime Director Flehr

10.13.2172

ACKNOWLEDGMENTS

Though many would consider it to go without saying, I would be remiss if I were not to thank my friends and family first. Without your steadfast foundation, the worlds I build would rest on tremulous ground and my words would ring hollow. Thank you for the support, quiet and cacophonous, known and unknown, past and future.

I would especially like to thank Claire for her serial ministrations of verbal confidence. Without your indefatigable enthusiasm, the walks through the woods of anticipation would have been agonizingly arduous.

I would like to thank the wonderful women at SparkPress for their patience, diligence, and for the chance they took on cultivating what I hope will be an auspicious career of the page.

Finally, and foremostly, I would like to thank you, my readers. Each of you is an unexpected treasure and, though I may never be able to repay the debt I have accrued from you lending your eyes, ears, and spending the time to ponder my words, know that your curiosity has made me feel wealthier than the richest sultan to ever live. Thank you.

ABOUT THE AUTHOR

© Adrianna Werneke

Patrick Meisch is a high school science teacher who has harbored an ambition to write ever since his literature classes influenced him at a young age. He is passionate about educating future generations of people who can make a difference on topics such as climate change, resource management and sustainability, and responsible use of technology. His writing is often used as a vehicle to broach these topics in an engaging format. He lives, works, reads, and plays a lot of video games in Minnesota. *Those the Future Left Behind* is his debut novel.

SELECTED TITLES FROM SPARKPRESS

SparkPress is an independent boutique publisher delivering high-quality, entertaining, and engaging content that enhances readers' lives, with a special focus on female-driven work. www.gosparkpress.com

A Place Called Zamora: Book One, L B Gschwandter
$16.95, 978-1-68463-051-6
If an eighteen-year-old boy must risk his life in a motorcycle race to the very edge of a forty-story rooftop, his bike better be the one with brakes. That's what Niko faces in this dystopian story of love and survival: a race to the death that, if he survives it, will get him the girl of his choice and a kingdom of wealth laid out for him in an endless buffet. Except prizes like these come with strings in a city where corruption permeates everything, and there is no escape. Or is there?

Gatekeeper: Book One in the Daemon Collecting Series, Alison Levy
$16.95, 978-1-68463-057-8
Rachel Wilde—sent from another dimension to bring defective daemons in for repair—needs to locate two people: a woman whose ancestors held a destructive daemon at bay and a criminal trying to break dimensional barriers. Helped by a homeless man with unusual powers, she uncovers a rising shadow organization that's changing her world forever.

Sky of Water: Book Three of the Equal Night Trilogy, Stacey L. Tucker
$16.95, 978-1-68463-040-0
Having emerged triumphant from her trials in the Underworld, Skylar Southmartin is stronger and gutsier, and can handle anything that comes her way. In the gripping climax of the Equal Night Trilogy, she uncovers one last secret no one saw coming—one that Vivienne, the Great Mother of Water, hoped would stay buried for another 13,000 years.

Echoes of War: A Novel, Cheryl Campbell $16.95, 978-1-68463-006-6
When Dani—one of many civilians living on the fringes to evade a war that's been raging between a faction of aliens and the remnants of Earth's military for decades—discovers that she's not human, her life is upended . . . and she's drawn into the very battle she's spent her whole life avoiding.